THE MISDIRECTION OF FAULT LINES

Published by Peachtree Teen
An imprint of PEACHTREE PUBLISHING COMPANY INC.
1700 Chattahoochee Avenue
Atlanta, Georgia 30318-2112
PeachtreeBooks.com

Edited by Ashley Hearn
Design and composition by Lily Steele

Printed and bound in February 2024 at Sheridan, Chelsea, MI, USA.
10 9 8 7 6 5 4 3 2 1
First Edition
ISBN: 978-1-68263-580-3

Library of Congress Cataloging-in-Publication Data

Names: Gracia, Anna, author.
Title: The misdirection of fault lines / Anna Gracia.
Description: Atlanta, Georgia : Peachtree Teen, 2024. | Audience: Ages 14 &
    Up. | Audience: Grades 10-12. | Summary: Three Asian American teen girls
    look for direction in their lives as they compete against each other at
    an elite tennis tournament.
Identifiers: LCCN 2023050573 | ISBN 9781682635803 (hardcover) | ISBN
    9781682636398 (ebook)
Subjects: CYAC: Tennis—Fiction. | Contests—Fiction. |
    Friendship—Fiction. | Self-actualization—Fiction. | Asian
    Americans—Fiction.
Classification: LCC PZ7.1.G7115 Mi 2024 | DDC [Fic]—dc23
LC record available at https://lccn.loc.gov/2023050573

ANNA GRACIA

THE MISDIRECTION OF FAULT LINES

PEACHTREE
Teen

*FOR ALL THE FRIENDS WHO CAME INTO MY LIFE BECAUSE OF TENNIS,
HOWEVER BRIEF OUR TIME TOGETHER WAS,
I'M GRATEFUL TO HAVE MET YOU.*

*AND SERENA WILLIAMS, WHO CURRENTLY ISN'T BUT
DEFINITELY SHOULD BE FRIENDS WITH ME.*

THE BASTILLE INVITATIONAL

Congratulations on your acceptance into the qualifying draw of the Bastille Invitational! It is a thirty-two-player single-elimination tournament played on red clay. Four players will earn entry into the main draw.

Qualifying check-in will take place on Wednesday, July 5, from 10 a.m. until 2 p.m. Please note that if you are not checked in by the deadline, you will be replaced by an on-site alternate. Competition will begin on Thursday, July 6, with the quarterfinals taking place on Saturday, July 8.

Should you be one of the four players to qualify for the sixty-four-player main draw, Sunday, July 9, is a rest day. Competition will resume on Monday, July 10.

Enclosed in this package, you will find a rulebook along with your room assignment. One of the time-honored traditions of the Bastille Invitational is having players room together in the villas on-site. Parents/guardians and/or coaches, should you travel with one, will be housed in a separate facility. We hope you enjoy this experience and that the connections you form here will be lasting.

The winners of the 12U, 14U, and 16U singles draw will earn both USA Tennis and ITF points, as well as a possible spot at the BJK Cup. The winner of the 18U singles draw will earn a wild card into a WTA 125 tour event, as well as USA Tennis and ITF points.

We look forward to a great tournament. Please route all questions through the main office to be directed as necessary.

Aces!

Dick Duncan
Director, The Bastille Invitational

WEDNESDAY, JULY 5TH

DAY BEFORE THE BASTILLE INVITATIONAL

1
ALICE

"DID YOU MAKE IT TO THE BASTILLE?"

I am so busy staring at my bizarre surroundings that I barely hear my brother's question through the phone. I hadn't expected central Florida to look so . . . French.

"Hello? Alice? Can you hear me?" David's voice strains with tension, as though I might have simply vanished without a word.

"I'm here," I confirm, giving a wary look at the imposing wrought-iron letters that have been twisted and dropped immediately upon entrance to the campus.

Bastille.

Not *the* Bastille. Just *Bastille.*

I'd known the place would be French-like. What I did not anticipate was stepping directly into a non–French person's fantasy of what France would look like. Right down to the cobblestone paths, I am in the middle of the scene in *Beauty and the Beast* where Belle insults everyone around her and visits the library in a town where no one else reads.

"We're so proud of you. I hope you know that."

My older brother clears his throat, surely giving himself more time to think of things to say as I wander through plaza after plaza of villas, each with a different Joan of Arc fountain in its center.

They're not called dorms here, these villages of miniature structures that burst out in all directions from their central gathering point. Each house in this plaza, marked *Place de la Concorde*, has four doors, all painted pale blue to contrast with the pinkish color of the building itself. The upper-level rooms have tiny balconies out back, the villas cleverly arranged so that they open into tall cypresses and other green shrubbery instead of each other. It gives the illusion of privacy, even as the buildings are crammed so close together you can nearly span the distance between them with your hands.

I'm accustomed to the dense housing of an urban environment, with San Francisco's mere forty-seven square miles housing nearly a million people, but the number of players Bastille is able to squeeze into these little villages is impressive even to me.

I shift the strap on my shoulder, thinking of the hot-pink sleeping bag inside the bag I'm carrying. Surely the color alone will mark me as an outsider here—a kid's color—borrowed from the little sister of one of David's friends. I see a few players towing carts of proper bedding from their cars, apparently unsatisfied at the prospect of living the actual camp experience. Everyone here moves with such assurance of where they're going and what they're doing.

I'm stalling.

Finding my assigned villa will lead to my going inside, which will lead to making this entire thing real. As it is now, I am simply a visitor, wandering the grounds in admiration.

My eye snags on a familiar face. With thick, glossy brown hair and a smile that would make dentists weep with joy, Violetta Masuda is unmistakable. So is the man next to her—with the wavy blond hair and dimples that vaulted him onto posters across America, it's Cooper Nelsen. He was once considered "the next big thing" in American men's tennis, until multiple knee injuries forced an early retirement.

So this is where he ended up.

They turn my way and, without thinking, I fling myself behind the closest Joan of Arc. Here, she is spitting gracefully into a concrete basin while proudly holding the French flag. In this sculpture, unlike the painting that clearly inspired it, her breasts are covered. It's perhaps the one detail that finally pulls me back to the reality of the moment.

Crouched behind a fountain with sweat trickling down my back and into my pants, I am hiding from people who have no idea I exist. From my low post, I have an almost unobstructed view of them. It's clear they are close by the way they interact, easy bumps and touches without hesitation—like they've had a lifetime of knowing each other. Funny then that he's never made an appearance on her social media.

I'm so immersed in watching them that I forget I still have my phone held to my ear, David waiting for me on the line.

"Alice? Are you still there?" he asks.

I grunt my agreement, not wanting to draw the attention of those crossing the plaza—this one marked *Place du Capitole*. No one seems to even look at the trees or the statues around them as they scurry to their villas. Perhaps they have all been here before.

"How are your hands?" David asks. "Did they survive the flight?"

I flex my left hand, watching each finger stretch out in front of me, pretending I don't know what he's really asking. In spite of his teasing tone, I know there's worry behind his question. "Present and accounted for."

He lets my sarcasm go without a response. He never used to do that.

I watch Violetta and Cooper hug goodbye, her arms lingering just a fraction longer than his, then stand and stretch my legs with relief once they're out of sight. My entire body is slick with sweat, my curly hair uncomfortably plastered to the back of my neck and my phone screen fogged from my body heat.

"Listen," David continues, not bothering to ask my permission for this unsolicited pep talk. "I know this is scary, but you can do this. We believe in you. You're going to be great and we'll be cheering you on the whole way."

We. He keeps using the plural pronoun, as if he speaks for the rest of the family.

I drag a finger through the water in the fountain, hoping it might cool my body and therefore my mind. But it's warm, like everything else here.

"Is Ma there?" I ask.

David awkwardly clears his throat. "She just stepped out to run some errands. She wanted to talk to you, I know she did. She's just busy with it being summer and all. You know how it is, people wanting their houses deep cleaned while they're on vacation. I'm sure she'll call you when she can."

A cloud passes over and temporarily darkens the sky and I wonder if it's a sign David is lying, like a penance for trying to keep light where there should be none. He's always been the upbeat one, cracking jokes and prying smiles even from the grim lips of Ahma, who smiles less now than she did in the *before*.

I hear David's faint breath through the receiver and I wish I could extend this conversation, maybe forever—anything to keep me from having to actually find my villa and go inside. But David and I have nothing else to talk about; nothing except the one thing we *never* talk about.

"How's the weather down there? You have everything you need? Have you met your roommates yet?" His voice is brimming with false cheer.

I wander into Place de l'Étoile, where another Joan of Arc fountain awaits, this one of her in full armored glory and wielding a sword. Instead of Joan herself spitting water, this one spouts out the tip of the sword. I wish my villa was in this plaza—I could use a battle-ready Joan of Arc on my side. Instead, I'm like the Joan in the previous courtyard, all soft and vulnerable and exposed to the elements, spitting water uselessly while the troops around me fight.

Yeah, yeah, she's an inspiration or whatever. I'm tired of being inspirational.

"It's a thousand degrees and the air is so muggy I could squeeze it for drinking water," I reply, checking the temperature of this fountain's water. It, too, is warm.

"You pack your hand sanitizer?" he asks.

He's trying so hard. I can almost *feel* his effort through the phone. But no matter how hard he tries, he can't replace what I've lost.

"I'll be fine," I reassure him. It's comforting to know I still have the ability to lie.

"I just don't want you to get sick," he frets. "Who knows what kind of germs you're touching? It's *Florida*."

I almost let out a snort of laughter, but I don't want to let him off so easily. His questions aren't about Florida any more than they are about germs. But if he won't simply come out and say it, neither will I. I'm tired of being the only one who refuses to pretend everything is okay.

We are not okay. *I* am not okay.

"I'd better go." The unfinished parts of my sentence stick in my throat, grasping for air I'm unable to give.

"Give 'em hell, Alice."

2

VIOLETTA

AFTER SAYING GOODBYE TO COOP, I FLOAT THROUGH THE DOOR ON A CLOUD of happiness until I remember who my assigned roommate is. Suddenly, my favorite aspect of the tournament is personal torture—having to share this space with Leylah Lê.

She's stomping around, slamming drawers as she unpacks, like she *needs* me to know how much she hates me without saying so. Spoiler alert: I already know. The past two years of silence from her was message enough. I hope she loses in the qualifiers and goes home before the main draw even starts.

A wave of guilt hits me but I shake it off.

I decide to be extra sweet just to get under her skin.

"Is there something I can help you with? It seems like you're having trouble opening and closing the drawers."

Leylah ignores me completely, slamming the next drawer shut even louder than before.

"I didn't quite catch that, can you repeat it?" I ask.

I chuckle to myself when she mutters under her breath. It doesn't matter that I don't hear what she's saying.

There's a light knock and after waiting a beat for the person to enter, I answer the door. The girl standing there looks down so all I can see is the top of her head. Thick, dark curls. The kind I need a curling iron and two different products to imitate. Even then, I could only dream of having curls like this.

Post idea: changing hair texture temporarily vs. permanently

She finally looks up and I see a spray of freckles across her flat nose. She keeps tilting her head back, back, back, until she finally reaches my eyes.

Hers widen at the sight of me and a little gasp escapes. "I'm rooming with Violetta Masuda?"

I can't lie—my ego swells a little at the recognition.

"That's me." I step aside so she can get through the narrow door. "And you are?"

"Alice. Alice Wu." She says it almost reluctantly, like she would have preferred never to have told anyone.

Her lack of enthusiasm sends mine into hyperdrive, my voice bordering on shrill. "Come in, come in!"

She sets her bags down in the entry and surveys the room I'm showing off like Vanna White. Instead of regular-looking dorms, Bastille's rooms are more like long, narrow studios, with a sofa and coffee table in the middle and the beds, dressers, and built-in shelving at the far end. A side door leads to the single bathroom and every room has tall, narrow windows that open, the upstairs apartments getting tiny terraces.

A lot of the players complain about the heat when they first arrive because it's not like the newer academies that outfit every space like a hotel, but it's actually not too bad because the stone floors keep things fairly cool. I think the charm of it all outweighs any other drawbacks. It's like being in a different country here.

"There are four rooms to every building," I explain. "So sometimes you'll hear the people upstairs or next door, but it makes you feel like you're really living in a tiny city instead of an independent campus in the middle of Florida."

That had been a big selling point to Audrey when we moved out here. Ever since I can remember, she's been pushing for me to be more independent.

Alice nods, her eyes still roving hungrily across everything like she might have missed a detail on her first few perusals.

"There are usually only two people to a room during the school year," I babble on, uncomfortable with the silence. "But they put four to a room during the tournament. My last roommate just moved out, which is why it's only the three of us now. I live here full-time," I add.

"That explains the decorations," Leylah mutters.

I see Alice take in the twinkle lights and dangling paper stars I've strung from the ceiling, along with some more homey touches like fresh throw pillows for the couch and an area rug for the middle of the room. "They're nice," she says quietly, and I'm tempted to stick my tongue out at Leylah.

"How far did you travel?" I ask. The Bastille Invitational is open internationally, so there are always some players who come from halfway across the world. So far, I've met people from twenty-two different countries.

"Just from San Francisco," Alice answers.

I look back toward the entry, where she's brought only a small duffel, a tote, and two racquets. Most of us go on court with more than she's got for an eleven-day trip.

Maybe she doesn't plan on staying the entire time.

Some players can't wait to take off to their next location after a loss, but most people stick around for a few days afterward to hang out. The big tournaments are usually the only places we get to see one another and Bastille is always extra exciting because it has everyone: all ages *and* both boys' and girls' tournaments. It's one of the toughest to get into because it's by invitation only and the admissions board never reveals exactly what the criteria for it are.

Bastille (the academy) even brings on a team of coordinators to help the students that live here with their applications to Bastille (the tournament). Playing here full-time doesn't guarantee anything except an error-free application.

It's archaic and time-consuming, but I also assume it's the only way Leylah got back here. Last time I checked, all her ranking points had expired.

"Is this your first time in Florida?" I ask.

A nod.

"Did you come out here by yourself? Or do you have a coach or a parent at one of the hotels nearby?" Bastille is one of the only truly independent tournaments where all players stay on campus while adults are relegated to off-campus housing. It makes it more like a summer camp than a tournament—another reason it's so popular.

"It's just me," she says after a hard swallow. Her fingers trail along the wainscoting on the walls, her eyes still scanning the area.

Back and forth, back and forth. She seems restless.

I press on. "Is this your first Lī tournament?"

"For fuck's sake, can you just waterboard her and get it over with?" Leylah bursts out. "It'll be faster and a lot less painful than whatever the hell it is you're doing now."

Alice startles a little at Leylah's abrasiveness, but I wave her off. "She's always like this," I explain. "You get used to it."

Leylah looks at Alice for the first time. She jerks a thumb in my direction. "*She's* always like *this*. Make sure you *don't* get used to it."

Leylah's tone is so sharp it actually stings a little.

"Excuse me for trying to make friends," I say defensively.

"News flash, *Violetta*. Not everyone wants to be friends with you."

She says my name with hard *t*'s, making fun of the fact that I insist people pronounce my name correctly. If *I* had the last name Lê, I wouldn't hesitate to correct someone every time they mispronounced it as *Lee*. It shouldn't surprise me she doesn't think it's worth her time. If she had my name, she'd probably let people call her *Violet*.

Post idea: staying true to your roots

I glare at her back while she finishes unpacking. Unlike Alice, Leylah packed like she's moving in. I'm sure she assumes she'll make it all the way to Bastille Day (the finals). Knowing her, she'll probably do it.

But she looks thinner than she did two years ago, bordering on ballerina-thin. Her bones practically poke through her coppery-brown skin that never burns, not a single ounce of fat to be found anywhere. She could walk straight into a runway casting without an issue, she's so tall and skinny. Plus the frown.

I pull myself up straighter and suck in my stomach a little.

As she moves—always keeping her back to me—I eventually spy the tiny insulin pump on the back of her arm, poking out of the sleeve of her T-shirt. I don't know exactly how they work, but I've seen enough commercials to know they're supposed to make being a type 1 diabetic easier. Also, they're very, very expensive.

Not that her family can't afford it.

Alice has chosen to escape us both, already safely tucked away in her bright pink nylon sleeping bag on the top bunk.

"Are you . . . going to sleep?" I ask, pulling out my phone to check the time. San Francisco is three hours *behind* us; there's no reason she should be ready for bed. "You're going to want to hold off for a little or your body will be jet-lagged tomorrow," I advise.

"Let me guess, you're offering to keep her awake out of the goodness of your heart?" Leylah snorts. "She just got here. Maybe you can wait a minute before you try to sabotage her."

Sabotage? Is that what she thinks I did?

I prop my hand on a hip. "How is an offer to help considered sabotage?"

"Don't be fooled," Leylah calls up to the top bunk. "Violetta plays the long game."

I roll my eyes. "Why am I not surprised you managed to make yourself a victim again?"

"Why am I not surprised you don't think you did anything wrong?"

"In telling Alice to stay awake?"

She glares at me.

"Alice. I need to go check in. You coming?" Leylah speaks to her like a dog. Simple commands, short questions.

Alice is fully buried in her sleeping bag with only her curls peeking out so her voice is muffled. "No, thank you."

"You know you have to do it before two o'clock, right? If you miss it, they'll assume you're not coming and replace you."

Now it's my turn to be skeptical. "Leylah Lê is suddenly a philanthropist?"

"I consider it a public service, getting her away before you can sink your claws in. And don't call me that," she snaps.

My "claws," as Leylah refers to them, are barely even past the tips of my fingers. They're painted the same shade of neon pink as Alice's sleeping bag, which is probably why Leylah sees them as over-the-top. God forbid a girl like anything *girly*.

Poor Alice. No doubt she hid just to escape our bickering. I hate that Leylah turns me into this person.

Post idea: courteous avoidance

I remind myself that I have the upper hand right now—I'm not the one who needs to qualify just to get in. I can afford to be magnanimous.

I put on my best sunny smile, hoping my eyes don't give me away. "I need to go there too, so we can all go as a group!"

Of course I don't need to, but I'm not going to let Leylah turn Alice against me when I haven't even gotten the chance to win her over. Besides, it's a friendly gesture to lead them and point things out since I live here.

Leylah's glare tells me she doesn't agree.

"Alice?" I gently prod the lump in her sleeping bag. "Alice? Are you ready to go?"

After what feels like an eternity, she finally pops her head out. Her eyes dart around furtively. Like what? We've come to apprehend her?

"Are you ready?" I prompt. "To check in?"

She looks down at her hands. "Um . . ."

Leylah claps her hands—twice, loudly—right in front of Alice's face, cutting off her thought. Her head snaps up and Leylah says, "Get your ass up. We're leaving."

3

LEYLAH

IT'S FUNNY, WATCHING VIOLETTA CHASE ME OUT THE DOOR.

At least it would be, if it weren't so goddamn annoying.

She's decided to play tour guide, explaining every building and its history like she's devoted hours of her free time to memorizing these facts.

Which she probably did.

Never mind that no one asked her to. Or that I used to come here every year, just like she did.

Alice doesn't even look like she's listening. She's hunched into her shoulders like she might make a run for it at any moment. But it's clear she has great spatial awareness, judging by the way she easily sidesteps and ducks Violetta's hand flailing. Even with both hands stuffed in her pockets and her head down, Alice seems to sense every fling of Violetta's overdramatic arm gestures.

Huh.

I'm glad she's not competing in my age group. Court sense is *my* thing.

V keeps talking, telling us both stuff we don't care about. "This is the Mont Saint-Michel—the library—because the actual Mont Saint-Michel was known as 'the castle of knowledge.'"

Violetta points to the next building. This one's not a castle. It's definitely more modern, bright white with a big dome on top. I recognize it as the Observatory, aka the place to avoid because it's where everyone else goes.

Violetta, naturally, perks up when she sees it. "That one over there"—she points for Alice's benefit—"is L'Observatoire."

Yes, she says it with a French accent.

"In total, there are twenty-five observatories in France, but this one is modeled off *L'Observatoire de la Côte d'Azur, mais oui.*"

She speaks French now. That's a new thing to dislike about her.

"I'm not a hundred percent sure why she chose this specific building to copy—"

"Who is 'she'?" Alice asks, thankfully cutting off Violetta.

I didn't even realize Alice was listening; her face is always pointed somewhere else.

"Oh, sorry. The lady who built this place. She called herself..." Violetta snaps her fingers together, trying to come up with the name. "You know," she says, eagerly snapping at me. "What was her name?"

"Why the hell would I know?"

Violetta sighs and deflates. I'm a huge disappointment for failing the pop quiz she just sprang on me.

"Anyway," she continues, "this super-rich woman one day decides she wants to build a school, but she's obsessed with France, so poof! Everything is modeled off something or somewhere in

France." Violetta gestures to the perfectly manicured landscaping around us. "See? Even the gardens."

I'd forgotten about these. The one we're currently walking through has been cut into fancy curlicues (I'm sure there's some official term I'm not using) with flat grass in between, the low hedges lining the walkway shaped in perfect cubes. It's somehow both satisfying but disturbing because it's *too* perfect. Part of me wants to snap a branch off just to see if anyone would notice.

"The French players hate it here," Violetta continues with a laugh, and I wonder how many players from France she really knows. "It's just a random mishmash of different architectural styles and time periods and probably stereotypes of some kind, but I like it. It's got this sort of cozy feeling, like we're all sequestered together in this tiny French village."

Her overly purply eyes look all faraway and dreamy.

"My high school has a trip to France every year for kids who take French," Alice says. It snaps Violetta back to this planet.

"You've been to France?" she gasps.

Here's the thing: Violetta presents herself as this perfect, worldly social media *influencer* (I throw up a little in my mouth just thinking the word). But I know for a fact she's never been outside the US. And of the trips she *did* take within the US, I'm certain she's never seen anything other than tennis courts and the hotel they were staying at. Audrey's not big on sightseeing.

"I didn't go," Alice says softly. "A little out of our price range."

Violetta nods sympathetically. "I get that."

If I don't win this tournament, I might have to join that conversation. Mom has made it more than clear they won't be funding any more tennis from here on out. I *need* to win this tournament.

"Well, it's not France, but the Observatory *is* air-conditioned," Violetta offers. "There's no actual telescope to look at the sky or anything—the inside is like a big common room with table tennis and TVs and couches and whatever to hang out. I guess because you go in there and 'observe' the other people? Either way, I can introduce you around if you go."

"Thanks. Air-conditioning isn't big in San Francisco."

I notice Alice didn't actually accept the invitation. She seems mostly focused on discreetly mopping the sweat off her forehead. She's wilting in the heat.

Even knowing we won't play against each other, I can't help assessing her strengths and weaknesses. Maybe I *should* go to the Observatory to scope out the other players. No one knows who's all been admitted until the draws get posted.

Violetta is still talking. "When the school ran into issues, Dick Duncan and some others stepped in and convinced the woman who owned it to turn it into a tennis academy instead. Bastille is one of the few that only focuses on tennis instead of expanding into multiple sports. It's part of what makes it so exclusive."

The only thing separating V from a paid tour guide is the embroidered polo and little handheld flag. Oh, and that none of us asked for this tour.

"It's also named after a jail," I can't help adding. I may be shit at school but at least I remember that. Violetta isn't the only one who knows stuff.

She rolls her eyes. "It's a *metaphor*. Like the players who broke out of here would be free to not only pursue their dreams, but look forward to their new life." She folds her hands over her chest. "*We're* the prisoners on Bastille Day."

I stifle a laugh. Violetta is putting on a full Shakespearean production to sell this narrative to Alice because if she thinks about it for more than five seconds she'll realize how stupid and offensive it is.

"The French don't call it Bastille Day," Alice murmurs. "They call it the National Holiday or just the Fourteenth of July, the way we call Independence Day July Fourth."

It's obvious Violetta didn't know that but she nods anyway, her chin lifting higher. "Yes, right. Like I said, the founder wasn't actually French."

We arrive at the row of check-in tents in front of the courts, and Violetta finally stops talking. My brain sighs in relief. Some people like that scratchy sort of quality her voice has, but it mostly makes me want to cough. Like there's something stuck in her throat.

"Whatcha you doing back here, Violetta?" The woman behind the check-in table has a big smile and a mild Southern accent.

I guess I never think of Florida as the South.

"I hope it's not to register in another age group," she continues. "You already got two!"

Alice turns to Violetta in something like awe. "You qualified in more than one age category?"

Violetta lifts her chin like she's the fucking Queen of England (not Camilla). "Number one seed in 16U and number twelve in 18U singles. Number six seed in 16U doubles."

I nearly choke. No wonder she didn't seem happy to see me.

She probably *liked* having me gone.

Without me there, she probably won everything. And now even that's not enough for her. Now she wants to try to conquer *two* age categories because she just has to have everything.

She's greedy.

"Look at you, Leylah Lee," the woman croons. "You probably don't remember me, but I've been watching you since the twelve and unders."

Of course I don't remember her. I'm pretty sure the last time I was here I vowed to come back full *Carrie* style, raining knives and fire on everyone—adults included.

It doesn't matter how friendly she is. No sampeah for her.

"Janice," Violetta says smugly. Like it's some kind of accomplishment to remember this random woman's name when she fucking lives here full-time. But that's Violetta: always going for the easy win.

I finally decide to acknowledge Janice with a nod and she chuckles. "Always was an intense one, weren't ya? Here's your doubles partner's name and contact info if you want to get in touch with her today or tomorrow. Match times are on the draw, darlin'."

She points her pen to her right and I make my escape. Even just a few steps away, I can already breathe more easily.

It's not just that Violetta smells like a lavender-soap factory—she sucks up all the oxygen in a room. I'm taller but up close, she feels bigger. As in, she's a three-dimension human while I'm still in stick-figure mode.

I get told by every oum in Massachusetts that I'm too skinny and to put some meat on my bones. Meanwhile, Violetta has actual curvature on her body, highlighted by the fact that her entire wardrobe is made up of spandex or other stretchy fabrics. We can wear the exact same outfit and you can't even tell. I know this for a fact because it's happened.

Don't get me wrong: I'm fine with my body. It's everyone else who isn't. And it's easy to say 'screw them' when you're not surrounded by a bunch of teenage boys who constantly whisper about Violetta's boobs or Violetta's legs because they don't consider you enough of a person to *not* whisper about it around you.

Or *to* you.

Point being: boys are stupid.

I shove Violetta out of my mind, focusing instead on the gigantic draw tacked up in front of me.

I used to love this part. Seeing my name in huge letters and imagining it moving across the board as I advanced. But right now I wish everything were smaller. I wish no one else could even see this. Because I'm in the *qualifiers*.

I'm pissed.

Worse, I'm embarrassed.

Unlike in the other areas in my life (read: school), I'm fucking awesome at tennis. Really fucking awesome. Little-kids-have-asked-for-my-autograph awesome. In my mind, it's never been a question I would eventually turn pro. Now it all rests on this fucking *qualifier*.

Three extra opportunities to choke and lose the only thing I care about.

Again.

My chest tightens and I have the urge to punch the nearest wall.

"Goddamn fucking cocksucker," I mutter to myself.

Swearing helps.

I repeat every single curse word I can think of, at least half of them in different languages. (A side benefit of tennis being a global sport.) Some feel better than others. I'm not a huge fan of the ones that talk about fucking someone's mom or calling someone a whore, but a satisfying *fuck off* is pretty great in any language.

"You're like a Duolingo of swear words, huh?" A boy is now beside me.

A cute boy.

A short boy. Well, shorter than me.

A cute, shorter-than-me boy who is grinning at me like we know each other already.

We don't.

My face accurately conveys this.

"Faen ta deg?" he asks. "It means *fuck off* in Norwegian."

I don't know that one. But fuck him for butting into my personal conversation.

"I'm Noah, by the way." He taps his name on the board. He's also in the qualifiers.

It's clear he's waiting for me to introduce myself. I do have enough social skills to understand this. I just don't care. Because this is how you get sucked into conversations with someone you don't actually want to talk to. And after sizing up Noah Edelman, I already know I don't want to talk to him.

His grin hasn't slipped. It tells me he's used to conversation-bombing people and expecting them to reply.

This is the problem with cute boys—they know they're cute, so they're used to having everything handed to them.

Negative 100 points. Noah Edelman is starting at the bottom of the Grand Canyon.

I give him a dead-eyed look and turn back to the draw. I try to keep my focus on the names near mine. I will never stop being bitter over these three extra rounds. I swear to god, if *fitness* costs me the trophy, I will burn Dick Duncan's office to the ground.

"Ah. You're one of those," Noah says with a knowing nod.

Gross. A subtle neg. Like I'm going to sit here and try to convince him to like me. Boys learning to read has set back an entire generation of trauma healing.

I hear Violetta and Alice getting closer.

Well, no, that's not true.

I only hear Violetta with her scratchy, laryngitis-y voice. But like I predicted, Alice is behind her. She's practically hiding, but V lunges forward and Alice is left standing there like a zoo animal.

"Noah!" Violetta cries, flinging her arms around him. She says his name like he's the *exact* person she's been hoping to run into. She tugs Alice next to her like a rag doll. "Alice, you have to meet Noah. He's one of the best people I know."

Somehow in all this, I've ended up squished against the wall. I am literally being held against my will by Violetta.

"Noah, this is Alice's first time at Bastille. She's from San Francisco and has the cutest tote from her public library—it's got this illustration of little kids fishing off a pier except instead of fish, they're catching books."

What an odd, highly specific detail to remember about someone we met approximately five seconds ago. I'll give her this: Violetta is very good at making people feel special.

"Leylah, this is Noah."

I am currently a very large bug squashed on a windshield. Excellent timing.

He's subtracting 5 points from me on looks right now.

I don't care about his point totals.

Goddamn it.

"He's the current reigning champion of both UNO and BANANAGRAMS." She giggles, which earns an eye roll from him. "He's also from New Zealand."

"I *moved* from New Zealand," he corrects. His accent sounds bland American. Nonspecific. "I'm from California, but some of my mom's family lives in New Zealand so we moved out there for a year."

Of course Violetta has made with friends with someone twenty-six time zones away. She probably times her messages through some preset program to make it sync with his schedule.

"Noah, Leylah. She's from Massachusetts."

Really? That was the most personal fact she could come up with?

And why didn't she tell *me* Noah was a good person? Or does she assume that trait isn't important to me? I was friends with *her*, after all.

I smile a little to myself at my clever burn.

Plus 5 points. Too bad she won't hear it.

"Are you from *Boston*?" Noah attempts a horrible Boston accent.

He's still trying to engage me in conversation. Maybe he has a death wish.

Violetta answers for me. "Lowell. They have a whole Cambodian community there. Her mom's Khmer and her dad's Vietnamese, which is wild because their countries were at war, like, when they were each still living there. They're basically a Romeo-and-Juliet-type love story."

What the fuck? Why is Violetta introducing me like I'm some kind of pageant contestant to this boy I don't even know? My background is none of his business.

Still, he quirks an eyebrow at this news. "A Cambodian community. In *Boston*?"

Someone needs to tell him to stop attempting accents.

"Lowell," I correct. If Violetta keeps talking to him, who knows what else she'll tell him.

"Isn't that near *Boston*?"

"What's your point?"

Noah shrugs. "I just like using the accent. But also, I thought Boston was known for being hella racist. Must be a tough place for anyone who doesn't look and sound like Marky Mark."

He's trying the accent again. No wonder he and Violetta are friends.

"Marky Mark?" Violetta asks, wrinkling her nose in confusion.

"Mark Wahlberg," Noah answers. "You know, the guy who did a bunch of hate crimes as a teen and is now one of the top-earning movie stars? It was a whole thing in 2020." He pauses. "And 2023."

Violetta gasps theatrically. "Seriously? I didn't know that!"

I don't want to be involved in the conversation. I really don't. But I'm also tired of Boston jokes and I don't even live there. "Everywhere is racist," I say. But I can't help adding, "But yeah, Mark Wahlberg went to jail for beating a couple of Vietnamese guys."

To us, it's not just a crime from a long time ago. It's personal. Mark Wahlberg movies are expressly forbidden in our house. So is anything from Tina Fey.

"I can't believe more people don't know about this!" Violetta exclaims. Turning to Alice she asks, "Did you know that?"

I don't care about any of this. I don't care about Mark Wahlberg or Tina Fey, about Boston, about what Alice does or doesn't know. I definitely don't care about Violetta's soap-opera dramatics or this boy I plan on forgetting the second I step away from here.

Besides, Violetta's already claimed him.

Good.

I don't bother excusing myself or saying goodbye as I leave.

4

LEYLAH

BECAUSE THE UNIVERSE HATES ME, I RUN INTO NOAH AT THE PRACTICE COURTS a few hours later. We're allowed to use the courts at the alternative site but no one wants to drive five minutes away when there are courts on the grounds. There's probably a number of us here without cars too.

He's sitting on the ground tying his shoes, but looks up at me with the same stupid grin he had earlier and snaps his fingers. "Leylah."

"Congratulations." I crane my neck, looking for someone else—anyone else—I can hit with. It sucks not having a coach who travels with me. It means I'm going to have to go looking for someone every day.

"Hey, how do you pronounce your last name? I saw it had one of those little hat thingies over the *e*."

I could explain that in Vietnamese *ê* is in fact a completely separate letter from *e* but I really don't care to. Google is free.

Instead, I give him another dead-eyed stare to help rush him along.

It doesn't work.

Noah hops up and bounces on his feet a couple times, followed by a number of high-knee jumps. Then side-to-side trunk rotation. I have to step back when he starts stretching and loosening his leg ligaments.

This boy is doing a full warm-up directly in front of me.

"You about finished?" I ask sarcastically.

A few more high-knee jumps before he answers. "I don't have cooties, you know." His voice is on the edge of panting. He definitely jumped more than he's used to in an attempt to impress me.

I don't hate it.

"You'll be safe, I promise," he says. "I'll try not to rub my boy germs all over the balls before you touch them."

We both realize the accidental *rub balls* comment at the same time and his lips twitch but he manages to keep a mostly straight face.

Plus 1 point for holding it in.

Noah Edelman has self-control.

I crack open a brand-new can of four balls. The satisfying snap and hiss of the released compressed air is even more satisfying than cracking my joints. When people talk about mindfulness and appreciating the small things, this is what I think of. I'll bet the kids here never think about missing the smell of new tennis balls.

I take a deep inhale of it before thrusting the entire can into his hand. "I don't like holding them." I just barely avoid saying the phrase *I don't like holding balls* at the last second.

He doesn't so much as flinch. Just stuffs them into the pockets of his shorts.

Three in the left, one in hand.

I feel weird.

Plus the other 4 points to him for taking all the balls.

Minus 1 to me for watching each and every one of those balls go into his pocket.

We start at the service line.

I know it's the standard warm-up most players use but I hate it. I hate it even more when he gives me exactly four hits before asking, "So what's up with you and Violetta?"

I mishit my next shot. "What's up with us? There is no us."

"You were both making weird faces earlier whenever the other person talked."

He's about to dig for more information about her. Maybe he'll ask what her favorite flower is or what kind of guys she likes or whether she has a boyfriend because he can't ask her without sounding like a creep.

I concentrate on making sure my warm-up short court shots are impeccable. No drop shots to dive for, no overhit lobs to gently deflect. Every forehand is a model of net clearance.

My stiff posture must give something away.

"So is it you don't like her or she doesn't like you?" he asks.

"Why are you so nosy?"

"Is it nosy to ask personal questions about two people I don't really know?"

"Yes. And I thought the two of you were friends."

"We're acquaintances."

"Then why'd she hug you?"

"Now who's asking personal questions?"

I shoot him a death glare and transition us into volley-to-volley rallying. Maybe now he'll be too busy to keep talking.

It's too much to hope for.

"To answer your question . . . ," he begins.

My reply is flat. "I really don't care."

"I think you do."

"I don't."

He keeps talking anyway. "I met her at a tournament last year. She's friends with my buddy Kevin Do."

"I know Kevin."

Kevin Do is a Vietnamese Kiwi who spends his summers (well, his winters) at Bastille. Violetta kept him in the divorce. Violetta kept everyone in the divorce.

"The plot thickens," Noah says with a waggle of his eyebrows.

"Oh god, stop. Fine. Violetta and I are assigned to the same villa. Are you happy?"

"Are *you* happy about it?"

"Do I seem happy about it?"

He cringes. "Shalom to your roommates. That's gotta be a tense room to land in. They really aren't as big as the pictures online make it seem."

I think of Alice and how she already seems mildly terrified of both of us. "It's supposed to give us the Parisian experience or something. Living in actual Paris would probably be cheaper."

"True, but would Parisians have this delightful fashion sense?" He gestures down to the ominous prison bars on his shirt, the words *break free* printed across it in bright, tennis ball–yellow. The back says *The Bastille Invitational*, followed by a list of the names of everyone who participates.

I already checked—both my first and last name are spelled wrong.

"At least this year we didn't get one of those stupid soccer bags with the rope straps that cut the hell out of your shoulders," I say. "They're completely useless."

"The bags? Or soccer players in general? Because either way I agree."

"Big talk for a guy that's what, five eight, one fifty?" *I* could probably tackle him, let alone people who actually play contact sports.

Noah puffs out his chest. "Five nine and a *half*," he emphasizes. Squeezing a biceps, he adds, "This is one hundred sixty-five pounds of pure muscle. I'm like a . . ." He trails off, trying to think of an adequate comparison.

"Rabbit?" I supply.

"Okay, I think we're ready to move to the baseline!" he announces.

I turn my face as I scoot back so he can't see the smile I'm smothering. He may not be the hottest guy I've ever laid eyes on, but his personality is moving him up the ranks.

Damn it. No ranks.

Minus 5 for even thinking of him like that.

I focus on moving my feet and hitting my strokes as cleanly as possible. Not to impress him—I want to impress everyone who's out here and might be watching me. They need to know I'm back and ready to pick up where I left off two years ago.

Once we've gone through a full warm-up—ground strokes, volleys, overheads, and serves—he calls over, "Wanna play some points? Ten-point tiebreak, maybe?"

I don't like playing boys. Their serves are usually a lot faster than what I'm used to facing—it's not exactly fair to go up against someone who regularly serves 115 mph.

But I'm also not going to admit that I don't want to play him because I'm worried I might lose.

"No serves, first two baseline shots down the center," I counter.

"First three," he calls back.

Fine.

We both take the tiebreak seriously and Noah cuts the chit-chat.

I win 10-7.

I expect him to make a bunch of excuses or demand an immediate rematch, but he just grins and holds his hand out over the net, waiting to shake mine.

I roll my eyes. "You're making this way too formal."

Still, I accept the handshake and he squeezes my hand just a little tighter and a little longer than a regular person would. "You wanna grab some food?" he asks.

I make a face. "Like, together?"

He clutches his chest. "Yowza. You really know how to eviscerate a guy's ego."

"You say things like *yowza*. I don't think you *have* an ego."

"I'll have you know that word was added to the dictionary a full five years ago," he says, shaking a finger at me.

This boy is an absolute fucking nerd. Teachers probably love him and he gets straight As. For some reason, this ticks his point total up toward a neutral zero.

I need to get out of here.

I kick off my shoes and stuff my feet into my slides, trying to exit as fast as possible. Already, I've spent these past few minutes thinking about *him* instead of scouring the internet for information about my opponent like I'd planned to do.

Mom and Dad are suspicious of TikTok (China), but you wouldn't believe the stuff people post about themselves. Sometimes that can translate to an on-court advantage. I'm hoping my first opponent is one of those people.

Still, Noah's waiting for an answer. "You've gotta eat, don't you?" he asks.

I do need to. In fact, I need to ASAP because I just worked out. Already, my phone is chirping with a warning that my blood sugar is low. Conversation with Noah *definitely* doesn't come before my physical health.

But I have to know. I don't examine why. I force down exactly two-and-a-half dusty, gritty glucose tablets to buy a few extra minutes. Just enough to get my question answered.

"What did you mean by *one of those?*"

Noah scrunches his eyebrows in confusion.

"Earlier," I say. "When we were looking at the draws. You said 'Oh, you're one of *those.*'"

Noah chuckles like he has a private joke with himself and I instantly regret asking. "I take it back," he says, waving his hand to cancel it. "I take it all back."

Now I *definitely* want to know what it is.

I've spent a lifetime weathering criticism. I just want to know. "Tell me."

"Why do you want to know? I already took it back."

Why *do* I want to know? Wasn't I about to feed myself?

"Fine, don't tell me," I say, turning to leave. "I don't care."

"Wait wait wait, don't leave."

I turn expectantly.

"If I tell you, will you come with me to grab food?"

"No."

My answer is automatic, like a reflex.

"All right, fine, I'll tell you anyway." He sighs. Someone should teach him how negotiations work. "I thought you were just your average mean hot girl."

No one, in the history of my entire life, has ever described me as *hot*. Cute, maybe, when I was a kid. Pretty, when the oums are trying to convince me to "soften up." But never hot.

I'm actually stunned into silence.

I want to know what he thinks now—why he changed his mind. But I have too much self-respect to ask.

He answers anyway. "Then I saw you play. You're the farthest thing from average."

He's looking at me like, well . . . like everyone else looks at Violetta. It's weird and uncomfortable. Like my skin is itchy and too tight. Especially because he said it was about my tennis and not my looks. Somehow this feels more personal.

I hate it.

Before he can say another word, I grab my things and flee without saying goodbye. *You're the farthest thing from average* echoes in my head all the way back to my villa.

THURSDAY, JULY 6TH

QUALIFYING TOURNAMENT,
ROUND OF 32

5
ALICE

I PROCRASTINATE ALL MORNING, PUTTING OFF THE INEVITABLE: MY FIRST match. I fiddle with my hair in the mirror, wrangling my curls into some kind of low bun, dozens of bobby pins holding down the fuzzies around my face. It's easier to occupy my mind with this trivial thing I never care about than to let myself think of stepping on court again after all these weeks.

Yesterday, I was tempted to just never register, but my roommates strong-armed me and now I'm stuck.

Roommates.

I am roommates with Violetta Masuda.

I know social media is not real life, but Violetta seems so similar to her online persona, it makes me think she is the only "recognizable personality" to be her genuine self on camera. I've seen so many of her videos and now being in her space, I feel like I already know her.

Of course, she doesn't know me. Because I am the kind of person who leaves their account blank, using it only to watch the lives of others. I'm nothing more than a starstruck teen while Violetta is practically an adult, living independently and making all her own decisions. She even earns her own money!

I think about this as I cross the grounds, winding through the patterned gardens until I reach the check-in tent—the row of them down to just one today—where every player seems to fall into one of two camps: a child with a parent or coach, or an independent teen, like Violetta.

I am neither.

Instead, I'm a child without an escort, unwilling independence foisted upon me without warning. I'm already approaching tears by the time I reach Janice, the woman from yesterday. "Oh!" She gives a little noise of surprise when I tell her my name. "You should've checked in earlier, darlin'. You're at the satellite site today. La Santé."

She pronounces it *luh san-tayyyy*.

Another prominent French prison.

"It's really just a high school, but you know they had to rename it something fancy to match the tournament," she winks, oblivious to my growing alarm.

I don't do well with surprises these days. I clutch my hands to my chest to keep myself from going into panic mode, where the only thing that soothes me absolutely *cannot* be done out here.

"What does that mean?" I manage to keep my voice only a tiny bit shaky.

"It means you've got to take the shuttle over there, but . . ." She checks her watch and frowns. "It looks like you just missed it. You'll have to wait another fifteen to twenty minutes for it to come back." She pulls out a paper map and slaps it down in front of her. "The good news is, it's really only about a six- or seven-minute drive, which should give you plenty of time," she says, highlighting the route with a blue pen.

My throat goes dry and it takes everything inside me to keep my mouth shut. But I have to tell her. "I don't have a car," I whisper, fighting back the tears that are all too ready to burst out at any moment.

I had no idea the tournament was going to require transportation. It was probably in the materials they mailed me upon acceptance, but I never even opened them. David was the one who found the envelope and mailed the deposit.

Acting in what he thinks is my best interest. Like a parent.

"What'd ya say, darlin'? I need you to speak up."

I swallow thickly. "I can't drive," I say, loud enough to hear now that my voice is shaking. Once again I am the child, unprepared for the realities of a situation. I allow myself to bite down on the tip of my left thumb to relieve just a fraction of my anxiety. From the outside, it will just look like I am a nail biter. Nail biting is a socially acceptable habit.

Janice gives me a sympathetic look. "Not sixteen yet, huh? You must be one of those late summer babies."

It's not like I'll get my license even once I am old enough—we don't own a car.

"There's no one who can get you there? Maybe a parent or a friend? Your coach?"

I shake my head again.

No parents. No friends. No coach.

Janice sighs, and I feel my cheeks go up in flames.

"I'm sorry," I whisper.

Coming here was a huge mistake. I am on the verge of turning around and running away when a man steps forward. "We can take you," he offers, gesturing to the teenage girl beside him. "We're running a bit late ourselves."

His smile is kind, even though he turns out to be the father of my opponent.

I follow them to their car, a moment of awkwardness when he reaches for my bag and sees that it's a free canvas tote from the SF public library and not a quilted black Chanel bag like his daughter has. Still, he places it into the trunk with care.

He seems like a good dad. Doting, careful, generous. Inside the car, he cranks the air-conditioning to give us a seven-minute reprieve from the heat and lets his daughter change the radio stations until she lands on a song she likes. He hands her a banana and she obediently peels it and begins eating, no doubt a regular pregame ritual.

I wonder if her dad is her coach and if so, what they talk about before a match. Baba would always keep it short—a directive of what my focus was that day. I'd get one text from him that would say something like:

Hit only second serves for the entire match
If the ball lands inside the service line, you must go
to the net
No overheads today, run down all lobs

Maybe this is why I remained an outsider on the team—always speaking a different metaphorical language. They never understood the point of these challenges. They played only to win.

I wish more than anything to have one of those odd directives right now.

Knowing it will be blank, I pull my phone out anyway.

No missed calls, no new messages.

My wallpaper is a picture of him in his tennis "uniform": a red windbreaker from St. Aiden's, my high school, navy blue joggers, New Balance sneakers, and a big hat with sunscreen flaps. He looks half coach, half beekeeper, and my heart squeezes just looking at this flat representation of him.

It's not until we stop that I realize I've been sucking my thumb—something I used to do only at night but seems to now plague me every hour of the day. When my opponent looks back and catches me in the act, her eyes widen and I hide my hand, but it's too late.

She knows.

We walk in awkward silence to our court, her mind no doubt full of thoughts of how childish or weird I am. She's probably wondering if I'll do it during our match and whether the balls we'll share will be wet after I've touched them.

All through the warm-up and racquet spin, I can see her eyes returning again and again to my left hand, observing my thumb in all its wrinkled glory. I'm so embarrassed, trying to cover it, that I barely notice when we officially start the match. I lose track of the score several times and the entire first set passes in a blur.

The second set starts much the same way, every shot of mine seemingly the wrong one. My slices float like they're filled with helium and my lobs linger in the air, always long enough for my opponent to get into position to put it away. Every shot I hit lacks power, every target I aim for off by feet, not inches. Even the court itself is a challenge—the clay foreign to me, every move precarious as I slide across the red dirt like an unprepared satellite on Mars.

All I can think of is what Ba would have said to focus on. I come up with nothing.

Her dad watches quietly from behind the chain-link fence, politely cheering her winners and keeping perfectly within the bounds of propriety. I suppose I thought it would be more like a jungle out here, with every player ready to rip your throat out for the win. Even when I hit the odd good shot, both she and her dad applaud my effort.

Looking at the score again, it's not difficult to see why they are able to be so polite.

I wade through the red clay, my feet seemingly underwater as my opponent hits winner after winner past me. I've become a ghost on the court, simply moving back and forth to fetch balls as she puts on a clinic of how to dismember another player in broad daylight. There is no joy to be found on this court. I am out here only because I have nowhere else to go.

I retreat further and further into the recesses of my mind, all my energy going to keeping my thumb away from my mouth. I never used to be like this.

I am so detached from my surroundings, it takes me a moment to comprehend that my opponent is lying on her back, clutching her knee and crying. There's a huge bare patch of clay trailing behind her, clearly marking the spot where she began to tumble.

Maybe my memory is like the red clay and I can go back in time to see the exact point at which it all started to go downhill.

A trainer is summoned and my opponent is examined on the ground, too weak to stand and make her way over to the chairs on the sidelines. I fetch her water bottle and tell myself I'm doing something helpful. Her dad paces anxiously behind the fence, not allowed to step on court. I wish I could give him an update.

Minutes go by and eventually the doctor who has joined the party declares her too injured to go on. She sobs openly, her dad finally able to rush on court and carry her to the car, her head buried in his shoulder. I follow quietly with her bag, her dad too polite not to offer the ride back to Bastille.

This time the air-conditioning is muted, nothing heard over the noise of my opponent's sobs. I don't know if it's because of the pain from her injury or the indignity of losing a match she was certain to win. Maybe both.

I manage to keep my thumb out of my mouth the entire way back, instead leaning my head against the window to watch the landscape go by as I clench my fists. This will probably be my only opportunity to leave San Francisco, so I had better try to at least remember something about it.

Right now, it's all a blur of red clay and Joan of Arc. And Violetta Masuda. At least I've met her.

When we arrive, I leave with a polite thanks and wishes for a quick recovery, speeding away to return the balls and report the results. Janice congratulates me on the win as if I've done anything to deserve it. This time, I am unable to summon a thank-you.

Instead, I slink away in shame, watching from behind a potted plant as Janice writes my name in on the board. I hear the gasps of shock and whispered questions of my identity, everyone wondering who exactly I am and what I've done to merit my place in this tournament.

I am no one.

And I've done nothing to deserve this.

I huddle lower.

I'm crouched low behind this plant when he spots me. Again, I've been caught with my thumb in my mouth. I don't even realize I'm doing it.

"Ms. Wu, I presume."

The past-middle-aged man is dressed in an uncomfortably tight white polo, Ray-Ban sunglasses dangling from his neck. He looks like a Bond villain if the crime were to take place at a country club.

"Stand please."

He speaks only in commands, even his questions said as assumptions to be agreed with. The principal of St. Aiden's sounded the same way. Maybe it's just the way white men in positions of power speak.

"Dick Duncan. Head of both Bastille and the Bastille Invitational." He considers offering a handshake, but pulls back and gives me a once-over. Even without consulting a mirror, I know what he'll see—hair smooshed and askew from being pressed into the back seat, dusty ankles, and a face red from both the heat and the embarrassment of overhearing others talk about me.

The evaluation is relatively fast, no more than a flick up and down my person. But even still, I can see his thoughts on his face. He wears the same generic half smile the ladies in Noe Valley use when they accidentally make eye contact with Ma while she's walking between houses with her mop and bucket of supplies. It's always accidental. It's clear they would prefer to ignore her but her presence is too conspicuous, so they exchange the bare minimum of pleasantries to avoid giving actual acknowledgment. As if treating her as an equal would somehow diminish the quality of her cleaning they've hired her for.

Mr. Duncan is giving me that same look right now. It says *You are only here by my permission. Be grateful.*

Dick Duncan is the male equivalent of a Lululemon mom.

I can already feel my blood heating.

"I see you're wearing our annual tournament shirt." He nods at the white T-shirt I'm wearing, a picture of the actual Bastille across the front. The neon-yellow words across it read *break free* in a hostile font generally reserved for vampires and slasher films, so it appears Violetta was right about its meaning.

I had chosen an extra-large with David in mind, but remembered I was upset with him, and was also too cowardly to go back and exchange it. So now its excess length is stuffed into the waistband of my shorts, the excess material puffing out from my body, shaping me into a mushroom.

"We have a dress code here at Bastille," Mr. Duncan continues, his posture more upright and his back stiffer than any ballet teacher's in the history of humankind. "If you consult the handbook that was mailed to you, you will see that we don't allow T-shirts of any kind on the court."

"Then why do you give them to us when we first get here?"

I may have been a little dazed yesterday, but I clearly remember being handed this T-shirt before even getting my match time. "Free" with the price of admission and cost of boarding at the tournament. Rich people really are the stingiest.

The tournament director reacts clearly to my tone, which is neither hostile nor wondering—but his lips thin anyway. "Those are meant to be a souvenir. A keepsake for players to remember their time here, however long or short it may be."

He pauses on the word *short*. Barely perceptible, but I understand his message.

This is an adult who demands to be in charge. The teachers at St. Aiden's were like that. My old school, before St. Aiden's, was collaborative and informal—teachers went by their first names and class input was always taken seriously. At St. Aiden's, the teachers teach and the student learn. There is a clear line between the two, and I am never unclear about the fact that I am not an equal there.

I go from being a child at home to a child at school to now, a child at tennis.

"Then wouldn't it be a better idea to give them out at the end?" I ask. "To preserve this beautiful artwork?"

I don't mean for the words to come out quite as sarcastically as they do, but my mouth has a mind of its own right now and that mind is intent on speaking its truth at all costs.

The T-shirts are atrocious.

Dick Duncan frowns and I see the lines deepen in his face. They shout that he's spent a lifetime in the sun, his skin baked like worn leather.

"When we admitted you into the invitational on the recommendation of Nancy Conrad, we were under the impression you would conduct yourself in accordance with our rules and regulations. If that's going to be a problem for you—"

"No problem," I rush to say. I even duck my head a little, to show deference. The less of my face he sees, the better I am able to feign remorse. Yet another trick I picked up at private school, watching and mirroring the other scholarship students to remain under the radar.

He eyes me with the skepticism normally directed at teenage boys of color walking through corner stores or crowded together on a street. At least once a week, I see police officers parked outside Clancy Liquors, questioning a boy on the sidewalk. I always want to scream at them, to tell the boys to stop going somewhere they're treated like this. But I'm not one to talk—coming to Bastille, already knowing it would be like this.

I wonder if anyone around even notices me; notices the way I've been singled out for this scolding. I am a newcomer here, the other players just a collection of convenience store owners questioning my intentions.

I thought I'd lost my capacity to feel, but humiliation is less an emotion and more an experience. And right now I am having a solitary, immersive experience with Mr. Duncan's disapproval of me.

All I want to do is go somewhere to hide and suck my thumb until I fall back into blissful sleep, where nothing has changed— Ba is home, I'm at my old school, and David doesn't look quite so tired.

Instead, I stand stock-still until Mr. Duncan decides he's done inspecting me. His frown deepens as he says, "Consider this a warning, Ms. Wu. If you breach the dress code again, there *will* be consequences."

6

LEYLAH

I CHECK IN FOR MY MATCH AND JUST MY LUCK, DICK IS THERE AT THE TENT. Between him and Violetta, I may never know peace.

I hear him scold Alice for her wardrobe, and her surprisingly sassy comeback. Maybe it's too early to write her off as a loss to Violetta. Alice contains hidden depths.

My mouth moves before my brain can process what it's doing. "Found someone new to bully, Dick?"

His name feels crisp. *Dick.* Like my mouth can't wait to cut off the end of his name.

He gives me the sickening smile he wears like a clown mask. I just know behind all that leathery skin is a rotting carcass of evil.

"Ms. Lee." He makes a big show of checking the shiny watch on his wrist. Alice sees her opening. She shoots me a grateful look before fleeing in the opposite direction. "You're late. According to the match time listed on the draw, you were due to check in two minutes ago."

I'd run back to the villa to grab another on-court snack in case my match goes long and my blood sugar runs low because it's hotter than usual today, but I'm not about to give him the satisfaction of explaining that. He's one of those people who would just see it as "making excuses" anyway.

I smile back, just as fake. "Thanks for the update, Dick, but I'm still within the ten-minute grace period."

Guess who else knows the tournament rules?

Five points for me.

Dick frowns. "That is meant as a courtesy, not an invitation for you to bend the rules to your will."

"I'm not bending the rules." I ball my fists to remind myself of how much it would actually hurt to punch him in the face. "The rules literally give you a ten-minute grace period. Which I'm using."

"It is meant for players stuck in an emergency situation, Ms. Lee, not because you cannot keep track of the time."

I'd say my body going into diabetic ketoacidosis would be an emergency situation but there's no point in arguing. Dick is probably already looking for ways to penalize me for daring to come back to this tournament at all.

I check in with Janice, the only friendly face here. She tells me my opponent already has the balls and is waiting on court 22. The farthest court from the tent.

Of course.

"Ms. Lee?"

I reluctantly turn to face Dick, who is determined to get off one last blast. I'm so irritated I can't even enjoy my unintended joke. "I'm sure I don't need to remind you of our code of conduct here," he says. "But if you require a brush up, I'm sure I can find another copy for your study."

I don't know how I'm keeping a straight face right now because I fucking despise this man. However much I despised him yesterday, or even two years ago, is nothing compared to how much I despise him right this second. I actually wish I could reverse time to the beginning of this conversation so I could be sure to despise him enough while he talked at me.

Two-years-ago Leylah would have said something. But this-year Leylah can't. Free speech here is a fucking luxury because I can guarantee I've never said anything on court worse than any other player, but I've never seen anyone penalized like I was.

Michelle Obama and her "when they go low, we go high" bullshit—it's the same thing my parents preach.

Respectability.

Perception.

There's no opting out of representing your community.

"Was there something you wanted to add?" he prompts. He's giving me the chance to toss myself overboard so he can save himself the hassle of shoving me himself.

I point at the giant clock behind his head. "Wouldn't want to run past the grace period. We both know just how *gracious* you are."

Okay, so this-year Leylah still splurges a little here and there. It's not like his opinion of me can get any worse.

Dick glares at me under the guise of a concerned adult. "No need to worry, I'll be watching the clock closely."

"Wish me luck!" I call out as I go. I cackle to myself all the way to court 22, thinking of how Dick finally admitted aloud that he wants nothing more than for me to lose.

7

VIOLETTA

IT'S FUNNY. EVEN THOUGH SHE'S MY MOM, EVERY TIME I SEE HER—FOR just a fraction of a second—it feels like I'm seeing her for the first time. Thin eyes, delicate frame, dark brown hair, and creamy-white skin. She's the poster child of what most people expect to see when they say "mixed Asian American."

But it's not just her exterior—Audrey Masuda radiates power. Confidence. Without knowing anything else about her, you would undoubtedly guess she was a celebrity. Maybe a CEO somewhere. Socialite. There's just an . . . aura . . . about her.

But then I remember why she's here, and my joy dips.

I thought I'd have more time to prepare.

"What are you doing here?" I ask, stepping off the court with the rest of my practice group.

The invitational takes over the red clay courts, so our practices have been relegated to the hard courts and green clay for the rest of the week. It's cleaner, at least, but more physically taxing. The heat is bothering me today and I'm sweating more than usual.

If I'd known she was going to ambush me, I would have at least made sure my hair was smooth and my neck free of pooled sweat.

Swea*ting*: perfectly normal for someone, say, playing tennis.

Sweat*y*: someone who is wet and possibly stinky.

Audrey arches a perfectly shaped brow—thanks to the magic of microblading—lifting a medium-size brown paper bag and showing off her perfectly respectable beige fingernails. "Do I need an invitation to bring you lunch?"

I paste on a smile. "Of course not. Thanks for bringing food."

Something tells me she won't have brought fresh chocolate chip cookies from Burgundy, aka the cafeteria. Those cookies are my favorite thing about Bastille, hands down.

She raises to her tiptoes, resting her hands on my shoulders as she gives me air-kisses on each side. It's very European. I wonder if she first started doing it when she joined the tour or if she did it to impress my dad. Or maybe she learned it from *her* dad, who was also white and European. Either way, it's definitely not Japanese.

The familiar scent of her cigarette smoke and musky perfume overwhelms me. Audrey's convinced anything even remotely fruity smelling will make her seem unserious, but I don't tell her she currently smells like an elderly person, still clinging to perfumes of the distant past.

I'm slick with sweat, but I pull out the lavender-scented lotion I always keep in my bag anyway. I sneak a quick inhale before spreading it across my hands and arms. It feels greasy and oppressive, but it does the trick. I can no longer smell the cigarettes and perfume.

"You should be wearing your visor," she chides. "You're starting to get too dark."

I look down at my tanned skin wondering on what planet I am considered "dark." At best, I look like a typical California white girl who sees the sun. If I dyed my hair blond, no one would even believe I had Japanese ancestry. As it is, I'm only linked to Audrey by last name and our matching brown hair. The idea of changing it seems . . . wrong, somehow. Like a betrayal.

"I was hoping to get freckles," I admit. Though maybe I *am* too dark to get the pale spray of little dots across my nose and cheeks like Alice has.

"Freckles are nothing more than sun damage, darling," Audrey frowns. "And wrinkles and skin cancer can happen at any age."

I'm saved by a voice.

"*Benvenuta*, Ms. Masuda," Leylah singsongs in a falsetto. It's a nice touch, using a greeting she knows will remind Audrey of my biological dad, an Italian player who used to bring me to Cinnabon once a year when he passed through Connecticut but never contacted me otherwise.

Post idea: favorite cheat day spots

Audrey's smile looks strained. "Please. Just Audrey. You know that."

If there is anything Audrey hates more than being reminded of my dad, it's being reminded that she's old in any way. Hence, Leylah's use of "Ms."

She leans in to offer even closer air-kisses, which I delight in watching Leylah endure. "I did hear you'd be coming, but seeing you here in person is a different matter entirely," Audrey says. "It's been what, two years?"

I should have known Audrey wouldn't let Leylah slip in an insult like that without retaliating. Leylah might have accused me of playing the long game, but Audrey is the master of it. Hold until the right moment, then twist the knife.

It's almost its own form of art.

But Leylah keeps her face perfectly serene. "I'm sure you remember the date better than I do."

Leylah can't even be within ten feet of me without snarling but somehow stays totally composed with Audrey. All the while, I'm sweating lavender and wishing I were somewhere else.

Audrey pats her arm. "Well, you're back now. And in the qualifiers!" She adds this last piece with a bright voice, as though it's the good type of surprise.

I see Leylah swallow, her jaw tightening ever so slightly. It's barely noticeable, but I see it. *This* was the twist of the knife.

But Leylah recovers. "Well, I already won my match today, so only two more to go. By the time I face Violetta—if she makes it there—I should be in top form."

She turns her smile on me like a serial killer who's found her next target. In all the years we've played against each other, I've only ever beaten her once.

"I'd love to stay and catch up," Audrey lies. "But I'm afraid Violetta only gets so much time for lunch. These coaches here keep such a tight schedule, you know." She pauses. "Well, you can imagine."

I need to end the bloodbath. I grab Audrey by the arm, not concerned with wrinkling her silk blouse. "I'm starving, let's go."

Leylah makes some kind of sound of agreement. "Mm. Enjoy your salad. I'm going to go eat a giant bowl of pasta in the cafeteria."

Pasta is my favorite food. I'm not sure Leylah can even eat pasta, the high carbohydrate count essentially a sugar bomb. Which is how I know she said it just to mess with me.

Not wanting to let her have the last word, I call out to her retreating form, "It's called Burgundy because of the cuisine!"

8

VIOLETTA

AUDREY AND I GRAB TWO BENCHES INSIDE THE LOUVRE, WHOSE FAMOUS glass pyramid has been stripped to just its outer framework, creating a sort of pergola under which to place benches. The entire structure is located within the Monet garden, which is the prettiest spot on campus, with scores of wildflowers growing from every direction. I don't typically spend time here, but it's Audrey's favorite spot and I don't want to do anything to upset her more than she already is.

I mentally send a sarcastic thanks to Leylah for leaving me to deal with it.

Audrey pulls out two boxes from the bag she's brought. My stomach sinks as I realize it is, in fact, two salads. The fact that Leylah guessed correctly irritates me.

I'm determined to turn this into a positive. Even if this particular salad has kidney beans as its only protein.

Post idea: the benefits of a predetermined meal schedule

I try not to think about Leylah's pasta, but fettuccini Alfredo is calling out to me, trying to lure me into Burgundy. *You can have chocolate chip cookies for dessert*, it whispers.

Audrey must see the look on my face because she remarks, "Carbohydrates will burn through your system too quickly. This will give you more sustained energy; not to mention it's much healthier. A little thank-you wouldn't be misplaced."

"Thank you," I automatically reply, but my focus is still on the salad in my lap. I hate kidney beans. The texture is all wrong and they have practically no flavor. They're the unflavored oatmeal of the bean world.

"Oh, what is it now?" Audrey asks with an eye roll.

I debate telling her. She already thinks I'm ungrateful for her coming today, I don't want to then complain about the food she brought.

Post idea: acclimating to new foods

"Well?" she prompts.

I relent. "I don't like kidney beans." I don't point out that she knows this about me.

Audrey huffs an exasperated sigh and thrusts her salad into my hands, taking mine off my lap. "Goodness. So much drama over something so little."

I didn't think I was making it dramatic at all, but I *am* grateful that whatever it was, it got me a much better-looking salad with black beans and charred corn. We eat in silence as I stew over our earlier interaction with Leylah.

She and Audrey never quite got along and I know what'll happen if I bring her up, but I can't help myself. It's like I *need* to talk about her with someone, and Audrey is the closest thing I have to a best friend.

"Did you notice how skinny Leylah was?" I use my baiting voice—the one that's meant to entice gossip. "She looks like she did right before she got diagnosed."

Leylah had been so stoic when she told me about her type 1 diabetes diagnosis. Matter-of-fact. No tears, no drama over the unfairness of it all. Just tunnel vision ahead, to how she could best manage it while continuing to train.

Until she couldn't.

"Mm," Audrey murmurs. "Nimbler feet. She's already quick but with a lighter frame, she could do a lot of damage at the net. You'll need to look out for that."

Five minutes ago, Audrey was doing her best to cut Leylah into bits. But now that it's just the two of us, she wants to remind me of how much better Leylah is than me—or *was*.

"Getting a little ahead of yourself," I mutter to myself.

Audrey hears me anyway and pins me with a stare. "It would be unwise to underestimate her, darling. I think you know that better than anyone else."

"I'm not underestimating," I protest, annoyed that I brought her up in the first place. I definitely knew better. "I just don't need the extra stress when I might not even have to play her."

Audrey tsks as she wraps up the other half of her salad. No matter the meal, she always eats only half. Precisely. The other half goes straight into the refrigerator, to be eaten as the next meal. She calls it a remnant from the early days of being a single mom—falling back on her training and willpower to stretch her dollars as far as they could go—but I think we both know she does it to maintain her figure. It's also why she picked up smoking.

"You can't afford to stress. If the two of you are rooming together, she'll be tracking every single thing you do. You'll need to keep your composure or she'll pounce on it immediately." She carefully reapplies her lipstick—a bright cherry red—using her phone camera. I tried to wear it once and I looked like a clown.

"My other roommate is in the 16U draw," I offer, hoping to now change the subject away from Leylah. "Her name is Alice Wu. She's Taiwanese and very, very sweet. I think this is her first time away from home."

Audrey waves away the information. "Don't get too attached, darling. She's probably one of those players who qualify for one big tournament in their life, and this is it. Don't waste your time on a nobody who likely won't even make the main draw."

I frown at the double standard. "But you just said to focus—"

"Not everyone is Leylah Lê, darling. And I don't want you to *focus* on her; just be aware. Friends close, enemies closer, et cetera, et cetera."

Is Leylah my enemy?

She's certainly not my friend.

"I'm so *aware* of her I've hardly been able to concentrate on anything else for the last twenty-four hours," I grumble. "It feels like I'm living in a tiger den, trying to avoid getting eaten."

"That's always been your weakness," Audrey says. She gently blots the invisible oil on her forehead before dusting finishing powder over it, returning her skin back to its perfect porcelain complexion. "You lack that killer instinct with her. Maybe observing her this week will teach you how to better assert yourself."

My mom thinks I'm spineless. Cool.

"She didn't hesitate to cut you," Audrey continues, "so you should be just as eager to attack. If there's a tiger den, *you* need to be the tiger."

"Okay, got it." I just need her to stop talking about Leylah. Anything to get her to stop talking about Leylah.

But she doesn't stop. It's like I'm not even here, the way Audrey drives home all the ways I fall short. "She always maintained that champion's mentality, no matter the occasion. I know you think of yourself as *likable* and that's wonderful, darling. It will be helpful with the sponsors. But your number one desire should be to win. Not just on the court but always. This is crunch time and we can't afford to laze about."

"I'm not *lazing about*," I snap. "I'm playing two different age categories—singles *and* doubles—while still keeping a full social media schedule. What else do you want from me?"

If we weren't having lunch together, I'd be spending this time shooting and editing segments for next week when I'll be too busy playing. Already, I can feel my muscles tensing at the thought of all the things I need to get done in the next few days. My schedule is so full, I can barely afford the time off I'm taking for this lunch right now.

Audrey waits until I've fully calmed down before she peeks over into my box. I've eaten every single bite—I couldn't seem to help myself. "I suppose I really *should* get you that salad next time," she says with a resigned sigh. "No sense in wasting money on something you won't eat."

I don't tell her I wish she'd bring pasta next time.

We rise and she gives me the same cheek kisses as before. But instead of pulling back right away, she keeps her hands on my shoulders. I'm trying desperately to breathe only through my mouth and not my nose, but the smell is getting through anyway. My stomach is starting to revolt.

"This is your year, darling. I can feel it."

She waves goodbye and I rush to the closest bathroom, needing to get this food out of my body as quickly as possible. Not until I've forced out every single bit of it do I finally stop smelling Audrey's perfume.

9

ALICE

THE REPRIMAND FROM MR. DUNCAN ABOUT MY CLOTHING SHAKES ME up more than I'd like it to. Maybe because everyone has been handling me with kid gloves lately, but I am privately outraged at his thinly veiled threats.

No one threatened me so directly at St. Aidan's, but the shame feels the same anyway. The knowledge that I am out of place—easily identified as the person who doesn't belong. Even without a name tag, Mr. Duncan immediately knew who I was. He'd probably been searching for me since my application was approved, lying in wait to ensure I knew I wasn't welcome.

At least at St. Aidan's, the coach never mentioned Nancy Conrad. We both knew she was the reason I'd been "recruited" to the team in the first place, being a prominent donor of the school and all, but he'd been friendly enough. He'd introduced me to the team not as a scholarship recipient, but as a regular transfer student—a sophomore looking for tougher competition and better visibility with college coaches.

It's always been Baba's dream for me to play college tennis; it was the whole reason I'd applied to the Bastille Invitational in the first place. I was sure I wouldn't qualify, even with all-conference honors.

I wander through the plazas again, looking at each and every Joan of Arc fountain until I've exhausted them all. My favorite is the simplest one—Joan in soft clothing instead of armor, her hand cupped around an ear, listening for something. I feel that way now, just waiting for a higher power to tell me what I should do with my life.

I have never felt as weak as I do here, mixed in among people like Violetta and Leylah, who are both so sure of who they are and what their purpose is. Leylah is Joan with armor, charging into battle, while Violetta is Joan in her gentle peasant clothes, triumphantly holding up the flag. I am the Joan who is waiting, listening, unable to move forward without guidance.

But without Baba, who's left to guide me? Who would I even trust to do so?

I've always been a little more disconnected from the world than most people. I find safety in solitude and prefer quiet to noise. But even that has not prepared me for this place, where I am constantly surrounded by people but feel lonelier than ever.

We have nothing in common, these other players and me. Some, like Violetta, make friends in an instant, constantly social-izing and staying busy with their own interests. I noticed Violetta was up late last night, replying to messages to her account, reaching out to the tens of thousands of followers who care enough to check in on her every day.

I steer clear of the Observatory, where other players have already started to gather as their matches wrap up, instead heading for the beach. It's a little over a mile to get there, but I barely feel it. The hills of San Francisco have made me into a flat-surface Olympian, able to walk to any destination on a whim.

David used to be the spontaneous one, always urging me to go with him on a run somewhere new in the city. I always said yes, even if it was all the way across the Golden Gate Bridge, because I trusted him to get us home safely.

Today I am forced to be my own navigator.

I run across the sand, reveling in the feel of my feet sinking and hoping it will swallow me whole. But it doesn't and I reach the shoreline, scattering the birds, yelling at them with this pent-up anger that has nowhere else to go.

Baba is gone. And it seems he took the rest of us with him.

Mama, David, Ahma, and I all exist as ghosts, unable to take up physical space as our auras float past and through each other. David calls, but he's only a facade of himself, talking to a facade of myself. Mama doesn't call at all. I wonder, as I skirt the edge of the water, whether I even leave footprints in the sand or if this is just another activity—like school and finals and even packing for this trip—where I go through the motions like a shadow on the wall.

I run faster, the frothy rim of the tide clinging to the hem of my shorts as each step kicks up spray. The drips on my legs evaporate quickly, leaving behind the coarse salt that chafes the insides of my thighs as they continue to swipe past each other.

The pain fuels me.

Since Baba has been gone, all I experience is pain. Stabbing, aching, throbbing, burning, fiery pain. I feel it every time I think of him and every time I don't think of him; every time I wish he were here and every time I realize he isn't. I feel it when I curl up into myself and suck my thumb, wondering if there will ever come a time when I no longer need to. Pain reminds me that I'm still alive—that I am choosing to stay alive when others do not and have not.

Whatever lesson it was Baba wanted to teach me with this, all I've gotten out of it is this anger.

My lungs are burning, the gulps of hot air searing my lungs with each breath. A stitch has worked its way into my side, spearing me all the way through like a pig on a roasting spit. I have been stabbed and seared, his death a surprise only to me, for I am the pig to be celebrated around in the Wu household. One-fifth of our household is no longer with us, but we must act as though nothing has changed. We are all adhering to the dream of a man who deserted us. Betrayed us.

Betrayed me.

Salt is running down into my eyes and I can't tell if it's the ocean or my own sweat, but I swipe it with the back of my hand and keep running, pressing through the hot needles that have taken over my skin. I am so hot now I'm shivering.

I never sweat in San Francisco. At least, almost never. But I am not myself here. I am a representative of the Wu family, showcasing all they have sacrificed to get me here. The judgments of others are judgments of them, of how I have been raised and bred, trained without the aid of expensive coaches and prestigious tournaments.

I am the poster child for underdogs, the feel-good story that gets people excited about sports for a moment before returning to their daily lives. Except this story is my life and I no longer want any part of it.

All that sacrifice. For nothing.

The sand is kicking up onto the backs of my legs and sliding its way down into my shoes as if stowing away for an adventure, my footsteps falling more heavily into the ground with each step. My muscles are weakening, their sounds of protest growing louder, and I can almost imagine myself tumbling down into the sand—the tiny shards of what was once stone cutting across my skin, bleeding the pain out drop by drop.

I push myself farther, just another hundred feet—then another hundred feet past that. I can barely breathe at this point, my swollen lungs pressing against my chest, trying to find another fraction of an inch to expand and find air, my heart beating so loudly it surpasses even the waves. But I feel them. They burn so brightly in my chest, like the illuminated sunlight of a Renaissance painting, casting a glow on my entire being.

Maybe this pain will kill me.

But guilt rushes in before I can stop it—the black hole that sucks away all emotions, reminding me that death is never a simple choice. And that as angry as I am, I could never force my family to endure this kind of grief again.

The shame of thinking it—even for a moment—crushes me and I stumble. My legs give out like those of a collapsed table, the contents atop it spilling over the edge and onto the ground with a mighty crash. Nothing breaks, and yet everything breaks. In the sand, I am now a still life portrait—a scattered assembly of everyday household objects that mean nothing to the viewer and everything to the person who painted them.

10

VIOLETTA

AUDREY AND I TOURED A NUMBER OF ACADEMIES WHEN WE DISCUSSED my leaving school to go full-time. I'd spent six weeks one winter at IMG and another two at Evert, but Bastille was always my first choice. From the moment I stepped on campus and saw the colorful villas meant to replicate Colmar, I thought this place was magical. I still do, to some extent.

But what really sold me were the windowsills. The deep, wide framing of each window, every single one of them painted a bright white. Along the back wall of my room, the sill is one long continuous bench—just low enough for me to climb in and out of. I took one look at those, the sunlight streaming in like in a photograph, and knew I *needed* them in my life.

I use them every day, like my own version of a prayer altar. Sometimes it's to exhale out the window so the entire room doesn't smell like weed, sometimes it's to take pictures for my social media—my presence inside the huge frame lends a little extra glamour to all of my photos. Sometimes I even sit in it like a cat would, warming myself in the sunlight that streams through the panes.

I'm sitting there now, reminiscing about life before I moved here as I dutifully direct my exhales outside, when Alice staggers in. Her face is a shade of red I've never seen before and her eyes are glassy and unfocused. I do my best to quickly hide my oil pen and fan the air around me to dissipate the smell but I don't think she even notices me.

"Alice! Are you okay?"

She collapses in the doorway and my heart stops.

Not again.

I don't hesitate. I jump off the windowsill and sprint toward her. Even steps away, I recognize the smell of vomit on her breath. It's one of the reasons I always carry mints. "Alice, can you hear me?" She's hot to the touch. My heart racing, I pick her up by the shoulders and drag her limp body into the shower as quickly as I can, even though both of us are still fully clothed.

The effort leaves me strained and panting, but I manage to turn on the tap. Still kneeling over her, cool water raining down, I try to revive her by tapping the sides of her face. "Alice, it's Violetta. Can you hear me? Alice? Alice?" Adrenaline is overriding my buzz, all my muscles tense as I hope my slaps are as gentle as I think they are. "Shit, I should have called 911."

It's what I should have done two years ago.

The memory of seeing a collapsed body floods my brain and I wonder for the millionth time how I could have frozen in that moment. Why my first instinct *hadn't* been to call 911.

It plays over and over as I slap and shake her, until Alice finally opens her eyes.

"No . . . ambulance," she says weakly. "No! Ambulance."

At least she's conscious now.

I heave a sigh of relief and lean back against the cold tiles of the shower, but my heart is still thumping wildly in my chest. "What happened?"

Alice's eyes are mostly closed like she's half asleep, but she manages fragments of words. "I tried . . . go running . . . too hot . . ."

Considering it's about one hundred degrees outside and she lives next to the ocean, it's no wonder her body overheated! If I know that, why doesn't she? Shouldn't she have felt herself getting faint? Even when I'm high, I'm aware of myself enough to not get hurt. Can't anyone be responsible for their own health?

"Of course it was too hot for you!" I explode, pushing off the wall with renewed energy. "This is the worst time of day to work out! You need to go either before the sun comes up or after it goes down. And why were you running so much in the first place? Don't you have a match tomorrow? You could have at least used one of the treadmills in the exercise room." I let out a breathy curse, pushing my hands through my hair in disbelief that history could so closely repeat itself. "You almost scared me to death!"

A ghost of a smile appears, curving her lips upward. I think it's the first smile I've seen from her. "Sorry."

We both sit with heaving chests, our breath eventually slowing as water continues to run over us. From this distance, the spray of freckles across Alice's nose and cheeks is much more visible. The symmetry of the pattern across her face is so balanced I can barely believe they're real. It's like I'm looking at her through a filter, the most perfect proportions already selected for each feature and tidily organized on her face. I feel a faint stab of jealousy.

But I spend so much time staring at my own face, it's nice to finally have a moment to stare at someone else's. She has a sort of porcelain-doll look—pretty but fragile—only to be handled with extreme care. She came here alone. Maybe this is what both of us needed: the chance to explore a different kind of life.

Her eyes are downcast, seemingly focused on a spot just beyond our tangled feet. "Noooooooo," she groans, pulling off her shoes which sends a cascade of sand down the drain. "My shoes."

Oops. "Sorry," I apologize. "I was just focused on getting you cooled down as quickly as possible. Maybe I overreacted?"

"No, no. You saved me," Alice says. "Thank you."

She gives me a grateful smile and her eyes soften, like she can see how badly I needed a crisis to solve—needed to prove that I could really do it all. Whatever happened two years ago is ancient history and today, I saved someone who needed it.

Being a doctor must be amazing.

"Do you want me to call someone for you? Maybe your parents?" I don't want to seem like I'm prying. But also, I am prying. Just a little.

"Par*ent*," Alice corrects. "Just my mom. But no. I'll be fine."

I wonder what happened to her dad—whether she lost him recently, or whether he's always been out of the picture like mine.

"Is it just the two of you?"

Alice shakes her head, but her movements are still lethargic. It's a slow shake, almost like she's unsure of her answer. "I have a brother, David. My grandma lives at home with us too."

My heart sinks a little. She has a whole family back at home. She's not like me at all. I push the selfish thought away. "That must be nice, having a brother."

Alice goes quiet and I wonder if there's tension there too. I prod just a little more.

"Are the two of you close?"

"We used to be." She seems sad, turning the soggy shoe over in her hands. "I guess I'll have to buy a new pair at the pro shop tomorrow," she says, more to herself.

It's then I notice she's holding court shoes and not running sneakers. She went running in her court shoes?

"Do you run a lot at home?" I ask tentatively. Maybe she'd just forgotten to pack them.

Alice shakes her head. "I hate running."

Well, that explains the shoe choice. I just wonder what pushed her to do it today. "Running isn't my favorite either," I say truthfully. "The only way Coop gets me to do it is to go with me. I know it's important for training, but it's so boring."

"Coop . . . like Cooper Nelsen?" she asks.

I can't help the smile that forms at the thought of him. "Yeah. He came on as a coach here a little over two years ago. Just before I started full-time."

"So is he like a . . . dad . . . to you?" she ventures.

I make a face. "A dad? Cooper? Ew, no. As far as I'm concerned, I have no dad. Coop and I are just friends."

"Friends," she repeats slowly. "Isn't he kind of . . . old?" Alice's head tips to the side as she studies me. Her gaze is steady and unnerving. I hadn't planned to answer questions about myself.

"We're only nine years apart," I say defensively. "Considering I've been on my own for the last two years, we have a lot more in common than you think. He's been through all of this before, you know?"

"Aren't the other girls who go here going through the same thing as you?"

I don't know how to explain that I don't make close friends anymore. "It's not the same," I say. "Coop and I aren't competing so there's no conflict of interest. I don't have to worry if he's going to turn on me or stop being friends with me out of nowhere the way other girls do, you know?"

Alice frowns. "Not really. Do people do that? Drop their friends out of nowhere?"

I'm saved from having to answer when the door swings open and Leylah's head peeks in. Her eyes pop out as she takes in the scene. "What in the *Grey's Anatomy* is going on in here?"

Only now do I notice the water is still running. I reach up and twist the knob to turn it off. "Alice passed out. Heat exhaustion."

Something flashes across Leylah's face, but it's gone before I can figure out what it is. She gives a small nod—an acknowledgment that I've finally done something right in her eyes. It shouldn't matter, but I'm pleased anyway.

"How are you feeling?" she asks Alice.

"Better, thanks to Violetta."

Leylah opens, then closes her mouth, as if she considered saying something but decided not to. Instead, she disappears for a moment and reappears with a suger-free sports drink and a banana.

"I only have blue flavor," she says, handing it to Alice. "Drink the whole bottle and eat the banana—you need potassium."

It's silly, but part of me is annoyed that Leylah is here, taking charge. Everything she's said is probably right, and I'm sure she knows more than I do about managing blood sugar. But it bothers me that she swooped in here, thinking she fixed things. *I'm* the one who got Alice into the shower to bring down her temperature. And I did it a lot nicer too.

Alice moves to stand and I rush to help her up. "Let me get you a towel," I say. But Leylah already has it in hand, offering it to her like a bathroom valet.

I notice she doesn't offer me one.

"Can you hand me my towel, please?" I ask.

Leylah tosses it to me without looking and it partially unfolds in the air, my face hit with a not unsubstantial part of it. "What were you doing that made you pass out?" she asks Alice.

Alice and I exchange a look before she answers, "Running."

Leylah looks at us like we're hiding something. And it's silly, but it kind of feels like we are—like we shared this moment together, just the two of us.

"Well, you need to rest," Leylah advises. "You have two matches tomorrow."

I clap my hands in excitement. "Ooh, that's right, doubles starts." Doubles is my favorite. "You got paired with Alyssa Avila. She's from Argentina originally but I think she lives in Spain now? Not a very big hitter."

Audrey wouldn't be happy about me sharing intel but I doubt it'll tip the scales. They're still in the qualifiers. Besides, Oksana and I are the number six seed in the 16U doubles main draw so I can afford to be generous.

Alice nods and exits the bathroom to get dressed, leaving Leylah and me to stare each other down.

It's almost weird how little her face has changed. Same sharp eyes, same sharp cheekbones. Even if she weren't currently frowning at me—which she is—she'd still look this severe. Exactly the opposite of Alice. Maybe this is what Audrey means about keeping a killer instinct at all times.

Post idea: staying calm when silently threatened

I can tell Leylah's struggling with the decision of what to do next—stay and protect Alice from me, or escape. A weird part of me wants her to stay, just so I can prove what a good friend I am. *Look! I might have saved her life! And she's grateful for it!* But I'm not going to be the first one to break. I stare at her, daring Leylah to say something, until she finally does.

"Make sure she stays hydrated," she says gruffly before stalking back out.

I hear Leylah grab her bag before shutting the villa door and give a sigh of relief.

11

LEYLAH

VIOLETTA IS LIKE A SAUNA—HER PRESENCE SUFFOCATES EVERYONE AROUND her for no goddamn reason even though people insist it's healthy. Even after she leaves, the whole damn space smells like lavender. Like she's forcing us all to think about her all the time.

I breathe easier outside.

I feel guilty about leaving Alice in that condition, but I physically could not be there anymore. Seeing Violetta save Alice and then sticking around after? Making sure she was okay?

The ugly parts of my heart threaten revolt.

I walk faster, swinging my arms and picking my feet up off the ground, keeping my brain busy as I wind through campus. This way, there's no room to think about anything else.

There are kids at the pool, aka the Riviera (yes, like the French one). They're screwing around and diving in, ignoring the NO DIVING signs everywhere. I'm not exactly the poster child for rule following but I'm at least smart enough not to bash my head in four feet of water. Laid across the grass are more groups of kids, lounging around like they have nothing better to do than watch the sun set.

I guess they wouldn't. It's a regular summer for them.

Because they couldn't get into the invitational, I remind myself.

Any hint of whatever I was just feeling evaporates and I walk even faster. If I walk fast enough, I might even be able to treat myself to a slice of dried mango. (Side note: it's completely unfair that a serving of dried fruit has more sugar than whole fruit, which is why the entire field of chemistry is a scam.)

Without really thinking, I find myself at the courts. It makes sense to stay now that I'm here. Playing will keep me occupied. It'll also prep me for tomorrow. And I can always use the extra practice on my kick serve.

Except the doors to the shed are locked. Excellent. Perfectly lit courts but no access to the balls.

It's so absurd I can't help but laugh out loud. I'm surprised at how good it feels. After two days of muzzling myself so I don't get kicked out of here, my mouth is finally getting to stretch out.

I force myself to keep laughing. There's really no joke to fuel it so it feels robotic and wrong. But it takes some of the heaviness off my chest so I keep going. Just recklessly heaving sounds into the air where anyone can hear them.

Someone's laughing with me.

I whip my head around, eyes wide. I'm almost relieved it's Noah. At least now I don't have to feel embarrassed.

"Why are you stalking me?" I demand.

"Why are you laughing?"

"None of your business."

He shrugs. "Then it's none of yours why I'm here."

Noah approaches me until he's just inches away. He smells like soap.

Average mean hot girl runs through my head.

He leans toward me and I hold my breath. His arm reaches around me . . .

To unlock the shed.

"Excuse me," he says belatedly, his grin so close I can smell minty breath. Does Noah Edelman walk around with mints like Violetta does? Or was it just for now?

I make a sound of disgust so he knows how uninterested I am as he rolls out a carriage full of fluorescent-green balls. "How'd you get that key anyway?" I ask. "Just so you know, I'm not getting kicked out of here for you if it turns out you stole it."

"What makes you think I'm going to share with you?"

My draw drops. "Seriously?"

"If you were the one with the key, would you share with me?"

"Probably not," I admit.

"You're consistently honest," he says.

I can't tell if he thinks that's a good thing or a bad thing.

Noah plunges back into the shed and comes out with a stack of orange cones. "I tell you what, I'll share under one condition. No wait, two conditions."

I sigh loudly. This ought to be good.

He walks around setting the cones inside the service boxes, each side mirroring the other. "Yesterday, you made me play with no serves and I agreed. But I want redemption. And a question of my choosing."

"Ugh. I knew your ego wouldn't be able to handle losing."

"Absolutely. What five-ten, hundred-seventy-pound pale-as-a-vampire Jewish boy *wouldn't* be walking around with a gigantic ego? It doesn't get much better than this."

"Yesterday you were five nine and a half and a hundred sixty-five pounds," I point out.

He grins. "So you remember."

"Not by choice," I insist, but it's no use. He won that one and we both know it.

"Keep telling yourself that," he says in a singsong voice. "We both know I'm a catch."

Unsurprisingly, I'm a terrible loser.

"I'll probably *catch* something from you," I mutter bitterly. It's the best I can come up with quickly and even then it doesn't really make sense. We're not hooking up.

Noah arches an eyebrow at me. "Someone's thinking a little far ahead. Slow down, girl, we just met."

I'm mortified. Arguing that I was *not* thinking about hooking up would make this situation worse. I dive headfirst at a subject change.

"You can have your rematch," I say magnanimously. I will not be embarrassed in front of this boy. I just won't.

"I didn't ask for a rematch," he clarifies, one pointer finger raised. "I asked for *redemption*."

"You are a ridiculous human being."

"Like I said, I'm a catch."

I shake my head but the fact is, I haven't been angry since he showed up.

He makes a big show of loosening up his arms and legs, like he's ready for real athleticism. "First, my question."

"I don't remember agreeing to answer any questions."

He raises an eyebrow. "Is Leylah Lê the kind of girl who reneges on an agreement?"

Noah's been asking around about me, it seems.

I hesitate. "Fine, but don't call me that."

"Why not?"

"Is that your question?"

"Come on, you won't give me a freebie?"

I throw his own question back at him. "Would you?"

He spreads his arms wide. "I'm an open book. My mom is a therapist. I've spent my entire life answering questions about myself."

This explains a lot about Noah.

"My name isn't really Leylah," I tell him.

"Okay, I'll admit I didn't see that coming."

There's no way to explain this without explaining *everything*, but I try to keep it as short as possible. "My first name is Ha. In Vietnamese culture, your last name comes first so my name shows up as Lê, Ha, except most people don't understand that—or how to pronounce the Vietnamese alphabet. So I would always get called like, Haley or Leah because people are ignorant and lazy, which was still better than the racists who think it's hilarious to just laugh "Hahaha" like they're the first person to ever make that joke. I started going by Leylah because it was the closest thing to my actual name. That way I didn't have to spend half my life correcting people and it saved me a lot of fights."

"So you go by Leylah . . . and your last name *is* Lê . . . but I shouldn't call you Leylah Lê. Do I have that right?"

"Is this another question?"

"You didn't answer! You gave me the backstory of the story."

Noah Edelman is paying too close attention.

I sigh wearily, so he knows just how much this is inconveniencing me. "Asian Americans have split opinions on whether we should adopt a 'western' name to make our lives easier. Let's just say certain types of people, who it's not a problem for, can get a little high and mighty about it. So saying 'Leylah Lê' reminds me of what a race traitor I am."

I say it all with my usual edge of sarcasm, but I know that's what Violetta meant when she first found out. I just don't give a shit how people pronounce my name anymore. It's not my job to expose greater America to Asian names.

"And that certain type of person . . . is currently your roommate?"

I narrow my eyes. I don't like the way Noah's looking at me. All I did was answer one question and now he's staring like he can perceive me. "I answered your question," I say briskly. "Now what? First to knock down all their cones?" My fingers are itching to grab a ball and hit it. Hit *something*.

His finger raises again, calling a halt. "Ah, but this time there are stakes."

I'm so happy to not talk about *identity* I don't even bother to shoot down this new idea.

"What do I win?" The truly important question.

He looks me straight in the eyes. "What do you want to win?"

Loaded question. Nope, next.

"What do *you* want?"

Noah smiles. It's not a nice smile. It's a sneaky fucking smile. "I asked you first," he finally replies.

I search my brain for something simple. Easy. No innuendo.

"You can do my laundry," I say.

Noah's smile widens. "You sure about that?"

My laundry currently consists of tennis clothes, bras, and underwear. Damn it. I wave the suggestion away. "Whatever, I'll decide after I win."

Noah shrugs, unbothered. "Okay."

I'm suspicious. I follow up. "Just like that?"

"You're not very trusting, are you?"

"I'm not trusting at *all*."

"Either way, it doesn't matter," he says, grabbing a ball. He fires off a quick serve, toppling the far corner cone. "I'm going to win and I already know what I want."

My heart stops. I'm frozen as he winds up, his legs dipping into a deep bend before exploding upward. The bottom of his shirt flies up and exposes a wide sliver of skin across his waist.

A flash of dark hair, then nothing.

It takes another serve before I snap out of my boy-induced coma.

"You cheated!" I cry.

Noah scratches his head. "Did I? You were watching me so closely, I would think you would've said something. Unless there's a reason you were distracted?"

I award him more points in my head. I sense I'm close to losing the head-to-head matchup.

He serves again and I stand frozen, watching, again. Another cone topples.

"Goddamn it," I mutter, stuffing my pockets with balls and keeping my eyes down so I can't get sucked back in. The overly crowded pockets feel terrible. But I'll lose precious seconds going back and forth between the ball carriage and baseline.

Clearly I'm not the type of girl who pretends to be bad at something so a guy can feel good about himself.

"You're dead meat, Edelman," I warn.

We serve in silence until we're each down to one cone. Mine is in an easier spot to hit. Or at least, it should be. It's a middle, into-the-body target, plenty of margin on the back end. But the fucker simply will not fall.

Noah knocks over his last cone, then drops his racquet and raises his arms like he's just won Wimbledon. He marches around me in circles, mostly humming the national anthem and filling in the words he knows.

I let him circle three times before I cut it off. "Enough gloating. What do you want?"

Noah makes a big show of thinking about it, stroking a nonexistent beard and pursing his lips.

Now I'm looking at his lips.

Minus 5 points for me.

I look away.

"A re-rematch," he finally says.

"Huh?"

"That's what I want," he says. "A rematch of our rematch.

Tomorrow night. Same time. So when I beat you again, you can't claim it was a fluke."

He could've picked anything. He could've made me do his laundry. Jump in the pool with all my clothes on. Humiliate me in front of Violetta.

Instead, he's choosing another night. With me.

I'm a walking zombie, undead with the knowledge that of all the things Noah wants right now, it's more time with me.

The not–average mean hot girl, whose tennis he likes.

He's standing too close and I'm getting that sauna feeling again. Except this steam smells like soap and not lavender. I'm tingly everywhere and my body feels too big for my skin.

I need to leave. Or at the very least, get away from Noah.

I practically sprint to the other side of the court, stacking cones and leaving them in a tidy pile. "You can pick these up on your way back to the shed," I call as I head for the exit.

"You're leaving?" He sounds disappointed.

I stop, but keep myself half a court away. I don't need him aromatherapy-attacking me again. "I have an early match tomorrow. So do you."

He grins. "So you looked up my schedule."

I roll my eyes.

Quick! Say something clever and exit on a high note.

"Double or nothing tomorrow night," I blurt out.

Minus a million points, Leylah. What the fuck is the double of whatever it was we just did?

Noah smiles and even from this distance, it does something to my chest area. "Perfect. I already know what I want next time," he says.

Sheer pride keeps me from finding out what that is.

Next time.

Throat dry and brain empty of anything useful, I turn and bolt. Like a coward.

FRIDAY, JULY 7TH

QUALIFYING TOURNAMENT, ROUND OF 16

12
ALICE

MY NEXT SINGLES MATCH IS AS MUCH A FAILURE AS THE FIRST ONE. THIS time, my opponent doesn't even make it to court, defaulting beforehand because of a sprained ankle that worsened overnight.

I'm disappointed.

Not because I feel ready to play, but because I have to play a doubles match with someone I don't know and the only practice I've had was my terrible performance yesterday. I'm also sluggish after my bout with heat exhaustion, despite Violetta making sure I stayed hydrated and rested.

Even here, I am so pathetic that others need to take care of me.

My doubles match goes exactly the way one would assume it would, considering half the team barely wants to be here in the first place, not to mention recovering from an ill-advised run. I play slightly better than yesterday, but my shots still hang too long in the air, giving our opponents multiple opportunities to put the ball away. My partner, Alyssa, gets pegged three times and I can see large bruises on her leg and torso before our match concludes.

I apologize and I apologize—it feels as though the entire match is just one big apology—but we lose and she's furious. Without waiting for me, she grabs her bag and stalks off the court, where her mom is standing by.

Yet another parent who is here to support their child.

I gnaw on my thumbnail as I exit the court, not caring that I didn't bathe it in hand sanitizer first. The cheap dollar-bin Walgreens brand that David sent along with me tastes so medicinal it's like being *in* a hospital.

Which I refuse to relive.

"It's so unfair!" Alyssa complains to her mom, who hastily grabs the heavy racquet bag from her daughter and shoulders it herself. "Why did I get paired with the worst person in the draw? No one's ever even heard of her! What's she doing here? How'd she even get in?"

"Very unfair," her mom agrees. "I don't know how the admissions board could've made such a mistake."

I slow, hoping to put more distance between us as we wind our way past the academy players practicing on the green clay. I don't need more confirmation of how I don't fit in here. As it is, I'm the only one wearing my high school team shirt—the only tennis top I own that *isn't* a T-shirt. I'm going to have to wash it tonight so I can wear it again in tomorrow's match. If I win, I'll be in the main draw. The main draw of the Bastille Invitational, one of the most exclusive tournaments.

It's so absurd that I laugh.

Alyssa must hear me because she spins around furiously. "Are you seriously laughing after you just tanked our match? Maybe this doesn't mean anything to you because you're a nobody, but some of us here are *real* tennis players, so why don't you just leave and go back to wherever it is you came from?"

I have never had someone say those words to me.

It shocks me more than I would have expected.

I feel tears coming and hold them off by digging my fingernails into my palms. Go back to where I came from? If only.

The last thing I want to do right now is go back to San Francisco.

The second-last thing is to cry in front of Alyssa.

Someone with a large red Wilson bag shoves past, knocking both Alyssa and her mom off balance so they trip over the short hedges that line the paths. It's Leylah.

"Oops," she says, the flatness of her voice indicating it was anything but an accident.

Alyssa's mom puffs her chest in indignation, demanding, "Apologize this instant."

"For what?" Leylah asks. She leans forward, her tone turning just a touch menacing. "Maybe this doesn't mean anything to you because you're a nobody, but some of us *real* tennis players need to use the path to get to our court, so why don't you just leave and go back to wherever it is you came from?"

Leylah is magnificent right now—a real-life Joan of Arc. Her short hair is pinned back, each of her angular features highlighted in the sun like a deadly weapon. Cheekbones, jawbone, collarbones, shoulders. Her fury is directed one way and it's all on my behalf.

Baba loved me.

Baba protected me.

But he didn't *fight* for me.

He could have fought his diagnosis. He could have done all the recommended therapies and taken all the recommended medications. He could have at least *tried*. Instead, he let it take him and now I'm alone.

Except right now I have Leylah.

I unfurl my shoulders a little, buoyed by the knowledge that someone out there sees me. Thinks I'm worth fighting for. I met Leylah Lê two days ago and now she's arguing with a parent on my behalf. No, she's *scolding* a parent on my behalf.

Alyssa's mom is trying to assert some kind of authority by standing tall and stepping closer, but she doesn't even reach Leylah's chin. By the look of disgust on Leylah's face, I'm half surprised Alyssa's mom doesn't simply wither away.

If I ever make it to seventeen, I want to be like Leylah.

"How dare you?" Alyssa's mom demands. "You can't go around pushing people, what if Alyssa had been hurt?"

"It probably wouldn't be much of a problem, seeing as she just lost."

The mom's eyes widen and even I swallow a little gasp. In my wildest dreams, I have never imagined speaking the thoughts in my head so frankly. I'm in the passenger seat of the most thrilling and terrifying ride I have ever been on.

"I only lost because of *her*." Alyssa decides to jump back into the conversation, bolstered by her mom's righteous anger.

Leylah leans close, but keeps her voice the same volume.

"Do you say that about all your partners or just the nonwhite ones?"

Alyssa's face blanches as she splutters a reply. "I wasn't—I didn't—"

"This isn't about race!" Alyssa's mom exclaims. Players on the surrounding courts have stopped and are now watching us. "You can't go around accusing people of being racist simply because you're *not* white! Besides, Alyssa is Latina. She was born in Argentina."

Leylah rolls her eyes at the attempt to justify Alyssa's words. As though being Latinx exempts her from racialized insults. "Okay, how about I tell her white Argentine ass to go back where *she* came from and you can tell me it's not a racist thing to say."

Leylah is the fully armored Joan of Arc, water spouting out of the tip of her sword as she stabs Alyssa and her mom in the name of justice. Struck motionless by gratitude and wonder, I can't even get the words out to properly thank her.

Alyssa and her mom bluster through snarled exclamations of Leylah's rudeness but quickly find their way away from us.

"You can be sure Dick *will* be hearing about this," the mom snaps.

Once they're gone, Leylah slumps and mutters a string of curses under her breath. It seems standing up to others is as tiring as I've always imagined it to be. I wonder who taught her to do it anyway.

"Are you going to get in trouble?" I ask.

"Probably."

I don't know what Mr. Duncan can do to penalize Leylah, but I can well imagine how the conversation will go.

"I'll go with you," I offer. "If you get in trouble, I mean. I'll come with. I'll try to make sure he hears your side of the story." Even as I say it, I can hear my suggestion grow less and less aggressive with each sentence. Still, I'm trying to help.

Leylah pats my arm like I'm a small child asking for an ice-cream cone, then readjusts the bag on her shoulder. "Don't worry about it," she says. "Let's just say I owed you one."

13

VIOLETTA

COOP HAS JUST PULLED THE BALL CART TO THE BASELINE WHEN RACHEL RUSHES in last minute, red hair flying around her shoulders and eyes wild. "You guys hear what happened with Leylah?" Rachel cackles as she pulls her hair up into a messy bun and reties her shoes—things she was supposed to have done before practice.

"I guess she like, shoved some girl's mom into the bushes and now everyone thinks Dick is going to kick her out of the tournament again." Rachel's reaction is pure glee. Part of me gets it—this is platinum-level gossip. And Rachel and Leylah have always hated each other. Even before *that match*.

I feel a little sick at the thought of Leylah getting forfeited a second time in a row.

"It's probably an exaggeration," I say, grabbing a ball and hoping Rachel will switch topics.

But Rachel is like a gnat; you couldn't get rid of her even if you tried.

"I totally see her doing it," she says, lowering her voice

conspiratorially. "Remember when I beat her in the semis here? I thought she was going to jump over the net and murder me."

"It *was* kind of a bullshit way to lose, especially in a semi," I can't help but point out. It was the whole reason Leylah had even been with me that night. After the infamous match, she'd been too angry to be alone. I'm still convinced the only reason Leylah didn't set fire to Dick's office that night was *because* she'd been with me.

Save me, I'm defending her now.

Rachel shoots me a sharp look after my rebuttal. "That wasn't *my* fault!"

"I didn't say it was."

Thankfully Cooper cuts in before Rachel can work herself up into one of her dramatic moods. "Super-invested in this conversation, but both of *you* are going to be out of the tournament if you don't sharpen up your serves," he says. "Let's go. Show me how much work you've done since last week."

He tosses a ball to Rachel and I watch as her arm kicks back and unleashes a flat serve up the middle. He nods in approval and tosses her another ball. "A little more toward the T. You want to really paint that line." She hits another. Then another. And another.

I'm not saying I deserve more coaching time than Rachel, but the serve I'm supposed to be working on is way more difficult than hers. I'm the one who needs the guidance. How hard is it to hit a flat serve?

Coop gently readjusts Rachel's arm and I pause for a second, fiddling with my skirt so I can watch the interaction. He's too close to Rachel for me to hear what he's saying, but I can see her flashing him a smile like her life depends on it. She always tries to flirt with Coop when he's on court with us. All the girls do.

I mean, I get it. The guy is tall, blond, and fit with a perfectly muscled body and a smile that gives off that little sparkle they put in toothpaste commercials. He's objectively hot. California hot.

The attention embarrasses him. He tells me so many stories about how other girls have tried to flirt with him. Because of that, he mostly avoids all the female players off court.

Except me.

Coop makes an exception for me. I can't go around saying we're the best of friends or anything because of how it would look, but he's not a creep. I just *happen* to be sixteen and he just *happens* to be twenty-five. It's not like we couldn't form a friendship with that big of a gap. Aren't there are like, a million stories about a little kid befriending some ancient, crotchety neighbor?

Post idea: how to seem more mature so people take you seriously

All of which is why I'm annoyed when I realize he's still with Rachel. I don't expect him to only coach me, but I *do* expect him to go above and beyond for me. The way I would for him. Because we're friends. And friends go out of their way for each other.

I wonder if anyone other than Cooper or Audrey thinks about me when I'm not there. Leylah probably still does, but only to throw darts at my face or something.

"You all right over there, V?"

Cooper's voice snaps me out of my weird memory haze and I shake it off with a flick of my hair. "I'm surprised you remembered I existed."

He hands Rachel one last ball and watches her hit it before turning back to me, a reluctant note to his tone. "Okay, okay, V, now it's your turn."

This is a game we play, in which he pretends that I'm being a diva and therefore *has* to give me extra attention. He puts on a good show for everyone else, but I know he secretly likes it. It's the whole reason we became friends. We started by just texting about tennis-related stuff and somehow it grew into . . . whatever it is now. Friendship.

I hit my serve, making sure to put a little extra oomph into the jump. I should probably always wear two sports bras to at least cut down on the . . . movement, but today I'm only wearing one.

I look to see Coop's reaction, but it's not ogle-eyed like I expected. When I'm playing on one of the show courts, let's just say my audience skews heavily male. I'm not stupid—having fans matters. Audrey may have been a promising player, but she made her money from endorsements.

His lips are pursed, brows drawn in thought. Maybe he didn't notice at all.

"Do it again," he orders.

This time, I focus less on my chest and more on my actual form. Still, my trusty Nike sports bra is pulling double duty today.

I wait to make sure it bounces in, then whirl around to Coop with a *take that!* kind of look.

He smirks, glancing down at my chest so I know he knows I did it on purpose. "Make sure not to drop that left arm too early," he says. "You're taking your head down with it."

A perfectly reasonable statement. No one hearing it would think anything weird. Rachel won't think it's weird. It's *not* weird, really. Just a harmless game.

I bat my eyelashes. "How low am I dropping it?"

I've switched over to the wide-eyed girl who needs his expertise—an inside joke about how so many of the girls here have crushes on him and how embarrassed it makes him. Except when we play the game.

An exception for me.

Accepting the challenge, he encircles my left wrist and hauls it up into position. "Here," he says, stepping so close to me I can feel the warmth off his body. "Make sure your left arm stays all the way up *here* until you make contact with the ball." He shoots a furtive look around before trailing his fingers down the inside of my arm, gone before anyone sees.

He takes a step back and raises his eyebrows. *Your turn.*

I glare and mouth *not fair* when Rachel's back is turned. The intimacy of the touch sent goose bumps across my body and now I'm in no position to serve, let alone fire back at Cooper.

Now *he's* the picture of innocence, hands up to deny any culpability.

We go back and forth, me having to take breaks to actually hit serves and him to give Rachel some attention, so nothing seems suspicious. Something tells me Dick wouldn't find it quite as funny as we do.

When he's finally free from Rachel, I take another turn. "I think I'm having problems with my right arm now," I complain. He has me hit a practice serve, which lands in, before he diagnoses.

"Hmm. I don't think it's your arm this time. Do it again so I can really take in your full form."

His lip twitches at the implied meaning and I'm so engrossed in pretending to need help I nearly miss hitting the ball altogether.

Coop takes pity on me. "You want to make sure you're getting a good angle on your shoulders," he says, both of his hands planted on me.

My shoulders are uncovered and the electricity of his hands on my bare skin sends even bigger goose bumps across my body. I'm embarrassed he can feel them. He's about to smooth his hands over them to send them away when Coach Anya yells his name. Coop drops his hands like they're on fire.

"Go find out what she wants," he whispers to me, meanwhile using me as a shield.

"You do it," I hiss back, both of us trying to hold our giggles so she won't see us.

"I'll make you a deal, you hit this next serve in and I'll go. You miss, you have to go."

Everyone is afraid of Coach Anya—even Cooper. It might be because she's well into her forties and seems to shout absolutely everything, but I think it has more to do with the fact that she even treats *him* like a student and not the respected coworker he's supposed to be.

I make the serve and he sticks out his tongue at me, leaving us to go see whatever the hell it is she's yelling about. With the main draw starting in just a few days, everyone's a little more on edge than usual. Well, the ones playing in 18U are, anyway.

Some, like Rachel, are dying for the wild card into a WTA 125 event that comes as the reward for winning the 18U tournament. She and a couple of the other girls have already tried a handful of the lower level ITF tournaments without much success. Skipping straight to the WTA tier would be a dream for anyone—it could take years to rack up those kinds of points otherwise.

I try to imagine playing a match at a professional tournament right now. Having crowds of anxious fans, many of them expecting me to be completely out of my depth. I'm just a teenager, after all.

It hits me. *I'm just a teenager.*

Suddenly, the pressure of just what this year's tournament represents seems heavier than usual. It's not like I haven't known all along where my career was headed—Audrey's talked about *The Plan* practically since my birth.

Go pro. Get famous. Sign endorsements. And never, ever worry about money again.

Somehow it hadn't really clicked that I could be starting . . . now.

I'm sure it's not just now occurring to Leylah.

If we're both tigers, she's the wild one and I'm the one that lives in the zoo. If I'm going to have to go head-to-head with her, I'd better work on my tricks.

I grab another ball and step back to the baseline with a sigh.

Keep your left arm up.

If I imagine Cooper standing here, watching my every move, it makes it a lot easier to bear.

14

LEYLAH

THERE'S A VERY SPECIFIC FEELING I GET WHEN I JUST KNOW I'M ABOUT TO BE punished by an adult. Like a Spidey sense for impending lectures. Everything's tingling but in a way that makes me sick to my stomach.

I wonder if Dick's called my parents yet. I guess if he had, Mom would have already called to deliver the "Three *A*s" lecture. *Action, attitude, accountability.* It's similar to the one I get at school, so Mom sometimes adds the *R*s for extra oomph. *Respect, responsibility, representation.* If both Mom and Dad are waiting for me, I get the all-you-can-eat immigrant-struggle buffet. Endless reminders about how they had it much worse and this means I must be grateful about everything until the end of time.

My muscles clench at the sound of Dick's office door unclicking, ready to defend myself against whatever the allegation is.

Just sit there and don't speak.

I tell myself the same thing every time.

Just sit there and don't speak.

Dick opens the door and gestures for me to sit on a wooden chair facing his desk. It's flat and hard, like a plank, uncomfortable no matter my position. It only puts me more on edge.

He settles into a white leather chair across from me, rubbing in his elevated status from behind his unnecessarily massive desk. I guess it's his version of an oversize pickup truck.

"Is there anything you'd like to share before we get started?" he asks calmly.

"Alyssa Avila broke the code of conduct so I hope you're talking to her next."

I really should stop giving myself the same pep talk.

Minus 10 points.

Dick pivots and spins in his fancy chair, his eyes focused on me like he's trying to figure something out. With a mustache, he'd be a perfect movie villain. Men with mustaches but no beard are always suspicious.

Finally, he speaks. "I assume your comment refers to the, ahem, *scuffle* over by court 15?"

Every word out of his mouth is pronounced crisply, like there's always a hidden microphone near him and he wants to make sure it catches everything.

"When Alyssa Avila said a racist slur to another player? Yes, that."

He sighs and it's a weary one. I'm familiar with this feeling too—I'm the last of the three Lê sisters. Every teacher who had already taught one of my rule-following, school-loving sisters gave that same sigh when they realized I spent my school day just trying to get through it as fast as possible.

"Do you care to comment on the alleged assault that took place immediately after?" Dick asks. He's a TV lawyer, trying to use as many words as possible.

"Assault?" I can't believe they're trying to frame that as assault. I put my hands out as a form of measurement. "The path is like, this wide. If she and her mom ran into my tennis bag, that's on them."

I'm dying to add that they deserved more than just tripping over a hedge, but I don't.

I award myself five points for my restraint.

"Are you aware that physical violence against another player or spectator both on *and* off the court is also considered misconduct? Gross misconduct, in fact. Punishable with a three-month suspension from all USA Tennis–sanctioned tournaments."

The bottom drops out of my stomach.

I'm reliving two years ago. My entire fate comes down to this one, single man who's made it more than clear he hates me.

This is *worse* than two years ago. We're in his office, alone, instead of on a court surrounded by hundreds of witnesses. When he fucks me over again, no one will even know about it. I'll just silently disappear and no one will come looking for me. It'll prove every assumption my parents have about me.

If I get kicked out of here for *assault*, forget turning pro. I'll never even be allowed to leave the house again.

Dick lets his threat linger, casually twirling a pen around his fingers.

It doesn't matter that Alyssa deserved it or that Asians are experiencing record levels of hate. Mine is the crime that gets punished because I was loud. He's essentially saying it's okay to privately criticize one person to their face but not a bunch of people publicly.

People who refer to me by my ethnicity or color sure hate when I do it back to them.

My tailbone is drilling a hole through the seat of this chair but I will it to stay in place another minute. I need this. Fuck, do I need this.

He can smell the desperation coming off me.

"You have a history of making things"—his face goes through an entire cycle of emotions as he settles on a word—"difficult."

He is absolutely referring to my semifinal against Rachel two years ago. The one he fucking *stole* from me.

I bite down on my tongue so hard it I taste blood.

Just sit there and don't speak.

"I like my tournament to run smoothly. *Without* physical altercations," he emphasizes.

I silently plot thirty-seven different ways to murder him, all of them involving physical altercations.

Number one, strangulation.

Number two, a stab to the heart with the very pen he's holding.

Number three—

"Do you understand what I'm saying, Ms. Lee?"

Oh, I understand all right. He wants me to cry mercy. He wants me to sampeah him at nose level. He wants to break me; to watch me finally fit into the little box he's already created for me.

I would sooner saw off each of my limbs, *127 Hours*–style, than let this man win anything from me. "Are you asking if I understand that you want me to stay quiet about the racism at your tournament so you don't have to do anything about it?" I ask.

Just sit there and don't speak.

Dick's jaw tightens and I can tell he's on the verge of losing it. If he disqualifies me (again), it'll mean I wasted the past two years. I've been working my ass off to get back here and I might lose it all over Alyssa fucking Avila?

"Do I need to repeat myself?" he asks mildly. There's no need to threaten me now—he's gotten his message across clearly already.

My stomach has long passed queasy. I could throw up on this man's shoes right now, I'm so sick. I'm going to have to walk out of here like everything is fine, living forever with the knowledge that I called chicken first.

I dig my fingernails into my palm and force the words out.

"I understand I should not have done what I did and I will focus on nothing but tennis from now on."

My voice is a corpse, brittle from being buried underground for so long. Dick smiles like he was the one who killed me.

"Glad to see you *can* take direction after all, Ms. Lee. If I have to call you back here again, it will be to pack your bags."

I don't bother telling him that he sounds like a bad reality-TV-show host, or that I might as well leave my bags here if I go. Unless I win this whole damn thing, there'll be no use for my racquets anymore.

15

ALICE

NO MATTER HOW HARD I TRY, I CAN'T STOP OBSESSING OVER THE confrontation with Alyssa as I attempt to scrub the red clay marks out of my shirt. I hadn't been certain during the match, but her comments afterward make me more so—she purposely tried to get me hit. Repeatedly. I managed to move out of the way of most oncoming slams, but stumbled on one and fell, earning the red blob that only seems to spread the more I wash it.

Part of me wants to excuse it, to assure myself her anger was just about the tennis and nothing else. But then why did she tell me to go back to where I came from? What would that have to do with our match?

I'm not so naive as to believe I'd go through life without ever encountering *some* kind of racism—even living in San Francisco—but I've never had it pushed in my face so blatantly. Even without a threat of violence, it's managed to shake me in a way I thought I was immune to.

I truly do not know what I would have done without Leylah's help.

As it is, I have no one to turn to in the aftermath. Who would I tell? And what would I say? Who could possibly understand what I'm feeling when I don't quite know what it is myself?

I turn my attention back to the stain. If Mama were here, she'd know how to fix this. She's the laundry person of the household. David and I split the cooking and cleaning, while Baba took on the mental load.

That seems to have fallen on David now.

I could call Mama. I could call and ask what to use to get this mark out so I can wear this shirt tomorrow, but I don't. Maybe because then I would have to admit that in my carelessness, I ruined my shoes and had to spend all of my emergency money on buying a new pair. That money was supposed to be for something special. I hadn't planned on spending it at all. We've already wasted enough sending me here in the first place.

I fight back tears just thinking about how many hours it takes at the grocery store to earn the money David spent on this trip. All so I could what? Stand by as opponents default around me and single-handedly lose a doubles match with someone who sees me as subhuman?

"Is everything okay?"

I startle at the sound of Violetta's voice, reminding me that I am but a guest in her permanent home. A guest she needed to care for most of yesterday, who is now clearly mired in another mess of her own making. I can't imagine what she must think of me.

"Sorry," I mumble to the decorative ceramic basin, now splattered with pale red droplets. "Do you need the bathroom? I was just trying to get this stain out."

I still can't look at her, standing just outside the doorway, afraid my face will show all its emotions. I'm sure Violetta Masuda doesn't have to deal with budgeting issues.

"You know, clay washes out better when it's dry," she offers.

I don't have time to let it dry.

"I didn't know about the dress code," I finally admit, my voice small. "This is the only non-T-shirt I own."

Violetta's purple eyes go wide and I see the shame in her face at stumbling upon such a sensitive topic. But a year at private school has made me accustomed to being the poorest in the room.

I never thought of us as poor before. We have a place to live, food to eat, and clothes to wear. I play an expensive sport. My parents work. We all ride public transportation. I know things get tight from time to time, but I'd never seriously worried about money.

Until I saw the bills.

Stacks and stacks of them, many marked PAST DUE in menacing red letters in all caps. As if they could resurrect Baba from the grave to pay his debts if they just threatened hard enough. But Mama is adamant she will pay what is owed, even as we teeter toward bankruptcy. David tries to simply sweep it all under the rug, wanting to keep even this a secret from me.

To them, their problems are not my problems.

"I could lend you something," Violetta blurts out. "I have tons of clothes."

I look between us, clocking the stark differences between not only our shapes, but sheer size. She's at least five inches taller, quite a bit skinnier, and everything she wears clings to her like it was made to highlight her fully grown-up body.

A social media star, I am not.

Still, my options are limited and she's offering. As long as I don't attract Dick Duncan's attention, I can manage being unfashionable for another day. It's not as if my St. Aidan's team shirt is stylish as it is.

"Thank you, that's really generous," I say.

Violetta leads me back to her closet and throws open the doors as if to allow me to peruse at my leisure. I can't bring myself to touch anything.

"This would look good on you," she says, pulling out a bright white polo shirt.

I shake my head, pushing it away gently. "I would just stain it."

She shrugs. "That's fine, I've never even worn it. This really isn't my taste. It's one of the freebies they sent me. You know, when trying to line up a sponsorship deal? You can keep it." She thrusts the shirt into my hands, hanger and all.

I stare down at it, my fingers running over the thickly embroidered crocodile logo on the front. It reminds me of the times Mrs. Conrad would hand me bags of clothes her daughter no longer wanted. Sometimes there were brand-new items among them too. In this case, it's a bit more humbling to receive something from someone your age instead of an obviously wealthy older woman who already thinks of you as a charity case.

That was how Ma had seen it, anyway. I remember the look on her face the first time Mrs. Conrad offered and I accepted. We never talked about it, but I knew from the way she bowed her head and looked away that she was ashamed I'd taken them.

"Thanks," I say, hoping my tone adequately conveys my gratitude. Whether or not Violetta pities me, the fact is, I need a shirt and she has selflessly offered me one that will at least somewhat fit.

"If you don't like polos I have some non-collared Dri-FIT-type ones in the back you can keep." She sticks her head farther into the closet, riffling through the items until she returns with another hanger. "Aha!" she cries triumphantly, holding high a caution tape–yellow shirt with neon-green ombré stripes across it on a diagonal. "Sorry it's not cuter," she apologizes. "Adidas was really pushing this line a couple years ago and it didn't quite take off. I think I have more in these same colors."

It's hideous, possibly even more than the Bastille Invitational T-shirt.

I take it anyway.

"Of course, you're welcome to borrow any of my regular clothes too," Violetta adds. "I'm not trying to only give you ugly stuff. I just figured the ones I actually wear might not be your style."

She gestures down to herself, dressed in a cropped turquoise top that's more bra than shirt, and a gauzy, see-through white skirt atop matching turquoise biker shorts.

I look down at my baggy T-shirt and shorts and decide there isn't a single universe in which I would put that on. Even my swimsuit doesn't show that much skin.

"Thanks," I say again, hugging the two shirts against my chest like found treasure. "But I don't want to ruin any of your nice clothes. These will work great."

Violetta scrunches her nose like a cat. "They're just tennis clothes. I have a million of them. And at least half of them will be out of style by next year anyway."

She's not kidding. Not only is the entire closet full of her items, but her drawers are overflowing, there are stacks of shoes under her bed, and additional clothes are flung across the chair at her desk. The space is positively bursting at the seams with her wardrobe.

"So you just get rid of them? Isn't that kind of wasteful?" The words tumble out before I can stop them and I clamp a hand over my mouth in embarrassment. The only thing more taboo than not having money is commenting on how others *do* have it and how they spend it.

Violetta appears surprised by the comment, likely having never calculated the thousands of dollars she uses and discards at a rapid rate. I, on the other hand, have spent a lifetime in David's hand-me-downs, carefully preserved by our in-home launderette.

"I guess I never really thought about it," she admits with a small cringe, and I feel guilty for having inadvertently shamed her. "I was always hustling for sponsorships and deals—reaching out to brands or doing promotions in exchange for gear because it felt like I was the only one who didn't have all the designer stuff everyone else did. At some point they started finding me— sending me stuff with the hope I'd post about it on my social media. I never considered turning anything down because I'd worked so hard to get to this stage in the first place."

Now it's my turn to be surprised.

"I had no idea."

Of course I wouldn't. I mentally scold myself for having made so many assumptions. I should have known better than to judge on appearances—San Francisco has more billionaires per capita than any other city in the world, yet it's impossible to identify them when they mingle among us in jeans and hoodies.

Violetta shrugs stiffly, seemingly uncomfortable with my reaction to this new information. "The only reason I could afford to come here in the first place was because I got financial aid and Audrey took a job in their marketing department so I got reduced tuition." She nods toward the bunk bed. "Leylah's easily the richest of us three."

Both facts shock me. I know even less than I thought I had. "Really?"

"Her parents are, anyway. Major American Dream success stories." Violetta visibly perks up and I know she is about to tell a story. Of all the content she makes, the ones with the personal stories are my favorite. "So you know her mom is from Cambodia and her dad is from Vietnam. *Their* parents managed to escape the genocide and war and all that, each family making their way to the US, where both of *them* grew up to become doctors!"

It's so common, and yet incredible every time it happens. Both of my parents were born, raised, and have never left San Francisco. It must affect us—affect how they raise us—Leylah a fighter, ready to traverse the globe and tackle the ocean if needed, while I have only just left my fishbowl for the first time. My world has only been school, family, and tennis.

"That's not even the wildest part," Violetta continues. Her excitement is so palpable I could be forgiven for thinking it was her own family history. "Her parents didn't even meet until medical school. Her mom had Leylah in like, her forties. They ended up inventing some kind of medical device and poof! Overnight life change."

"Wow. That's . . . a lot."

"Right?"

It has been clear from the moment I arrived that Leylah and Violetta previously knew each other but I had no idea to what degree until now. I don't know that level of detail about anyone else's family history except my own. Even then, I don't harbor the same kind of romanticization. Maybe because like Leylah, I've had two parents for most of my life.

"I don't want to talk about Leylah anymore." Violetta shakes her head like a wet dog ridding itself of water. "Tell me more about you."

"Me?"

What would someone like Violetta want to know about me? But her eyes are eager.

The question is, who am I? I'm not sure I know anymore.

Before, I would have instantly replied something about tennis. It was my whole identity. At St. Aidan's, no one knew anything about me beyond the fact that I played on the tennis team. And I was okay with that.

But then Baba was gone and it felt like he took that part of me with him. Baba was tennis and tennis was Baba. Without him, I'm just Alice. No other descriptors.

The other girls here have a hunger—the desperation that if you *just perform well enough*, you can mend whatever rift or hole exists inside to make yourself whole again. I see it in Leylah. I see it when I walk by the courts, watching the intensity of each player's focus as they warm up for matches, the strain of needing to win in their every shot.

I have a Ba-shaped hole in my chest that can't be filled by anything.

Violetta frowns in sympathy and hands me a tissue and I realize I'm silently crying. I don't know who I am without him.

"I'm sorry," I apologize, sniffling as I dab my eyes. "My dad died recently."

Her eyes widen and I brace myself for the same platitudes I've heard over and over. *I'm so sorry. Keeping you in my thoughts and prayers.* Or worse, *It's part of God's plan.*

But Violetta doesn't say any of those. Instead, she places a hand on my shoulder and I realize how long it's been since someone has touched me. I nearly lean into the contact, my skin starved for human touch.

"Do you want to talk about it or do you want to pretend like you never told me?" she asks gently.

I see the humanity in her eyes, looking at me as though my problems matter to her. The offer to press rewind on the entire thing is unexpectedly touching. I hate being prodded to speak— to perform my grief or outrage so someone else can feel good about themselves when they express their sympathies.

"He was my coach," I explain. "He taught himself how to play when I told him that was what I wanted to try. He would even do this thing where he'd text me funny little challenges before my matches. Like, there was this one where I had to hit everything as a backhand slice. I was running around my forehands to hit backhand slices. My opponent probably thought didn't know how to hit anything else."

The memory sends a little laugh through me.

"How did it go?" Violetta asks. "With the backhand slices?"

"I lost. I don't think it was even close. But you know what? I can hit a backhand slice from anywhere now."

A small wrinkle forms between her eyebrows. "I don't understand, why would he want you to keep doing it even if you were losing?"

"Because that was the assignment. And he wouldn't have given it to me unless he thought I needed it." I shrug. "He was the coach. I had to trust he was doing what was best for my overall career."

Nothing is more important than your own growth, he'd say. *Not even winning.* "He said it would make me more confident in my shots because I wouldn't get nervous about missing. To take away the fear of losing," I explain.

Plenty of time to win when you're on tour. Better to lose now doing the right thing instead of winning but ingraining bad habits.

I trusted him. His vision. And he was right—I wasn't afraid of losing.

The thought of his death tumbles me back to reality, where I realize I've been entirely too trusting of his "vision."

"He had Graves' disease," I continue, the need to tell someone this secret so heavy I almost can't keep the words from tumbling out. Maybe then it will stop this ache. "It's an autoimmune disorder. It's not usually fatal, but . . ."

My sentence drifts quietly away but that doesn't stop the thought that continues to cycle through my mind.

Would Baba still be alive if he'd spent the money on treatment instead of on my tennis?

Violetta remains silent and I find that it gives me space to keep going. "It was his dream for me to come here. We did my whole application together."

She bumps me with her hip and another frisson of something goes through me. "It sounds like he'd be really proud to know you did it."

I don't mention that Mrs. Conrad sits on the board of Bastille.

"He'd be happy as a dad, but I don't think the coach in him would be *proud*." I cringe, thinking about my performance in the previous matches.

Violetta dismisses my embarrassment. "So you had a couple of off days. So what? That can happen to anyone. It's amazing you're even back on the court, judging from what you say about your relationship with your dad. I don't know what I'd do if Cooper was suddenly not here and we're nowhere near as close as you two are! I'd probably give up tennis all together."

I appreciate the reassurance. Everyone left in the Wu family seems to be on team Keep Alice Playing Tennis, which makes it difficult when the player in question is currently suffering an anti-tennis crisis.

"You're very wise," I tell her solemnly. "You should be a life coach."

Violetta closes her eyes, pretending to meditate by turning her pinched thumb and third finger upward. She even hums a little *ohm* for effect before opening her eyes with grin. "A sixteen-year-old life coach."

How is it possible we're separated by only one year? Maybe I am as young as my family sees me after all.

"You feel older than sixteen," I say.

She smiles. "That's what Coop always says." Her smile is different when she talks about him. More guarded, but also more genuine, and I wonder once again if they're more than just friends.

"How old is he?" I ask. I grew up watching him play; listening to the commentators christen him "the next big thing" in American men's tennis. To me, he seems ancient.

It must show in my face because Violetta sighs in exasperation. "He's only twenty-five. And we're just friends."

A red flag unfurls in my mind. I've spent enough time in public spaces to know that adult men don't make friends with teenage girls for no reason. But I don't want to spoil my budding friendship so instead I change the subject.

"I noticed you always stay up late watching your phone. What do you watch?" I silently hope it comes off as more of a friendly question and not that of a parasocial fan looking for information. Surely we've crossed that line by this point.

Violetta flashes another one of her shy smiles and I am gleeful with the knowledge that I can now differentiate her expressions and emotions.

"Cooking videos," she says.

Now it's my turn to wrinkle my nose. "At night? Doesn't that make you hungry?"

Violetta shakes her head. "Never. Watching them makes me feel like I'm eating, so I never wake up hungry."

The words strike me as strange, but I am desperate to know more about her. Just being around her pulls me into her glow and makes me feel as though I could glow too—that I could somehow become someone other than the girl who lost her dad and sucks her thumb, if only I just learn the secrets to changing it.

"Can you show me?" I ask.

Violetta beams at me and I feel as though I've finally done something right. I have secured a shirt for tomorrow and now, instead of stressing over my wardrobe, I get to spend time with the person everyone wants to spend time with.

Maybe today hasn't been a complete waste after all.

16
LEYLAH

I'M STOMPING AROUND THE BEACH VOLLEYBALL COURT WHEN NOAH finds me. I've been here long enough to wear an actual track in the sand, deep enough to sprain an ankle in. Honestly, it would serve Bastille right if I somehow ruined it. What the hell is a beach volleyball court doing on a tennis campus, anyway? This place is like a fucking resort.

"You know, when I said meet me at the courts I guess I assumed we both knew I meant the ones for tennis," he quips.

This means Noah went to the courts, didn't see me there, and went searching for me.

I feel only marginally guilty about being a no-show. I've been so angry since walking out of Dick's office, I completely forgot about my date with Noah.

Tennis practice. Not a date.

I don't look at him as I continue pacing. If I don't burn off this anger, I won't be able to sleep. And I've done enough testing to know pacing works better for me than pillow punching.

It's not just Dick I'm angry at. I'm mad at my parents for putting me in this position. If they would just let me play full-time—like so many other kids my age are already doing—I wouldn't have to deal with Dick at all. I could just say fuck the Bastille Invitational and play all the other big tournaments. This place could be my version of Serena's Indian Wells boycott.

Instead, they only have tunnel vision for school. More school. Never enough school!

Noah falls in step next to me. He smells like soap.

I switch to breathing through my mouth instead. Noah doesn't get to spoil my perfectly rotten mood.

He clears his throat. "I don't like to get hung up on assigning blame or making accusations but I do think the standard is to apologize when you're the person who got the details wrong."

"Sorry," I grumble. But I don't slow down. I'm still plotting the other thirty-five ways Dick Duncan might die a grisly death.

Noah keeps walking with me but doesn't say anything else. Two laps. Three. Four. He says not a single word. What the fuck is his game? Finally I stop and face him. "Well?"

"Well what? I don't even know who we're mad at."

It's not at all what I expected him to say.

I expected him to get offended. Or mad. Maybe even another prompt to apologize. A better apology. Instead he looks like he always does. Goofy, relaxed, and wearing a T-shirt that fits so well I have to actively try not to look at him. I definitely didn't expect him to take my side. Especially with no details.

"*I'm* mad at Dick Duncan." It's important that he knows I

don't *need* his help. That this isn't me running to him to fix my problems or whatever.

"Okay. Why are *we* mad at him?" Noah makes it a point to stress the *we*.

I hate what it does to my stomach.

Minus 5 for him. He's not allowed to get *more* attractive.

"Because Dick Duncan is a dick," I tell him matter-of-factly.

Noah nods solemnly, like he's considering the information. "That's a stiff accusation."

There's not so much as a twitch in his lip. But there's no way he said that by accident.

I mentally return the five points I just took away. Then I give him a quick recap of the Alyssa Avila situation, followed by Dick's threats to disqualify me again. "In summary, fuck Dick Duncan."

"I'll pass, thanks."

Noah's quip is so quick, and so unexpected, I laugh at what is maybe the dumbest joke in existence. He looks pretty pleased and I don't blame him. I'm an easy audience for his corny sense of humor for some unknown reason.

"Does this mean I'm finally going to find out whatever the hell happened two years ago? I hear people talking about it but they don't actually *say* anything. I'm convinced the entire thing is some Mandela Effect at this point."

It's not a story I like to think about let alone tell, but I'm pretty confident at this point that Noah's reaction won't be anything like Violetta's or my mom's.

"Two years ago, I was in the semis here," I begin. "I should have won like twice already but the girl I was playing against was full-out cheating, so we were in a third-set tiebreak. She hooks another call so I flip out on her and the line judge gives me a penalty. So I turn to the judge like wtf and she gives me one of those 'I didn't catch it' bullshit whatever lines."

Noah sucks his teeth in understanding.

I keep going. "So I point out that it's literally her one fucking job and she gives me another penalty for verbal abuse."

"Ouch."

"It gets better," I warn him. "Then Dick swoops in—like the fucking vulture he is—and decides the person who really needs to be punished in this scenario is me, because I used some swear words about someone cheating me out of a match."

Noah silently tallies the point penalties in his head. "So you ended up losing what, a game?"

"We were in a tiebreak," I remind him.

The bitterness is still in my voice. No matter how hard I try, I can't seem to get over it. The unfairness of it all. Just one more fucking obstacle for me.

Noah closes his eyes as it finally clicks for him. He exhales slowly. "Wow. No wonder you hate him."

Last time, a lot of people thought I deserved what happened to me. Like Dick, they think my loud reaction to a quiet insult is the problem. That I should learn to deal with it like everyone else does. Except most people don't have to deal with it as often as I do.

I stick out. I'm a tall-ass brown girl who doesn't walk around smiling and people feel the need to *do* something about it. When shit happens to me, like the match two years ago, I don't have the luxury of assuming it's just bad luck.

Dick would never make that call against the likes of Violetta and anyone saying he would is lying to themselves.

"Hate doesn't even *begin* to describe how I feel about him. It's been simmering in there for *years*." That Mom took his side was maybe what pushed me past the point of no return.

Noah mimics gently swirling a wineglass before pretending to drink out of it. "Ah, this hatred has been aged, giving it a deeper, more full-bodied richness."

"Aren't you supposed to gargle it before swallowing?"

Noah dips his head so I can't see his reaction. "I'm a gentleman so I'm going to let that one go by."

It's probably for the best. "So, do your manners extend to giving me a two-ball head start since you cheated last night?"

He arches an eyebrow at me. "The way I remember it, you *chose* to watch me serve. Which worked out great for me. You got a show from *this*," he says, his hands sweeping down his body as if to say *ta-da*, "and I got the win. Happy endings for both of us."

It takes both of us an extra second to realize the unexpected opportunity for another joke.

My brain races, needing to be first. I can *win* at flirting!

"I can't believe you brought up happy endings just because I'm Asian," I say with a dirty look. "That's so racist."

He splutters for a second before he realizes I'm joking and laughs.

Plus 20 points for me.

I've definitely won this round and I want to end on a high note. At the same time, I don't want it to end at all.

"Are we doing double or nothing tonight?" I blurt.

He stares into my eyes and it takes everything in me to not squirm. I will not lose to Noah Edelman again. In anything.

Already he has too much power. Beating him in this will keep things more equal.

"Curious to know what the double part of the challenge is," he says.

Me too. I still haven't come up with anything.

He's still staring at me and I can't withstand the attack much longer. I need to make a joke. Break eye contact. Run.

Make this less meaningful than it feels.

For once, I take my own advice. I take off running, calling back, "First person to the courts wins!"

17

VIOLETTA

ALICE AND I ARE SQUISHED ONTO MY BED WATCHING COOKING VIDEOS when Leylah arrives back at the room, much later than usual and in a weirdly good mood. I almost don't recognize it, since she mostly ignores me and I'm busy with Alice, but she's too quiet for it to be anything else.

When Leylah lingers, it means she's looking to pick a fight over something: how annoying I am or how shallow I am or how I'm terrible person in some way. For someone who hates me, she seems to spend a not-insignificant amount of her time arguing with me.

With Alice next to me, it bothers me a lot less. But tonight Leylah dives straight into bed after her shower without so much as a snarky good night to either of us.

Trying to stay quiet, we bury ourselves under the covers and giggle every time we hear Leylah turn over until she finally wakes up from our noise and sends us out to the sofa. I should feel guiltier about keeping everyone up, since I have practice tomorrow and both Alice and Leylah have matches, but I can't. I finally feel like I'm at real camp—the kind where you go *only* to make friends.

"It's surreal to be hanging out with you," Alice says for what feels like the hundredth time. "It's like I know a celebrity."

My ego puffs at the compliment until I remember that I have nowhere to go but down in her estimation. Only showing the best side of yourself at all times comes at a cost.

"I'm just a regular person," I insist. "See?" I wiggle my nose, shifting the oversize purple frames on my face to prove my point. Only a few people have ever seen me without my contacts in, and I'm surprised to realize I'm not as nervous about Alice doing so. Maybe because exposing my physical flaws is easier than the deeper ones I know exist in multitudes.

She laughs. "Sure. A regular person who can make purple eyes look natural."

Even in the dim light, it's impossible not to notice my eyes aren't actually violet—that it's just another part of me that's been tweaked to better fit my image. I'm dying to ask Alice which version of me she prefers but I don't.

"Wait until you see me with no makeup," I threaten. "You probably won't even recognize me."

She shakes her head like I'm being ridiculous. "I've watched enough makeup tutorials to know those eyebrows are the real thing. I'll bet if you put that perfect eyebrow filter up to your face it'd match perfectly."

I've done it and yes, it matches. But I try to remain humble and don't say it aloud.

"What about you?" I ask, wanting to give Alice a compliment in return.

"What about me?"

"What kind of regular person has hair like yours? It's like a wig it's so perfect."

Alice fingers the shiny black curls on her head and I wonder if she got the genes from her mom or her dad. Every part of my face is, ironically, from my dad: the Roman nose, square jaw, even my skin tone. No wonder Audrey always seems pained every time she looks at me. All she seemed to give me was her hair.

And her career.

Stretching a curl between her pinched fingers, Alice admits, "I used to want straight hair."

We both laugh. I guess everyone wants what they don't have.

"Have you always wanted to play tennis?" I don't ask it as a way to scout her interest and commitment to the tournament. At least, I don't think that's why I did. I truly want to know more about her, but I can't help but file away every bit of information just in case.

If Alice suspects something, it doesn't show. She gives a sleepy sort of smile, resting her head against the arm stretched across the back of the couch. Her eyes, so often sad or haunted, take on a sort of wistfulness.

"Always," she says. "Or at least, as far back as I can remember. We live across the street from a court and I would spend hours staring out at the people there, cheering them on from inside our apartment. It felt like a special occasion, like I had a front-row view to it." She pushes a mass of hair out of her face. "What about you?"

"Of course," I reply, a little too quickly. "Both my parents were professional players. It's in my blood."

Alice shrugs. "Neither of my parents played. My dad learned just so he could teach me because I was so interested."

Every time Alice mentions her dad, my heart twinges a little. I learned long ago not to spend time wishing for things I didn't have—like a dad, for example. But to hear Alice talk about hers, I can't help but wonder what I missed out on.

I push the thought away, more than a little guilt gnawing at me. Even though I've never voiced any of this to Audrey, I still feel like I'm betraying her.

"I can't imagine what you've been going through," I say in what must be the most obvious statement of all time.

Alice casts her eyes downward and fiddles with the soft fringed edge of the blanket that's been folded across the back of the sofa. She doesn't say anything for several beats and I wish I could take back my words. Considering our conversation earlier, she's probably sick of being reminded of him.

But then she says quietly, "I thought I would be able to handle it better."

Who handles death well?

"I don't mean his death," she says, as though she's heard my silent question. "But that too. I expected to be sad. But most of the time, I'm just angry."

"At him?"

"At everyone. But especially myself."

I'm no stranger to being hard on myself, but I wonder what Alice has to regret. "Why?" I ask.

"He sacrificed a lot to get me to this point. He even agreed to step back as my primary coach during the high school season so I could play at this private school across town. Except now I'm here and I'm totally unprepared. I'm just wasting it."

Leylah said something similar—about this being her one chance at things. I know what Audrey expects of me here, but I also know it's by no means my only chance at it. So why do I feel the same kind of crushing pressure as they do?

"Why haven't I seen you at any tournaments before?" I ask. Maybe Alice's answer will give me a clue to things.

Alice gives a shy shrug. "My dad didn't know about all that stuff. Sports in San Francisco is . . . complicated. And expensive. It wasn't until we started busing out to Golden Gate Park to find more competition that we even heard about the junior programs. Even then, there wasn't a lot of time or means to get to any of the locations. The only USA Tennis-sanctioned tournament I played was because one of the girls on my high school team entered and she gave me a ride."

I try to imagine an entire year in which I only play one single tournament.

I can't.

"Are you good friends with the girls on your team?"

High school sports has always seemed like such a bonding experience. Granted, most movies and TV shows center around football or basketball, but Zonals has always been my favorite tournament because of the team aspect. Instead of competing *against* everyone in my section, we get an entire week to join forces against other sections, playing in teams we might never have experienced before.

12s Zonals was when Leylah and I really became friends.

Alice shakes her head and the sadness creeps back into her eyes. "Not really. I mostly keep to myself. Every once in a while they invite me to stuff but it always feels like a pity-invite so I never go. I don't really have anything in common with them anyway."

I am absolutely a pity-inviter. And I definitely pity-invited Alice to look through my closet for clothes after I saw her washing her shirt in the sink earlier. I thought I was being altruistic. Now I feel like a jerk.

Maybe I am the superficial facade Leylah accuses me of being.

I want to confess to Alice that I sometimes feel I'm wasting my time here too—that even with world-class training six days a week, year-round, I am still terrified I'll never be as good as Leylah. That I'll disappoint Audrey and she'll have given up her entire life for nothing.

But I can't bring myself to say those things aloud. I like that Alice still looks up to me as this person who's got their life together, and telling her otherwise would end up disappointing her too.

Maybe after I win this tournament. *Then* we can truly be friends.

SATURDAY, JULY 8TH

QUALIFYING TOURNAMENT, QUARTERFINALS

18

VIOLETTA

SATURDAY PRACTICE HAS NEVER BEEN MY FAVORITE. I'M NOT SURE IT'S anyone's favorite, frankly, but today I have an especially hard time dragging myself out of bed for it. Part of it is probably because Alice and I stayed up all night like middle schoolers at a sleepover. But another part is just . . . dread.

Why do we have to practice six days a week? Why can't we have time off to relax and do normal teenager things? Like drive around or go shopping or whatever it is kids on TV get to do. Even when we *do* get time off here, practice always looms in the back of our minds, threatening its comeback after only a day or two of rest.

There's never *really* a break.

I wish Alice luck at her match and head off to the courts, where the only thing I have to look forward to is seeing Coop. If not for Alice, I probably would have been throwing up from nerves and panic-texting him all last night. The main draws won't be released until tomorrow but already I'm nervous. Instead of feeling like there are more chances to succeed, like Audrey says, I feel like there are only more chances to fail. Four separate draws where I could lose. And not that I'm tracking it closely, but Leylah seems positioned to make the main draw in not only singles but also doubles.

Alice said she was angry with herself for her dad's death. Maybe some of my anger with Leylah is letting her bother me in the first place.

Practice crawls along like we have court sweepers dragging behind us, the green clay getting shuffled left and right. Coop has to remind me more than once to get my head in the game. "Monday's a big day." He gives my shoulder a little squeeze. "I want to make sure you're in top shape for it."

I try harder. For him.

At lunch, Audrey texts me to say she can't make it over to the courts, but reminds me not to "go wild with carbs" today. I slather my mashed potatoes in butter and eat an entire sleeve of chocolate chip cookies in response.

After lunch, Cooper arranges doubles practice for Rachel and me even though we've been playing together for so many years I can practically hear her thoughts by now. Besides Leylah, Rachel is the player I've known the longest. The first time she asked me to pair up we were ten years old. I said yes, and we've just been playing together ever since.

On the court, we're a great combination. She's communicative and always gives maximum effort. But also, I pair with her because I don't want to play against her.

"V, can you pay attention?" Rachel squawks, barely dodging

another high volley put away because I floated my return across the middle.

"I thought I'd go for a chip 'n' charge kind of shot," I offer.

Rachel gives me a look. "Since when do you have a forehand slice?"

I offer her an anemic sort of smile and she gives me another hard look. Between her sharp nose and close-set eyes, she looks a lot like a peregrine falcon, ready to attack at ninety miles per hour. "You are banned from using that shot in our doubles match," she says, the clay beneath her feet grinding loudly as she whirls back to her spot.

She's probably right. Neither of my slices are very good, despite spending hundreds upon hundreds of hours practicing them with Coop. It's still my biggest weakness.

I look over to him for reassurance, but he's on the next court, giving pointers to some of the 14s girls. They giggle behind their hands when he's not looking and I tear my eyes away.

The server double-faults and it's my turn to return again.

Without thinking, I attempt another forehand slice, which floats nicely just over the net player's head. She looks about as surprised I am that my clear mishit was so cleverly placed, and suddenly we're knee-deep in a long point. They lob back, over Rachel's head, and as I'm running to retrieve it, I attempt a slide that jams, rolling over my ankle.

I pitch my body forward to minimize the weight on the joint, hitting the ground with a thud. I just hope I don't get clay grit in my skin. Having to scrub out tiny particles of dirt from a wound is especially nasty business and always reminds me how lucky I am that Audrey didn't put me into contact sports.

Everyone rushes toward me after I don't immediately bounce back up. Even from a court away, Cooper is the first one to reach me. I can see the concern in his beautifully blue eyes.

He's worried. About me.

"What'd you hurt, V?" he asks, his familiar hands already on my shoulders. He helps pull me to a sitting position and I grab my ankle. He takes it in his hands and I wish the girls crowded around would give us some space.

"You think you sprained it?" he asks.

Coop is asking me to diagnose myself. He trusts me to do this. Because I'm mature and responsible enough to know my own body.

"Maybe," I reply, standing up and gingerly putting the slightest amount of pressure on it. It's definitely sore. And maybe I could walk it off, but that might damage my ankle more. Better play it safe. "I think I need ice."

He braces an arm around my waist so I can hobble my way to the training room. "Go back to playing," he orders the girls. "Daniella? Pair up with Rachel for now. She needs to practice for next week."

The Panthéon, aka the training room, is a bit of a trek from our court—a fact I both love and hate. I hop a little closer to Coop and he holds me tighter, trying to ensure I don't have to put any weight on my ankle. "I hope it's not too bad," I say.

"I'm sure you'll be fine. Looks like you took a good roll so hopefully you didn't land on it too bad." He grins at me and swipes across my back a few times to brush off the green dust. It's a full swipe, from the top of my shoulder to the absolute bottom of my back, nearly grazing my butt. It's probably unintentional.

"What did you get up to last night anyway?" Coop asks. "You came in dragging like you were hungover or something."

I nearly trip at that, too close to the times I *have* shown up mildly hungover. It's not often, of course, but I've definitely made the mistake of smoking too much before bed and waking up still drowsy and a little nauseous. Really, only a handful of times.

But Coop doesn't know about any of that. He may hint at it, but we've never actually talked about it. I guess he'd have to report it if we did.

"I made a new friend." I beam, my mood instantly improving at the thought of Alice and our long conversation last night.

Coop arches an eyebrow. "A male friend?"

I give him a little shove, despite the fact he's holding me up, and he laughs.

"Just asking!"

"Female friend," I assure him. "Alice. She's in the 16s. She's staying in my villa."

"Is she cute?"

I shove him again, hopping on one foot to stay upright. "You're a pig."

"I mean for you! What would I do with a sixteen-year-old girl?"

"I'm a sixteen-year-old girl," I remind him.

He wraps his arm back around my waist muttering, "Don't I know it."

Once again, I wish I were eighteen. I'm practically an adult already, living on my own for the past two years—the number is just an arbitrary line to pass.

Still, I know it's a line Coop won't cross.

"Do you miss being around adults?" I ask.

He gives me an odd look, but keeps us moving forward. "In what way?"

"On tour. I don't know. Just, your life before you came here. I'm sure the people you hung out with were more mature or whatever."

I'm not sure what I'm hoping to hear. It's not likely he'll tell me he likes being around a bunch of kids instead of other professional athletes that have their own lives and money and whatnot. But I hold my breath anyway as he thinks it over, his forehead wrinkling in the most adorable way.

"Tour life is pretty lonely," he admits. "It's a lot of travel and a lot of nights in very uncomfortable hotel beds by myself."

Is it just my imagination, or did he stress those last two words just a tiny bit?

"Adults are overrated," he continues with a shake of the head and a little chuckle. "I was practically a kid myself when I was playing. I have no business being around other adults."

"And now?" I ask. "Do you miss playing?"

"Nearly every day." His tone is grim and I can feel the pain behind his words. Audrey never speaks of that time in her life, or that I was the reason she had to give it all up. But even as well as she hides it, I know she must miss it as much as Coop does. Maybe even more so.

With Audrey, I distract her with the latest gossip. She acts like she's above it, but she's never once forgotten a fact I've told her about someone. I think being able to be petty and mean about stupid, trivial things is an outlet for her—a way to quietly compete against herself in compiling and weaponizing facts about my opponents.

I have the same instinct to cheer up Coop, so I shoot him a saucy grin before asking, "Which days don't you miss it? The ones you're with me?"

He barks a laugh and just like that, he's back to himself.

We hobble together past the stone columns out front of the Panthéon (not to be confused with the Pantheon in Rome) and I try not to think about the fact that our wellness center is located inside what's used as a crypt in Paris. Despite its grand size and lack of a creepy basement, I can never quite shake off the feeling that going inside it equates to death.

I suppose for athletes, injury and illness *are* death. Coop knows that better than anyone.

We reach the training room and he helps me up onto a training table, even going so far as to lift each of my legs so that they stick out in front of me. He waves off the junior trainer and goes to the massive ice chests along the wall, scooping ice from one of them into a clear plastic bag for me. "Tell me more about this Alice," he says over the crunch as he plunges the shovel into the ice. "You two stayed up late last night to what, pillow fight? Braid each other's hair? Swap secrets?" He waggles his eyebrows, dropping his voice to a low rumble that sends a little quiver through my insides. "Maybe your deepest, darkest, desires?"

I shoot a look toward the junior trainer, who seems too absorbed in her phone to have heard his remark. I shake my head at him in a warning. "Don't get jealous just because you weren't invited."

"Don't worry about me, I find ways of entertaining myself." He jostles the bag of ice in his hands, before cradling it and sucking the air out. He catches me looking at him and holds my eye, the twinkle in his that tells me it's just a game. But it feels like he's sucking the air out of my lungs through that bag.

I sit, speechless, as he peels off my shoe and sock, touching my sweaty foot to position the bag on my ankle before wrapping it tightly with the roll of cling film. His fingers graze my skin twice as he wraps it enough times that I could stand and the bag would remain in place. Goose bumps run up my leg and I suppress a shudder, hoping to pass it off as a reaction to the temperature of the ice.

When he looks up, we lock eyes and I fall into the unfathomable depths of his magnificent blue pools. More like he sucks me into them. From this distance, I risk drowning but I won't be the first to look away.

I couldn't even if I tried.

After what feels like both a lifetime and a split second, he breaks the connection. Patting the bag twice like someone sending off a taxi, his voice comes out rough and thick. "Sit tight, I'll check on you later, okay?"

He's gone before I can even answer the question.

19

ALICE

I FIDGET IN THE SOLITARY CHAIR OUTSIDE MR. DUNCAN'S OFFICE, waiting to be summoned in. He has insisted we all just call him Dick, but I can't bring myself to do that. For myriad reasons.

I'm still slick with sweat after my match, my thumb salty as I nervously rack my brain for why I've been called here. I lost. I'm completely out of the tournament. What could he possibly need with me?

My teeth gnaw on the familiar bump below my knuckle during the wait, not caring who sees me right now. I know there is no good news coming. No good news ever comes out of being summoned to speak privately.

The doctor who delivered the news had asked to speak to Mama privately, taking her down the corridor and away from where David and I could hear. After keeping Baba's illness concealed from me for over a year, what was one more day? She'd managed to choke the words out eventually, once the tears had stopped and she'd begun to worry there weren't enough savings to cover the cremation, let alone the lingering care expenses. Care that saw him die anyway, each bill an individual reminder of his passing.

And yet they bought my ticket to Florida.

Guilt gnaws at my stomach and I suck more furiously, the pain from my teeth well deserved.

The sound of a door opening turns my head and all I see are Dick's dark, hairy hands curling around the doorjamb like a horror movie creature, lurking in the shadows to pounce upon the heroine unexpectedly. I gulp but stand and enter, my own hands twisting themselves into the pockets of my shorts.

The office is large and well-lit, windows across two walls allowing sunlight to drown the entire space in a bright glow. I hear the faint hum of the air-conditioning but my body is too numb to register any meaningful drop in temperature. All my senses are currently consumed by the soft tickle of dust mites in my nose. I see them all, drifting through the beams of sunlight like the seeds blown off a dried dandelion.

If I could make a wish on them, it would be to start this whole day over again. Replay my match. Next time, I wouldn't hit that lob on such a crucial point in the tiebreak. I'd been *so close*.

"I imagine you know why you've been called here," Dick says in a smooth voice once I've taken a seat.

I shake my head, hoping to form words but unable to. Sitting here gives me flashbacks to that day. Is it home? Has someone else died?

"As you know, the Bastille Invitational is a very exclusive

tournament. You getting into the qualifying draw at all, with your background, was a feat unto itself."

"Okay," I choke out. Has he really called me here to gloat over my loss?

"We pride ourselves on hosting the best of the best here, so naturally I had concerns when your first two contests ended with . . . so little competition."

I know I don't have to defend myself to the likes of him, but I can't stop myself from blurting out, "My last match was *very* competitive. I lost 10-8 in the super-breaker."

Never before have I felt the need to boast about my performance, especially when shouldering a loss.

He steeples his fingers together, the wrinkles on the backs of his hands placing his age somewhere in the mid-fifties. "Now that the final four qualifiers have secured the empty spaces in the draw, this is the time that many players choose to take their leave. Of course, some stay on to watch the tournament, which is completely within their right to do as the cost of housing is paid in full up front."

He pauses, then unsteeples his fingers and leans toward me, the angle of his head catching the light and highlighting the deep grooves in his face. I'm grateful he has such a large desk to keep the space between us. "You do know how much the housing and meals cost for the tournament, don't you?"

I saw it when Baba and I sent it my application. He told me not to think about it.

"Yes."

"Then you would agree it's quite a sum to be spent on—what did you play, two complete matches?"

My brain is spinning, but I still cannot seem to work out why I'm here. Is he going to offer me some kind of second chance? Is there a secret consolation draw I wasn't aware of?

My heart lifts for a split second before it comes crashing down again.

"Despite some protests from the board, Nancy Conrad personally saw to it that all your expenses were covered."

It's as if a gunshot has been fired next to my ears. I hear nothing, the echo of his words ringing in my head. Mrs. Conrad paid for this? How is that possible?

Unaware that I'm not entirely listening, he continues. "In normal circumstances, these fees are nonrefundable. Everything is a flat rate so that those who continue to win are not penalized with additional expenses. However, we find ourselves in a—ahem—*unique* situation here." He clears his throat once more before forging on. "As Nancy Conrad is a respected and valued board member of Bastille, I am inclined to return a portion of the expenses on a pro rata basis, assuming you leave tomorrow."

I am slow to process the information. Ma and David *didn't* spend thousands of dollars for me to be here. But Mrs. Conrad did.

Any relief I feel in having saved my family the funds is clouded by the realization that I owe even more to the generosity of Ma's oldest client.

I can't imagine how Mama reacted to the news. In seventeen years of cleaning Mrs. Conrad's house, Ma has never once accepted a single gift from her. I can't seem to wrap my head around the fact that she took such a large sum on my behalf.

It does, however, explain how they were able to come up with the money.

"So you'll give Mrs. Conrad back her money if I leave tomorrow?"

He gives a brisk nod. "A portion of it. A large portion, seeing as we haven't yet hit the halfway mark of our ten-day event."

Another reminder of how disappointing my results have been.

"So . . . you think I should go home," I say slowly. I don't phrase it like a question, but it's what I'm asking nevertheless.

Mr. Duncan purses his lips like he's eaten something sour. "This is not about what I think, Ms. Wu. It is about you and your family's relationship to Nancy Conrad and whether you believe it is a wise investment of her money to remain at a tournament you have been eliminated from."

I almost miss Mr. Duncan's emphasis on the words *her* and *you* because I'm so focused on Mama—how she hadn't even wanted me to accept the scholarship to St. Aidan's, so how could she possibly have let Mrs. Conrad pay for my trip?

A galaxy of questions swirl around in my head, chief among them the decision of whether or not to leave early. I can't stomach the thought of wasting Mrs. Conrad's money, which is exactly what I would be doing if I stayed until Bastille Day.

It's just . . . last night was my first glimpse at happiness since Ba died. Even when talking about him with Violetta, I felt less sad than before. As if the emotions bottled up in me could be physically poured out and reduced—served to another person to consume and take away.

My presence at Bastille is selfish. Wanting to stay, to avoid real life just a bit longer and luxuriate in this fantasy while my family at home remains broken, is selfish. Even enjoying my time here, when Baba cannot, feels selfish.

But I can't seem to bring myself to agree to Mr. Duncan's terms either.

"Can I think about it?" I ask.

The sour face makes a reappearance, my continued presence somehow displeasing to him personally.

But he nods. A temporary reprieve.

20

ALICE

THE ENTIRE WAY BACK TO THE VILLA, I TURN MR. DUNCAN'S OFFER OVER in my head again and again. I could go home tomorrow. I could pay back Mrs. Conrad some of the money she spent on me, and spare Ma the embarrassment she is surely feeling over the whole thing. I've already lost. The chances someone will pull out at this point—opening up a lucky loser spot—are nearly zero. There's no reason for me to stay.

I should leave. Of course I should leave.

I cross each cobblestone plaza and bid the Joans goodbye, this probably my last time seeing them. The villas around each plaza are different colors and if the internet is to be trusted, the Bastille dorms do look reminiscent of the bright, half-timbered houses of Colmar. This is as close as I'll ever get to France.

I step into our villa and drop my racquets onto the stone floor, allowing them to clatter loudly. I've noticed both Violetta and Leylah do this. At first I'd thought it was perhaps out of negligence for their equipment, easily replaced if broken or damaged.

But now I see they do it to take up space. They assert themselves by making noise, and it makes me realize I've been quiet for too long.

I've been silent about my grief, about my anger, and about my needs. And right now, I need comfort. Support. Affection.

I need to touch another human being and know that they won't immediately disappoint me.

"Alice?"

Despite my mess with the equipment, I carefully toe off my shoes and line them up against the wall before turning my attention to Violetta. "How did you know it was me?"

"Leylah's way louder."

"I heard that," Leylah shouts through the bathroom door.

I find Violetta stretched across the couch, one foot propped on a pillow and strapped with ice. Whatever bad news I'd been carrying evaporates as I rush toward her. "Oh no! What happened?"

She waves off my concern. "Nothing serious. I rolled over it at practice."

"From sliding?" I guess. Moving on the clay seems to require its own set of rules, like antigravity or underwater.

"Enough about me. How did your match go?"

Reality comes rushing back.

"I lost." Saying it aloud reminds me that I will likely leave tomorrow, no reason for me to stay. Tears spring to my eyes and Violetta scrambles up from the couch.

"Your ankle," I protest before she smothers me in a hug. The contact shatters what's left of the emotional wall I've been clinging to and I sob into her hair. Violetta Masuda's beautiful, thick, shiny mane that creates its own current of air whenever she moves.

Except she's no longer *Violetta Masuda* to me. She's the person who welcomed me here, selflessly helped when I was in need, and now the only person I've let comfort me. This is no longer a fantasy, but a real connection I'm forming with a real person. I'm not sure I've ever had someone like that who wasn't related to me. The fact that Violetta smells like lavender is real. It forces to me think of my other reality, three thousand miles away, above a laundromat and across the street from a tennis court.

"It's okay, there will always be another tournament," she says, which only makes me sob harder. How do I go home like this? How do I explain to my family that this *thing* they've all sacrificed for—that Mama swallowed her pride for and Baba may have lost his life for—isn't something I'm sure I want to do anymore?

Yes, I went out and performed today. I even almost won. But ultimately my heart just wasn't in it.

I don't know how to do this alone.

Violetta lets me cry into her shoulder as she hugs me with one arm, her other hand running strokes down the back of my head as I finally exhaust the emotions I've been holding inside all these weeks.

I'm angry. I'm sad. I'm devastated. And I'm incredibly, violently guilty that it's taken me this long to finally cry the way I should have the moment I learned Baba had died. But more than anything, I feel so desperately alone.

"You're not alone," Violetta murmurs, causing me to pull back. I must have said my words aloud.

We both notice Leylah at the same time. When we lock eyes, Leylah freezes, her face and body position announcing she'd meant to sneak by undetected. "I kept waiting for a better time, but there wasn't one," she explains with a cringe. "Sorry."

I dry my face on my shirt—the polo from Violetta. It's now smudged with dirt and the fabric chafes my eyes, sore and dried out from the sunshine and crying. "It's fine," I assure Leylah. "I appreciate the distraction."

I'm slightly embarrassed to have called so much attention to myself.

It's okay to take up space, I remind myself. If I were either of them, I would have been understanding enough to let them cry on me. I force myself to acknowledge they probably feel similar.

So I tell them about what happened in Mr. Duncan's office. Still, I keep it short, aware of Leylah's financial status and the fact that I'm currently wearing Violetta's castoffs. I understand Mama's aversion to pity. But I'm not a victim of anything other than an overly generous patron and my own wasted potential.

When I'm finished, a wrinkle pinches between Leylah's eyebrows. "So you had no idea that this rich lady—"

"Mrs. Conrad," I correct. It feels disrespectful to let anyone refer to her as "this rich lady," as if she were nothing more than an ATM.

"Sure, whatever." Leylah agrees to get me to shut up. "My point is, why are you rushing to get her money back? It sounds like she has plenty of it."

Violetta fires off an insult, seemingly offended by Leylah's remark. "You *would* see this as completely transactional. Her family obviously has a relationship with this woman."

"Yes. A good enough relationship for her to drop thousands of dollars without even asking for credit," Leylah fires back.

"So you think she should just stay, even if it totally humiliates her mom?"

"Some of us don't live our lives just to please our parents."

In a mere two shots, though not directed at me, Leylah dismantles my entire world.

I came here for my family. *Because* of my family. Because they went behind my back and accepted this massive gift on my behalf without bothering to tell me. Because I felt responsible for making the most of Baba's sacrifice.

David insisted they'd all tried to talk him out of forgoing treatment—that Baba had said his gut told him this was the right decision. Dying was the right decision. Leaving me was the right decision. And everyone simply went along with it, carrying his secret for months so I could "live a normal teenager's life."

Just thinking about it enrages me. What normal teenager has a parent die?

I think of the kids I go to St. Aidan's with, who shoplift from stores or smoke weed in their cars after school, stealing pills from their parent's medicine cabinets. Are they normal? Or is it the kids who tag the boarded-up stores along Mission Street, riding the bus around the city with their music on full volume without a thought to other passengers? How about the kids at Bastille, who move away from their family and friends to train six days a week for a dream so improbable the whole of us are more likely to be struck by lightning? Are they the normal ones?

If my family is so eager for me to live a teenager's life, I should be doing ill-advised teenager things.

I want to shut off my brain. Just once.

"I want to do something reckless," I declare.

My outburst surprises the both of them, Leylah seeming wary. But Violetta's eyes light up, seemingly delighted by the existence of this side of me.

She opens her mouth but before she can say anything, Leylah cuts her off.

"No."

"What do you mean, no?" Violetta demands.

"I know what you're thinking, and *no*," Leylah says.

The two of them make a series of angry faces at each other, a full conversation taking place with their eyes. Every time I'm with the two of them together, it's like I'm missing half the script and I spend the entire time trying to catch up.

Left out once again.

"I'm in," I say, using the same voice of confidence I had when I decided thirty seconds ago to act like a "normal" teenager. I am committed to asserting myself in the conversation. Without a fully developed prefrontal cortex, it should be perfectly reasonable for me to make rash, foolish decisions with unwavering certainty.

Leylah is nearly frantic, her face pinched with intensity. "Don't do this. However you're feeling right now—it's not worth it, trust me."

"Alice isn't you," Violetta snaps at Leylah. "She doesn't have diabetes, she'll be fine."

"It's not the *health* aspect I have a problem with," Leylah retorts.

I really, really hope what Violetta has in mind isn't some viral trend of chugging two liters of soda or something equally horrifying. And she was too smart to suggest something like the crate challenge, wasn't she?

Despite my hard exterior, I'm rapidly losing confidence inside. Clearly Leylah knows something I don't. "Will someone please tell me what we're arguing over?"

"I'm not arguing," Leylah insists, throwing Violetta a final look of disgust before turning back to me. "I have better things to do with my time, and so do you."

She's probably right, but I shrug anyway. If this is going to be my last night here, this is how I want to spend it. This is who I want to spend it with.

Leylah storms out, slamming the door closed with a sharp *thwack*.

"What was that about?" I ask.

Violetta's scowl is replaced with a sunny smile. "Nothing, but forget about it," she says briskly. "Tonight is about you and fulfilling your long-lost dream to be reckless."

Her eyes twinkle with mischief and already I can feel the heaviness in my chest easing. It's only then I realize that despite all the turmoil, I haven't once needed my hands anywhere near my face. My thumb is dry and entirely wrinkle-free—a rare sight since I arrived at Bastille.

How could I ever have doubted her?

"What do you want to do?" Violetta asks. "Or maybe I should say, what are you *willing* to do?"

That she asked means everything to me, so used to being dictated to rather than asked. Knowing she sees me as an equal only reaffirms my attachment. *This* is someone who truly wants what's best for me.

"I trust you. You choose."

21

LEYLAH

HONESTLY, I'M PRETTY FUCKING SICK OF STORMING OUT OF PLACES. I only have so much energy every day. I should *not* be spending this much of it on Violetta.

It's not my business what she does.

Or what Alice does.

Especially if they do it together.

None of this is my problem. I need to focus on myself.

Yes, I would fucking *love* to see Violetta finally get in trouble for something. Especially when it's the same thing she got me in trouble for two years ago. Watching her fall from grace would be a life highlight. Not to mention seeing Audrey's reaction.

But I'm not a narc. Even if she deserves it.

So instead I'm at the courts again, not having anywhere else to go.

I wish Noah were here.

I shake the idea out of my head. He already said he was hanging out with his guy friends tonight. Which is fine, of course.

It would probably be weird if he cleared his entire schedule for me. Under the right circumstances, I could see Noah being one of those guys who would. Like, for someone he'd known longer than a couple days. Which is different than this. Naturally.

Ugh.

Minus 5 points for being pathetic.

This is exactly what I don't need right now. I could lie to myself and say I want him here because he's the one with the key to the ball cart, but it's better this way. Really. This way I won't be distracted.

I just wish I had more than six measly balls with me. Especially since two of them are already sort of dead.

Whatever.

I serve my six balls across the net, trying to narrow my focus to only this one task. I won't know who I'm playing until the draw is announced tomorrow so I need to prepare like it's going to be the hardest match of my life.

That's how I try to play every time—like it could be my last match. Except this time it's true.

The only reason I haven't been held back in school is because I ace PE every year and it boosts my GPA. I spent last year—my junior year—in freshman English and sophomore math. Even then, I needed extra tutors every time an essay was due. My entire summer has been nothing but makeup classes, and after this tournament ends, I'll be right back there. Until it starts all over again in the fall.

The thought of another year filled with underclassmen has me hustling to the other side of the net. The past two years have been hell, fighting on what seems like every front just to get back to this point. And now I'm six wins away from winning it all.

Six balls for six wins.

Freedom from school. *Thwack.*

Freedom from Violetta. *Thwack.*

Freedom from my parents and the person they expect me to be. *Thwack.*

"A little late to be out on the courts, Ms. Lee." Dick strolls up to my court, leaning his arm against the low side fence that lines one side. He's a one-man police department at Bastille—always a lurking presence, but only focused on certain people.

"There wouldn't be lights on the courts if we weren't allowed to use them at night," I say, using my racquet to point up at the lights. If I used my hands, I'd be tempted to flip him off.

Dick's mouth flattens but he doesn't have a good reply for that one. "It seems difficult with only . . . what is that, six balls?" He does a quick count to ensure the number.

"If you have a key to the shed, I'd happily use one of the buckets we're *supposed* to have access to but don't," I say sweetly.

"You could have easily asked someone at the front office to unlock it for you."

He says it like I'm supposed to fucking know that. Violetta hadn't included that in her tour.

"I'm asking you now," I say, my voice strained but steady.

Plus 5 points for keeping my shit together.

"I don't remember hearing a *please*, Ms. Lee."

"Fuck that," I say reflexively.

Dick twists his face into a little crinkled bundle of outrage. "Always with the colorful language."

I pinch a tiny bit of skin on my thigh and twist it. Hard. This is absolutely the last place I should be swearing. After yesterday's "chat," I would rather swear in front of my *parents* than Dick right now.

"That came out on accident," I say. It's the closest thing to an apology I can muster.

Dick sorts through his key ring until he singles out a tiny silver one. He holds it up and shakes the whole ring, the way people do to dogs. "I'm afraid I can't use this without a please." His voice is practically a singsong. "Your future is in your hands, Ms. Lee. Make sure you choose what's best for it."

Fuck this guy. Fuck every teacher, tutor, reading specialist, language coach, and whoever else who told me I was stupid and that I'd get nowhere in life. And fuck Violetta and my parents. If it weren't for them, I wouldn't have to be dealing with any of this right now.

Dick is like the teachers who sit me in the front row on the first day to "keep an eye on you." The ones who memorize every time I've done something wrong, but never anything I do right. The ones who decide that I'm oppositional—even when I'm not saying anything—just because I'm not all smiles and deference. Especially compared to the handful of East Asians at my private school. Every time I open my mouth, it ends in detention.

I'd love to know what "life skill" I'm being taught by sitting in an empty classroom for thirty minutes after school. How much do you have to hate kids to give up your own free time after work just to punish one?

If Dick were a teacher, he'd definitely hand out detentions.

Scratch that, Dick is the kind who would call the police on a student.

He jingles the keys again and I just know. I will never show respect to people like him, in any situation. It's the main reason my parents and I don't get along. Apparently having an intolerance for disrespect is considered "too American."

If Mom were here, she'd give in to Dick and say *please*.

If Mom were here, she'd say it was *my* fault Dick felt he needed to speak to me like that in the first place.

I make it a point to cross the court on the *other* side of the net, away from him.

He shakes the keys a final time, reaching toward his pocket like he's about to put them away. "Ms. Lee?"

I don't respond. I act like I don't even hear him. I don't deserve this shit.

I collect my six balls to serve back the other way while saying nothing.

I keep my eyes forward as I serve but he stays in my peripheral vision. By the time my second serve lands, he's gone.

22

LEYLAH

I STAY ON THE COURT FOR ANOTHER HALF HOUR JUST TO SPITE DICK.
Toward the end, I'm really more angrily walking back and forth
than actually serving, but it's the best I can do under the circumstances. At least I've done something productive with my time,
unlike *some* people.

I avoid going back to the villa, if for no other reason than it
might be filled with smoke. That's one of the things I remember
most about it: the smell of the smoke. It reminded me of skunk
spray. It'll take forever to air out the room, so I head for the
beach to wait it out. It'll be good to get away from Bastille for a
while.

It's not that I'm *sad* here, exactly. I never actually believed
I'd get to live at an academy like this. My parents are happy to
drop unlimited funds for my education (private school, private
tutors, supplemental materials, summer classes, and so on) but
not for athletics. That, I always have to earn. Without tennis as
my reward, I would have tried to quit school a long time ago.

Meanwhile, the rest of my family collect degrees like fucking Pokémon. Both my sisters graduated college in only three years—one of them is now in a master's program for aerospace engineering and the other is pursuing her PhD in biotech.

Mom's personal crusade is to change the stereotype that Southeast Asians are bad at school. I don't think she can forgive me for not being able to contribute to the cause.

Even before I can see the water, I hear the waves. Thinking about dipping my toes in the water perks up my mood. Maybe the ocean can wash away this storm cloud that hovers every time I think about what's waiting for me back home.

I slip off my shoes and socks and sigh as my feet sink into the sand. The sky is darkening by the second but the sand is still warm.

I wish Noah were here. The thought flits through my mind for the second time tonight.

It's not just that he always seems to cheer me up. It's that he isn't . . . put off by me. I'm not *trying* to go through the day angry—the world just conspires against me. But everyone acts like it's a mortal sin not to slap on a smile and make the best of it.

I don't want to make the best of it. I want to smash it the fuck down so no one asks me that anymore. Somehow Noah seems to get that about me. There's only ever been one other person who has.

The high sand dunes on both sides of me block my peripheral vision, like I'm in a straight tunnel down to the waves—Moses and the Red Sea and all that shit. I'm grateful because it makes my path easier. It'll be pitch-black when I try to head back.

I'm nearly to the water when I hear Noah's voice.

I freeze.

He's here. Right here. How is he right here?

I check my phone. Not too late to be out, but definitely too late to be at the beach. Obviously my case is an exception.

But then I hear *her*. That raspy laugh, like she's swallowed a hornet's nest.

I unfreeze and quickly scramble up the sand dune on my hands and knees until I see the dim glow of cell phone lights.

Below me are six bodies huddled in a sort-of circle, everyone sitting on the sand. I identify Violetta and Alice immediately, even from the back—V with her annoying laugh and Alice with her mass of hair. Squinting to adjust my eyes, I spy DJ's dark skin, Kevin's high bun, and Alexei's towering height. Even sitting, he looks like a flagpole sticking out of the sand.

Alexei and DJ are in the boys' 18U draw like Noah, while Kevin is Violetta's age and still qualifies for 16U. All three of them are goggling Violetta like she's god's gift to humanity.

That means the person squeezed between Alice and Violetta, blowing smoke into the air, is Noah. He laughs like he's exactly as happy to be here with them as he's been every time with me. He hands off whatever he's holding to Violetta, who gives a fake shiver before leaning into him and resting her head on his shoulder.

My heart drops through my stomach.

I should have fucking known.

Violetta has some internal radar that goes off any time someone might like me just a little more than they like her so she can swoop in with her big boobs and her shiny hair and her perky fucking attitude that makes boys feel like they have something important to say even when they don't. She's spent her entire life cultivating a personality designed to attract attention. I shouldn't be surprised when she gets it.

Two years ago, I *was* surprised when she kissed Peter. We'd all been high and my brain was moving at half speed so it took a minute to sink in, but I definitely saw her lean on Peter the same way she's leaning on Noah right now. It makes her so much closer to kiss.

I've gone over it a thousand times in my mind and I am absolutely certain Violetta kissed *him*, not the other way around. The lean was a precursor.

Everything after that is a blur.

Fruity, thirsty, dizzy, alarms. Blaring alarms. Waking up in a hospital to Mom and Audrey, then being whisked home with the threat of never letting me play ever again.

Violetta and that one kiss almost ruined my fucking life.

I can't believe I almost let Noah do it to me all over again. I guess this is what he meant by "hanging out with friends." He and his cozy little party of six laugh and joke and snuggle together as the wind comes in off the water. They're probably all high.

Backing away slowly, I hope my movements don't attract their attention. Getting caught here, like I followed them or something, would be so hideous I can't even imagine it. I never want to run into Noah Edelman ever again.

I sprint away from the beach, all the way to the villa, not bothering to put my shoes back on. Fuck Violetta for doing this to me again. And fuck Noah for falling for it.

If I'd been smarter this never would have happened.

23
ALICE

THE SIX OF US ARE SPRAWLED ACROSS THE SAND LIKE STARFISH, OUR faces pointed skyward. We'll all be tossed out of Bastille if Mr. Duncan or any of the staff happen to catch us here, but I find I can't muster the energy to be anxious about it right now. I've essentially been kicked out already, after all.

I have always wanted to see snow in person, and brushing my arms and legs across the sand to make an angel pattern is probably the closest I will ever get. My body sinks farther into the ground with each stroke and I imagine the tiny grains of sand working their way into the crevices of my body—clinging to the roots of my hair and hiding away in my pockets. I burrow my feet deeper into it, searching for the warmth that lurks beneath the cool surface.

Maybe the beach isn't a stationary location, but a moving, feeling thing that's *alive*, much like the ocean. Maybe it's not so much the ocean that rises and falls, pushing and pulling the sand with its tide, but the beach itself controlling the ocean with its subtle influence. The beautiful ocean, with its glittery brilliance during the day and cool, stormy depths after sunset. The beautiful ocean, that everyone flocks to and admires, its natural radiance reflecting off their bodies like gold just from sheer proximity. No one admires the beach except the ocean, and maybe that's where it draws its power.

Am I the beach? Could I be Violetta's beach?

My thoughts are interrupted as a face appears above mine, a light shining straight onto me. I throw my arms over my eyes to protect them and I feel the person direct the light away from me.

I reopen my eyes to Noah asking me, "You feeling all right?"

"I was making snow angels."

He raises his eyebrows, as if my answer is somehow strange. "We've all been calling you but you weren't answering."

I prop myself up on my elbows to confirm that the others are all indeed standing around, waiting for me. But for what?

Noah speaks to the others as if I'm not here, each person their own small dot of light in the dark. "Yeah, she'll want ice cream."

I don't know what's happening, but ice cream suddenly sounds delicious. I find myself wondering where we'll find ice cream on the beach and whether there will be cones, my mouth already anticipating the tactile crunch of each type. Sugar, snappy. Cake, crispy. Waffle, always soggier than expected.

I hear the sound of my own voice, full of wonder, before my brain registers that I'm the one who's asked. "How did you know I love ice cream?"

Noah grins, his brown eyes squinting at me in the fuzzy light. "Because you're high as fuck."

24
ALICE

BEFORE I REALIZE WHAT'S HAPPENING, WE ARE SANDWICHED TOGETHER in the back of a car like layers of a wafer. Noah has placed himself in charge of my welfare, for which I am grateful because the motion of the moving car has started to make me a bit dizzy. I am vaguely aware of DJ and Kevin next to us, but everything is fuzzy through the thin haze of smoke wafting about. My legs and toes tingle, like they're on the verge of falling asleep, and I brush them back and forth on something . . . furry.

Is this how the carpet feels in all cars? I've never thought to check.

Noah clears his throat behind me. "Can I help you?"

I furl my eyebrows. "Huh?"

"My legs? You're rubbing against them like a cat."

Heat rises to my cheeks and I duck my head in shame. "I—I didn't realize," I stammer. "They're so . . . fuzzy."

He laughs, unbothered by my behavior. "My mom will be ecstatic to hear one person in the universe thinks I've grown a decent amount of leg hair. Fingers crossed I get facial hair next."

Violetta twists around from the passenger seat to find me studying Noah's pale face intently. He's right—I can't see even a hint of stubble anywhere on his jaw despite my close proximity. I could probably stick out my tongue and touch his face from here.

"Letti, were you this munted your first time? I can't remember," Kevin says.

Violetta doesn't answer, instead continuing to study Noah and me. "Well, don't you two look cozy," she says with a sharp edge to her voice.

I, for one, am still fascinated by the utter lack of hair on Noah's face, especially when compared to Kevin, who's a full year younger but has the beginnings of a mustache forming at the corners of his lips. DJ, who is on the other side of Noah, has patches of dark hair that have been shaved off his chin and jawline.

"I don't have any facial hair either," I volunteer. "No body hair at all, really. I've never even shaved my legs."

Everyone's eyes zero in on my legs, Kevin even reaching across DJ to run his hand up my calf muscles for confirmation. "Chur, cuz, you must be doing those calf raises, aye? Your legs are too much. You've really never shaved them? You must've got those good Asian genes. Even I have *some* body hair."

Between my decidedly pear-shaped body and flat nose, I'd never really thought of myself as getting the "good" genes, especially when compared to every K-drama girl. "At least you got the good hair," I reply, reaching past Noah and patting Kevin's hair.

He undoes his bun and shakes out his dark hair, the locks falling to his shoulders.

"What, *this* hair, aye?" he asks with a pose. His Kiwi accent makes everything sound more fun. I've never heard anyone from New Zealand talk before. It's similar to the Australian accent but markedly unique, seemingly with its own vocabulary.

I run my hand through his hair to the crown, watching each finger plow a tidy row along his scalp before the hair closes in around it again. Fascinating. I do it again and Kevin shakes off a shiver.

"Ayeeee, I'm keen to trade spots with No-go here," he screeches, giving Noah a bump with his shoulder. Kevin has a nickname for everyone, it seems.

Violetta's eyes narrow at me and I wonder if maybe she forgot her contacts and is having trouble seeing me. "Are you going to feel up *every* guy in here?"

"If that's the case, can you give me a shoulder rub while you're at it?" Alexei jokes, hiking a thumb at his back. "You're welcome to feel all of my shoulder muscles."

Noah punches the back of the driver's seat. "What muscles? You know the only thing you've got going for you is being six foot six." He turns toward me. "Has he told you he's six six yet? I'll bet he has."

"I think he mentioned it," I murmur, trying to figure out why Violetta is being so strange. Perhaps she feels left out. "Violetta, you should like him," I encourage. "You two would look good together because he's so tall. And at least he's our age."

The car erupts into laughter and I am in a daze, like I've fallen into a high school movie where I've been taken in by the 'cool crowd.' Except Violetta is scowling, ignoring Kevin's needling about who it is she likes that *isn't* our age. Even though my brain is moving at half speed, I understand that I've said something wrong. I just can't remember what it was.

We drive and drive, seemingly forever, conversation and jokes flowing through the car without rest. I learn that Noah and Kevin met in New Zealand during the year Noah lived there and that DJ is not a nickname for anything, his name is simply Deejay, even though he still shortens it to DJ. Alexei speaks Russian and Kevin speaks Vietnamese, which sounds like a separate language all its own with his accent. Noah travels with his own stringer. Kevin is allergic to lilies. Alexei's parents own a house-painting company.

On and on they go, sharing their lives with me without demanding I do the same. I do volunteer some information. I'm afraid of dogs. I've never been skiing. My dad just died.

No one dwells on it except to offer me their own stories of loss. DJ is still grieving his recently deceased grandmother, who had lived with his family since he was a baby. Kevin lost two cousins to suicide and a third in a car accident. Alexei's parents defected from the Soviet Union when they were young, only returning to Russia a handful of times.

They offer these pieces of themselves, some funny and some sad, and I begin to see them as more than just moving scenery outside a train window. I can now identify these landmarks and their history, appreciating each new fact that enriches the view. I almost forget about the ice cream.

But then Alexei announces, "We're here!" and we scramble for the doors, trails of smoke following us out.

"That took forever," Violetta grumbles as the rest of us stretch our arms and legs and shake out the knots and kinks that developed from sharing such a small space.

"Just a little tiki tour," Kevin assures us. "You can't find ice-cream sandwiches made out of doughnuts just anywhere. Especially not this late." As if on cue, he points to a neon sign blinking OPEN LATE.

"Y'all better have brought your own money 'cause I ain't paying for none of you," DJ announces.

"I drove all of you here, so *somebody* needs to pay for me," Alexei says.

"Fuck off, it's *my* car, aye," Kevin points out.

"You couldn't drive, you're high!"

"Then why'd you let us hotbox the bloody thing, mate?"

I drop to the ground, crouching behind the car, when Noah squats down next to me. His voice is low and whispered. "What are we doing here?"

"Cops," I whisper. "What if there are cops?"

At home, there seem to be so many cops. But where Mama works, there are none. It seems they all take up residence at the south end of the city, even patrolling the buses that run half empty. Even when I am not breaking the law, like I am right now, I feel uneasy around them. Perhaps because they, too, speak only in commands.

Noah claps my shoulder and laughs heartily at my answer as he pulls me to standing. "Someone's reached the paranoid stage," he announces, and DJ lets out a whoop of celebration.

"Alley-oop!" Kevin says, mimicking a basketball shot—a fading three-point jumper. "Is this your first time taking a smoko?"

It's my first time doing any of this. Not just the cannabis, but the friends, the laughing, the camaraderie. I hadn't realized just how much I had retreated behind the safe fences of Baba's and my tennis court, not even attempting to widen my circle. After he was gone, I had no one to lean on.

I think of Leylah, who is also always on her own, and I wish I could invite her to be here with us right now. She hasn't lost a parent, but she's alone just the same.

I survey the new friends I've made, even if only for a night, as they take turns calling me "Alley-Oop" and affectionately touching my head, shoulders, and arms. I soak up the contact and the heat of their smiles, as if I can store them away to warm me at a later date. Right now, I feel none of the burdens that have been weighing me down.

The shot of happiness that goes through me lasts longer this time—long enough for me to realize that *this* is what I loved about tennis, and what I've been missing. Not just the game, but the connections it makes. It started with Baba and me. Then I arrived here and it was Violetta and me. Then Leylah and me. And now, Noah, Kevin, Alexi, and DJ as well. If not for tennis, these people would never have come into my life. I would still be in San Francisco, none the wiser that something like this could happen.

Maybe Baba knew I would need new relationships to keep my ties to the game. Without him, tennis became an empty sport— simply this thing I did. It's why even with my efforts here, I wasn't able to win a match. I don't know if I subconsciously sabotaged myself, preparing to grieve tennis on top of Ba, but I do know now the value of staying until Bastille Day.

Losing my matches and forcing through the guilt of doing this alone—this sport that belonged to both of us—was perhaps the best thing that could've happened. I broke free.

Crap. This means the atrocious Bastille T-shirt is prophetic.

Noah studies my faraway look and answers for me. "I think that's a yes."

Violetta shoos him away and protectively wraps an arm around my shoulders. "You guys shouldn't have been smoking in the car." She frowns. "It was too much for her."

I nearly melt into Violetta's shoulder, willing to forgo ice cream all together in favor of feeding my continued hunger for touch.

She cares. Noah cares. Even Leylah, who was upset at the thought of me doing this, cares. And with the exception of Leylah, they all give hugs.

I grin so widely my cheeks hurt and I pull Noah into a three-way hug with Violetta and me. "It's not too much," I insist. "This has been the best day of my life."

25

VIOLETTA

ALICE PASSED OUT IN THE CAR ON THE WAY HOME AND HAD TO BE shaken awake before we could sneak back into the villas, where she promptly passed out again. Leylah was asleep by then, buried beneath a pile of blankets. But hours later, I'm still lying awake, a stomach full of doughnut ice-cream sandwiches and a sick feeling I'm pretty sure isn't from the food.

I just wish I could sleep.

I usually enjoy the buzz in my brain after smoking. Faded Violetta is way more mellow than regular Violetta, who seems to be turned up to full saturation at all times. But tonight the weed seems to be having the opposite effect. Maybe because I used my pipe and not my usual oil pen, which produces so little vapor you can't even smell it thirty minutes later.

My mind continues to spin, thinking about everything that happened tonight.

There was nothing really going on between Alice and Kevin or Alice and Noah—I know better than most how mild flirting doesn't mean anything. I just wanted her to have fun and stay distracted, which she did. So why am I upset?

The guys folded Alice into the group seamlessly. Kevin even gave her a nickname! I should be happy for her, but instead I'm . . . jealous. Jealous that the guys acted like her best friends after knowing her for all of a day, Alice's easy charm winning them all over so effortlessly. She wasn't shy tonight, spending most of her night away from me and talking to the others like *they'd* been the ones to save her from heatstroke. Shouldn't *I* have been the one she leaned on for support tonight instead of Noah?

This is so fucked, I know. Even Faded Violetta knows.

Alice isn't *mine*. She's not a possession to own, or a person who answers to me. But all night I wanted to grab her hand and run away from the car screaming, "*Mine!*" Kindergarten behavior.

I never had to share Leylah when we were friends. No one else liked her.

I roll over to my side, poking my belly where I imagine the six doughnut ice-cream sandwiches I gobbled down, cycling around inside like a washing machine. Faded Violetta has the time and space to think up crazy shit like this because her brain isn't cluttered with the day-to-day of life. I think that's why I've been visiting her more often lately.

That, and she stays up later than everyone else. I can always count on her not to desert me. It's so tragic I could cry. My only friend: me, but the better version of me.

I grab my phone and without more thought, type out a message to Cooper.

Violetta: is there anyone in the world you love more
than me
Violetta: NO LYING
Violetta: ok other than your mom

I stare at the phone, waiting to see if he'll reply. It's past 3 a.m.
Of course he's not going to answer. We're not *that* kind of friends.
It was stupid. Now he's going to wake up to those messages and
think I'm just like every other annoying teenage girl.

*He's going to think I'm just like every other annoying teenage
girl.* Shit. No more friendship, no more special treatment. How
could I have been so reckless?

I'm going to wake up with no friends. Alice will ditch me for
being a weirdo who wants her to only be friends with me. The
guys like Alice better and will just replace me with her. Leylah will
be ecstatic. And no Cooper.

No one to make a particularly long day a little brighter. Or
make me excited to get up in the morning. Or make me feel alive.

I ruined it. All because I got high, ate too many doughnut ice-
cream sandwiches, and lashed out. Oh god, the PSAs were right.
Drugs *will* ruin your life.

I push to sitting, damn near hyperventilating. If I get caught,
I'm not sure Audrey will be as forgiving this time.

I hug my stomach. I'm sickened, imagining those six
doughnut ice-cream sandwiches slowly dissolving into my
bloodstream where they, alongside the weed, will proliferate
through my body. All the fat will coagulate in my arteries and
the weed will overwhelm my liver or kidneys and the effects

of all this will reflect in my performance level so everyone will know that I didn't take this tournament as seriously as I could've and blew it, all over a blue-and-yellow psychedelic pipe named Cheryl.

I scramble out of bed and dash to the bathroom, barely getting the door closed and the toilet lid open before I puke. When it doesn't all come out, I force the rest until there's nothing left but bile—my sign to stop. Without it, the food I *do* manage to keep down won't dissolve into my bloodstream and keep me fed. Even stoned, I understand that dying isn't the end goal here.

When I'm finished, I wash my face and brush my teeth twice, scrubbing my tongue to try to get the taste out. I'm still high— though less paranoid than I was ten minutes age. Maybe now I can sleep.

I climb into my bed, accidentally knocking my phone. It lights up with a message.

Coop: whatever it is you're doing I don't want to know about but GO TO SLEEP
Coop: IN YOUR OWN BED

I go to sleep with a smile on my face.

SUNDAY, JULY 9TH

MID-TOURNAMENT BREAK, NO TENNIS

26

VIOLETTA

I WAKE UP WITH A START, AFTER FINALLY FALLING ASLEEP AROUND four o'clock or so. My head feels like it's been filled with lead and there's a lingering queasy feeling over the way I acted last night.

But somehow, magically, Faded Violetta has made it through the night and whispers her wisdom to me.

It probably isn't as bad as you think it is.

I glance over to Alice's bunk for reassurance and my heart stops.

Her bed is startlingly empty, nothing but the bare mattress there. No sleeping bag, no pillow, no nothing.

Holy shit, she left without saying goodbye?

I swallow my panic, telling myself there's a perfectly logical explanation for all this. What it is, I have no idea, but no way Alice just left me without a word.

She's not Leylah.

But her corner is stark—bag gone, drawers empty. The panic grows. Even Faded Violetta is screaming at me to freak out.

She could have been kidnapped! Running from the mob! There's no other reason she'd be gone than you driving her away!

I'm a crazed soul after an earthquake, tearing apart the few square feet we have, looking for signs of life. This is my punishment from the universe. I was greedy and tried to hoard Alice and now she's gone. Audrey was right—I shouldn't have gotten attached.

This is how Leylah finds me—sitting on the floor with couch cushions piled around me like a fort. I don't know how long I've been sitting there, but when I see her I realize I'm not high anymore.

"What the fuck are you doing?" Her face tells me just how deranged I look right now.

"I . . . was . . . looking . . . for Alice." I trail off.

"Between the couch cushions?"

I shake my head. There's no use in explaining. "Did she go home?"

I can see Leylah debating in her head whether to tell me and my lungs nearly burst from holding my breath, waiting to hear the answer. She tosses the cushions back onto the couch in nearly the right places before flopping down across them.

"Why do you care?" she asks instead.

I'm thrown by the question. "What do you mean? You were trying to convince her to stay last night."

"I didn't tell her to stay. I told her there was no reason not to. Maybe she found a reason to leave."

The implication is clear: I am what made Alice not want to stay.

"You're acting like she was your best friend or something," Leylah mutters. Her voice sounds tight as she cracks open a blue sugar-free sports drink and guzzles it down.

"She was my best friend *here*," I reply.

"Yeah, well, that doesn't mean quite as much as you think it does."

I'm already tense—I don't have the stretch to absorb her little jabs today. I spring up to loom over her, hands on my hips. "What is your problem with me? You go missing for two years and when you show up you decide you hate me. Why?"

Leylah presses her back against the cushions to gain distance from me. "I wasn't *missing*, you knew exactly where I was."

"Sitting at home, thinking about how much you hated me, apparently."

She huffs. "Don't flatter yourself, I forgot you even existed until I saw you here."

"I'm sure you did." I fling my arms up like a ringmaster announcing the next act. "The great Leylah Lê, folks! She doesn't play by anybody's rules! She doesn't need anyone!"

"It's better than needing *everyone*! You can't function if you even *think* there might be someone out there who doesn't bow down and surrender to your very presence. God forbid anyone be allowed to like someone else more than they like *the* Violetta Masuda! No, no, you have to be the *most* liked. People have to *love* you."

She says my name the same way I said hers: presenting curiosities for the crowd. My oddity is I'm likable.

I bark a short laugh. "You're mad that more people know who I am? Or that they think I'm nicer than you?" It's almost funny, how simple the basis is for her dislike of me. All this has been because she resents having to smile and acknowledge other people?

I shake my head in disbelief. "Talk about needing to beat me in all categories. So what if people *like* me?!" If I could exchange online followers or comments that tell me I'm hot for Leylah's skills, I'd suffocate beneath all the trophies.

"So what?" she shoots back. "So you don't follow the rules either! You don't even have to use the same rulebook as other people! You don't *have* to work as much or try as hard because you're *special*. We're all supposed to just hand everything over to you just because you're pretty and predestined for greatness because of your mom."

My mom. Yeah right.

"It's not my fault I was born. It's not my fault she used to be a pro player. If you went into medicine and became some kind of inventor, people would say the same thing about you."

"I guess lucky for you I'm not very smart," Leylah snaps.

"Oh yeah, lucky me. Audrey is always going on and on about how I should be more like you. I'm so lucky that you're faster, you're taller, your serve is bigger, you're more focused on the court. She wants me to be you, and she doesn't even *like* you!"

That seems to stun Leylah. It sort of stuns me too. I hadn't meant to confess that.

"I'm the one who dialed 911, you know," I say quietly. "I know you think I hoped you'd die or whatever, but I didn't just leave you there. I called Audrey and she insisted on being the one to go with you to the hospital, but I'm the one who actually called the ambulance. Even though it could've gotten me in trouble too."

It's my olive branch. My offering.

I cared. I still care enough to tell you.

Leylah stares at me for a long second, then begins a sarcastic slow clap, the echo of it loud in the otherwise empty villa. "You're a real fucking hero. Tell me, did you decide to make the call right away? Or did you figure you could make out with my boyfriend a little longer since I was, you know, unconscious?"

27

LEYLAH

VIOLETTA DOESN'T SAY ANYTHING—SHE JUST BLINKS WITH A WRINKLE between her eyebrows.

I've clearly surprised her. She thought I didn't know. I can almost *see* the effort she's making, trying to decide how to respond.

She'll probably deny it but I know what I saw.

Finally she splutters, "I didn't know you thought of Peter as your boyfriend."

Of all the things she could say, of course it's the worst possible option.

Not an admission. Not a denial. Just a pivot to whether I was even qualified to be mad about it.

"Seriously? That's what you think matters here?" I demand. What matters is that Violetta stole the boy who liked me.

The *one* boy who liked me.

The one who liked me *better* than her.

"I . . . just . . . didn't think that was what you'd care about after all this time."

What does *that* mean?

"What else should I care about? How after I disappeared, no one came looking for me? Not even the person who claims to have cared so much that she called 911? After running to mommy, that is."

Violetta's laugh is short. Cynical. "Who, me? The girl who supposedly *steals* everyone from you?"

The way she says it—jazz hands next to her face on the word *steals*—makes me sound like a fucking lunatic.

"Sure," she continues. "Be mad at me. It's my fault that you never called or explained why you were just *gone*. And it's my fault no one else called you, even though you went out of your way not to have any friends. You think having a single human emotion about anyone makes you weak, but yeah, blame me for your isolation."

Her reply hits so close to the truth I nearly topple over.

It's part of the reason, after all, I've been avoiding Noah. I let down my guard for *one second* and somehow got burned by my nemesis in that sliver of space I left uncovered. I'm a goddamn Spartan out here, trying to fight off an army's worth of soldiers by myself. Of course I need all my armor on.

I flip defense to offense, pulling out my favorite weapon: sarcasm. Mean sarcasm. "It must be so hard being such a martyr all the time. Maybe you should make a post about bullying. You could partner with a Korean skin care company. *How to whiten your skin so the world doesn't see you as a threat.*"

I know *I* hit close to the truth by the split-second freeze-frame of her expression. She can deny all she wants that her life hasn't been more privileged than mine but it would be bullshit.

"You know, I'm Asian too," she snaps. "You don't get to corner the market on oppression."

This, I need to hear. I kick my feet up onto the coffee table, one crossed over the other, and gesture for her to continue. "Go ahead. Tell me all the ways you've had to struggle because of your background."

Violetta sinks down onto the coffee table, only inches away from my feet. I scoot them farther away.

"You know who my mom is," she begins.

Yes, Audrey Masuda is, for lack of a better term, a real fucking piece of work. She's like a cross of "tiger parent" and "dance mom." But Violetta is not going to win this argument.

"Do you have any idea what it's like to have a celebrity parent?" she gripes. "To have to follow in her exact footsteps, except somehow be better than her?"

She cannot be serious.

I tap my chin. "Hmm. What's worse: having a mom who's already played pro so she'll be able to tell you what to expect and how things work—not to mention support you—*or* . . . a mom who's a fucking *doctor* and *inventor* who expects you to go to college even though you need a million tutors just to get through high school, and who also thinks you going to college will solve all the problems for your entire community?"

I see her eyes flash, but she doesn't argue.

5 points to me.

"I'm not saying you're not Asian," I clarify, now that my blood pressure has stabilized a little. "I *am* saying that being a quarter Japanese and living at a resort in Florida isn't the same thing as being surrounded by a bunch of people that had to literally flee their country to avoid death. I don't just have to be a success story for my parents, personally, but for every Cambodian or Vietnamese American so *their* parents can point at me and tell their kid, 'You should be like that.'"

"I understand having to be a role model—"

"No! You don't!" I'm not just frustrated anymore—I'm flat out *mad*. She somehow turned around this *thing* I've had to deal with and made it about her. "Who the fuck do you think you're representing? The federation of girls who wear makeup while they play sports?"

It's mean. I know it's mean the second I say it out loud. But I'm too pissed off to stop.

"You have no idea what I've gone through!" I exclaim, setting my feet on the floor so I resist the urge to kick her. "You have a mom who sends you to *this* place, where you get to play tennis all day, whenever you want. You're practically already living a professional life. Meanwhile, I'm in school for six hours a day, learning fuck all, and wasting critical training years—all because I let you convince me to try pot once."

"How was I supposed to know how your body would react?!"

"Because you were supposed to be the expert! You told me I'd be fine and I wasn't!"

At this point, I might as well have confessed what I'm actually upset about—that I trusted her and she stabbed me in the back. Not just when she kissed Peter, but when she didn't take my side against Dick.

I watch my internal point total plummet, any advantage I used to have over Violetta totally obliterated.

I deserve the hit. All this, over a boy. Again.

Maybe I really am as dumb as my parents think I am.

This time, I don't storm out. Instead, I give Violetta the most pitying look I have. She cares so much. I don't have to.

"Alice is doing laundry at the Seine," I say. Then I watch Violetta scramble up and dash out.

For Alice.

28
ALICE

I ASSUMED I WOULD WAKE UP GROGGY THIS MORNING, MAYBE EVEN with a hangover. Instead, it was the opposite. I rose with the sun, and too impatient to wait for Violetta to awaken, decided to wash everything I brought with me. She was right—the clay was much easier to clean once it was dry.

I'm folding the last of my clothes, reveling in the lavender scent of Violetta's fancy detergent I borrowed, when I notice the time. The main draw will be getting posted any moment and I want to be there to celebrate Leylah once it does. She doesn't seem to be particularly popular here, which is a shame. There should always be someone present to celebrate your accomplishments. Before coming here, I can't remember a single instance of being left alone at a big moment in my life.

I decide to leave my things at the Seine for now. I can't imagine who would take the opportunity to steal a hot-pink sleeping bag or Violetta's outdated neon shirt. Laundromat rules here seem much more lax. I'm willing to take the risk.

It seems last night has sent me down a path of destructive recklessness.

The hushed whispers and buzz reach me even before I touch the stairs to the deck where the draws are hung. Something is happening.

Each step, the buzz grows louder, until I finally wriggle my way to the front, where Janice is blotting out a name on the girls' 16U singles draw.

"What do you think happened?" I hear a girl behind me whisper.

"Maybe she got disqualified," her friend whispers back. "I heard that happened to a girl a couple years ago."

I'm not familiar with the exact protocol for what will happen next. I know professional tournaments have lucky losers every once in a while—a second chance for a player who lost in the final round of qualifying—but I don't know how tournaments determine which player will fill the vacancy.

"Ms. Wu." Mr. Duncan's voice and sudden appearance by my side startles me.

I eye him warily. "Yes?"

"Follow me to my office. I have something I need to speak with you about."

The last time I was there, he insulted me and then tried to send me home. "Can't you just tell me here?" I step away from the crush to give us some semblance of privacy without having to be in an enclosed space with him.

His mouth thins. "As I said, I'd prefer to speak a little more privately."

For some reason, his summons doesn't strike the same fear in me as it did last time. What can he possibly do? Send me home a second time? *What would Leylah do?*

I flash him a smile, not bothering to make it sincere. "I'd prefer to not walk all the way to your office when you could just tell me here."

His lips turn down and his eyes get that contemptuous look again—the one that shows how he really feels about having to take my wants or needs into consideration. "Very well. As I'm sure you saw, there has been an unexpected opening in the girls' 16U draw. Under almost every circumstance, the lucky loser is chosen by ranking points. This would obviously not be ideal for you, as you have next to no ranking."

"Obviously," I echo. I have a sick sense of déjà vu.

He draws another breath, as if steeling himself for the next part. "However, the Bastille Invitational has always prided itself on *merit.*" His teeth are tightly clenched, as if the word itself is painful to say. "Here, we determine lucky losers by their game differential."

He waits for me to react, but I don't know what he's expecting from me. Is this just his way of letting me know I'm still not going to qualify? I already know that.

"Okay."

"Because of the retirement of one opponent, and the withdrawal of another, giving you what amounts to a 6-0, 6-0 win in that round, *you* have come out on top of that particular equation."

He's fairly shaking with anger, so it takes me a moment to register his words.

I'm the lucky loser.

I'm the one taking that blank spot on the draw, earning LI points, an ITF ranking, and the opportunity to play in front of college scouts.

Me. The person who didn't win a single match on skill.

I almost pity Mr. Duncan for having to deliver the news. No wonder he's so angry. First I snuck in under his disapproval on the say-so of Mrs. Conrad. Then I had the audacity to stay here when he basically requested I leave. Now I'm in the main draw. Mingling with the "real" players.

I nearly laugh at the thought. It doesn't even seem real.

"Is that all?"

Mr. Duncan—Dick, I now understand why everyone uses the nickname—raises a furry eyebrow at me. "I would think you might show a bit more excitement, Ms. Wu. This is an opportunity many players will never have in their lives."

I could smile. I could dip my head and thank him as if he's done me this great favor. But the fact is, he hasn't done anything more than inform me of what's already happened. The rules were in place and would have been carried out in the exact same manner even if I hadn't been here. But people like Dick don't care about trivial things like truth, only what suits their narrative. And in his mind, I am a onetime visitor, and someone he plans to quickly forget.

What he doesn't know is that last night sparked something inside me, something that has flared to life and is pushing to get out. I'm tired of being sad, of being tired, of being isolated. I am not the same Alice who arrived at the gates last week. Maybe Leylah is right and spite is the best motivator. I am absolutely going to prove Dick Duncan wrong.

I excuse myself as quickly as possible, needing a safe space for the riot of emotions brewing. The shock of it is wearing off and the enormity of what's happened hits me.

I'm going to play again tomorrow. I'm getting a do-over of this whole tournament. And if I'd decided to go home today, I would have missed it.

As I approach the Seine, I see Violetta waiting for me and it's too much. I promptly burst into tears.

She rushes toward me. "Alice! What's wrong?"

"I'm in the main draw," I manage to sniffle out. "I'm the lucky loser."

Violetta frowns. "Isn't that a good thing?"

I nod as the tears keep coming. Weeks and weeks of not being able to cry and now it feels as though I can't stop.

"I don't understand," she says.

"I don't either."

"How long ago did you find out?"

"Just now."

I see her mentally calculating, trying to figure out what might have upset me between then and now. But there is nothing to discover, no rational explanation for my emotions.

"Are you . . . do you . . . not want to play anymore?" she asks tentatively.

"No! I mean, yes. I don't know," I admit.

"Is it because . . . you were planning to go home today?" Violetta seems afraid of my answer. Not that it would matter even if I had.

I shake my head. "I knew last night that I was going to stay.

It's just ... I don't know. Last night, I felt like I was part of something—part of a group."

"You were," Violetta eagerly reassures me.

"But now ..."

"Now you're still here with us. Everything is the same."

But it's not.

"Last night, I wasn't still in the tournament," I explain.

"Okay ..."

I bite down on the tip of my thumb, trying to gather my thoughts into something coherent. I appreciate that Violetta doesn't rush me or jump in to tell me how happy I should feel about this. "It's like this: I met all these people and made all these friends and finally I got to a place where I was just happy to be here. But now I'm competing again. This second chance just fell out of the sky."

I look up at the ceiling, still unsure of exactly why I feel so topsy-turvy about this news.

"I'm grateful, of course. I know how lucky I am to get this. I'm just ..."

"Not happy?" Violetta posits.

"That's just it! I *am* happy! So much so that it makes me feel ..."

Violetta stares at me expectantly as I finally find the word weighing me down.

"I feel guilty," I whisper.

Even admitting it aloud does nothing to alleviate the turmoil inside me. How could I possibly be surrounded with so many wonderful things and yet still yearn for more?

Another tear trickles out and Violetta's eyes soften. "Maybe it's because your dad can't be here with you."

The words strike my soul and the dust blows away, leaving a deep throbbing feeling.

She's right.

My heart has been fractured and scattered and as I try to assemble it back together to celebrate this good news, I realize I can never achieve the happiness of before because Baba ran off with the last piece. Things will always feel incomplete because *I* am no longer a whole human.

But then Violetta wraps an arm around me and I feel the bleeding inside stop, as if her hands reached into my chest and physically plugged the hole in my heart. "Come on," she urges. "Let's go back to the room so we can veg out and watch cooking videos."

Her private way of tuning out the world, no additional substances needed. On our way back to the villa, I stop and let the Joans know I'll be staying another day. Maybe if I keep saying it aloud, it will finally feel real.

29

LEYLAH

TODAY IS ALWAYS MY LEAST FAVORITE DAY OF BASTILLE. WHO DO THEY think they are with this bullshit "middle Sunday" talk, anyway? Wimbledon?

I wander around campus, trying to figure out what the hell to do for a whole day. If I were at home, I could at least watch TV or hide in my room. But here, there's nowhere to be alone. I suppose I could park myself somewhere and stream a show, but I'm not really in the mood.

I'm not really in the mood for anything.

I make my way to the Observatory. If I can't be alone, the next best thing is to be surrounded by people I can actively ignore.

I push open the massive double doors to see the space crowded with what feels like hundreds of kids. Kids at the pool tables. Kids at the air-hockey tables. Kids at the Ping-Pong tables. Kids on every couch, chair, and bench. If not for the glorious air-conditioning, I would turn and run.

I wind my way between tables and around herds of people

standing, just seeing if there's anyone I know. Most of the people in here look to be in the twelve- to fifteen-year-old range, but I do spot Kevin and DJ at the Ping-Pong tables.

I head over.

Just to watch.

"Hey Ha Lê, cuz." Kevin bunches together all the syllables so it sounds like Hayhalay. He's the only person outside my family who gets away with calling me by my real name. Vietnamese privilege and all that. Even though he turned it into a Hawaiian-sounding nickname. Heihalei. *Aloha.*

I greet him back with his Vietnamese name, purposely said backward like he did with my name. "Hey Nam Do."

"Sweet as, you're just in time to watch me win." He turns his attention back to the game, calling, "Fourteen-ten."

He and DJ battle through a long rally, but it's obvious why Kevin is feeling confident. Some people's tennis skills just translate to the table better.

He tosses the ball across the net to DJ. "Fifteen-ten, me."

DJ rolls his eyes. "I can keep score, you know."

"Yeah right."

DJ turns to me. "You know this asshole changes the score-cards between every friggin' game on the court?"

"Only if I *win* the game," Kevin corrects him.

"That's worse!" DJ exclaims.

I'm with DJ on this one. "Yeah, that's obnoxious."

Kevin drops a jaw at my reply. "Aw, stink. You of all people. What's a bit of mind-gaming to win, aye?"

I wag a finger. "That's too far."

DJ whoops at his victory in the argument. "Speaking of winning, what's up with you and my boy Noah?"

My heart stutters, but I cover it well. "What does he have to do with winning?"

He shrugs. "Winning his heart? I dunno. I just wanted to ask."

At least he's honest. Unlike Noah, whose heart I definitely don't have.

And don't want.

They keep playing until Kevin finally closes it out. He celebrates by taking down his bun and shaking his shoulder-length hair free. "Fuck off and tell your mum it was a piece of piss," he says with his typical swagger.

"I can't wait to school you on the court."

Kevin snorts. "I'm Asian, mate." He taps his chest twice. "I *am* the school, aye." He points at me. "Tell 'em, Ha Lê."

"You're on your own. I suck at school."

Kevin shakes his head. "You're really messing up the stereotype, mate."

"You should talk to my parents—they have plenty of thoughts about it."

DJ hands me his paddle and Kevin ties his hair back up so we can rally to warm up. He hits the ball so casually it barely looks like he's paying attention to it. "You never told me you had tiger parents. What flavor?"

"They're completely obsessed with getting my grades up so I can go to college."

"Yeah nah, that's nothing. My parents are on me about *everything*." He ticks off his list of grievances. "Until last year, my schedule was chocka with tennis, swim team, school, *and* piano. I'm taking a weekend coding class in case my grades aren't enough. They have me writing practice essays for uni! They only let me quit piano this year because my dad was sick of having to post my keyboard back and forth to the States. Ten fucking years of my life without a single day off." Kevin gives me a look like, *Top that.*

"At least you're a boy," I argue, not yet ready to believe my parents might be considered mild in comparison. "At every event, at least one Cambodian auntie will tell me 'I'm not sexist, that's just how things are' while spewing the most sexist shit about how I need to be gentler or softer or whatever because otherwise I'll never get married. Literally every event."

"Why do you think I always travel with DJ and his mum?" Kevin gestures to his beat-up T-shirt, the collar and sleeves cut off. "Mine said this shirt shows 'too much armpit.' It's too skux for the girls." He shakes his head and his loose bun bobs back and forth. "Ayeee, too much armpit!" he exclaims.

"Maybe your mom don't want you looking like a slut," DJ says.

Automatically, Kevin retorts, "Your *mum's* a slut."

"Wow!" exclaims a voice behind me. "You guys got the trash talk started early!"

I don't need to turn around to know it's Noah.

Dressed in crisp white shorts and a matching white polo, he gives DJ and Kevin each a bro handshake. I take the time to assess him. It's absolutely cringe he's wearing a head-to-toe matching outfit—especially off court—but I have to admit he looks good. A lot better than me, that's for sure. I smooth my hair and straighten my top before I remember he was with Violetta last night.

I purposely make myself rumpled again. I don't care what he thinks I look like.

When he turns to greet me, I serve and start the point instead.

He joins the conversation while Kevin and I play, joking around with both DJ and Kevin—not even stopping during points. He tries addressing me a few times and I pretend I can't hear. Even still, I'm getting murdered so efficiently there should be a *Dateline* special about it.

I can't concentrate when Noah's around.

Minus 10 points to him for showing up and ruining my game.

In the middle of another point, Noah makes a joke about how badly I'm doing. Definitely not helping his case.

"I guess I should've challenged you in table tennis, huh?" he teases.

Kevin puts away a forehand winner. "Not even you let her beat you, mate?"

"No one *let* me beat anyone," I snap, not bothering to call the score aloud anymore. "It was easier then because there wasn't someone talking in my ear the whole time."

I direct a pointed stare at Noah, who acts like he's somehow confused about why I'm so snippy.

"Wow, I didn't realize we were playing the world championships of table tennis here." He gives a short laugh afterward and I don't know whether it's because he's truly joking or because I've made him uncomfortable.

Part of me wonders if I'm overreacting, but I tamp down the feeling. He deserves to be uncomfortable.

We keep playing. The points fly by as I lose the first set, switch ends with Kevin, and begin losing the second set as well.

This isn't going to help my tennis. Or my confidence.

Noah still talks during the match, but he keeps it to between points now. Still, I can't concentrate. He might try to talk to me at any moment.

Except he doesn't.

I consider bringing up my parents again, just so I'm not the (fourth?) wheel in this conversation but even I know that's pathetic. Also, I'd rather not think of them while I'm here. I'm facing enough pressure without the reminder that my entire life rests on this tournament.

I sneak one tiny peek his way. Just to see if he's even paying attention to me.

Kevin serves and I'm not ready, so I stop the ball and throw it back at him. "I wasn't ready. Redo."

"All good," he says. "You need time to check out your boy toy, aye." With his Kiwi accent, Kevin manages to stretch out the phrase *boy toy* to an exorbitant length.

"I think they're having a li'l lover's quarrel," DJ quips. "Leylah's been avoiding talking to him this whole time. Noah, what the hell did you do?"

"Thank you, Dr. DJ, for that armchair analysis," Noah says sarcastically.

"I'm just saying, look at her face—she looks *pissed*."

Noah shrugs. "Well, she *is* losing. By a lot."

"Yeah, nah," Kevin says with a wave of his hand. "She always looks like that."

They're just discussing me (and my RBF) like I'm not even here.

"Everyone shut up, we're in the middle of a match," I snap, and the guys all exchange looks with one another like I'm being totally unreasonable. I guess this is why they'd rather hang out with Violetta.

I can see Noah examining me with a tilted head, like he's trying to figure me out and it takes everything inside me not to look back.

I end up losing. I don't stay for a rematch.

30
ALICE

VIOLETTA AND I SPEND THE REST OF THE DAY AND NIGHT HUDDLED NEXT
to each other in her bed. It's only a single extra-long mattress,
but it's not difficult to fit the both of us side by side. Leylah has
been asleep for several hours now, her daily routine so well prac-
ticed that she's out the instant her head touches the pillow. We
undoubtedly should do the same, but neither of us seems capable
of being the one who ends it. Instead, we dive under the covers
and pull them over our heads like children hiding out in a cave.

I have vague memories of making forts with David in the
living room when we were little, the two of us pretending to strike
out on a grand adventure. We would visit everything from the
Redwoods to base camp at Mount Denali to our grandparents'
home in Taiwan—places we'd only seen in pictures. Sometimes
we would even sneak in prawn crackers, reveling in the little pops
and snaps that tickled our tongues.

Now I wonder if he just did it to humor me—playing pretend
with a child to keep my attention away from all the problems our

family had. It wasn't just Baba's disease—I found out afterward that he'd reduced his hours at work because of the pain, which meant less money and more bills. That David hadn't left school to take a gap year, but to get a job and help with the household. While I was at school, Ba would have to lie down—for hours, sometimes—just so he'd have the energy to play with me in the evenings.

Who knows what else they've hidden from me all these years?

I kick up against the covers in frustration, welcoming in a rush of cool air.

"Do you have any embarrassing habits?" I ask.

"What do you mean?"

I rub my finger over the bump on my thumb, deciding whether or not to share my mortifying secret. A few weeks ago, it felt like I might never trust anyone ever again. But Violetta has let me into her world and I want to show my gratitude by sharing my own life more.

"I still suck my thumb sometimes," I confess. "I stopped, mostly. Or I at least only did it at night, but ever since . . ." I still don't like saying the words aloud. It makes it more real, and right now I want to live in the fantasy we've created. "It's just a habit, you know? Like a defense mechanism or something. I can't seem to help it."

I wait for her to be disgusted.

But instead, she pauses before replying. "That makes sense," she says. "You've been through a pretty traumatic event. You're doing whatever it is you need to cope with it."

Traumatic. I haven't really thought of Baba's death in those terms, but it really was. Or, is. Even now, I feel the trauma of it nearly every moment of every day, along with the trauma of having been betrayed by my own family.

I am coping with trauma.

"I sucked my fingers as a kid," Violetta offers.

"Fingers as in plural?"

She wiggles her third and fourth finger on her left hand. "These two. That way the pointer finger and the pinkie act like braces, you know?" She demonstrates and I giggle a little at how silly it looks. I'm sure I look the same with my thumb.

"What made you stop?" I ask.

Violetta sighs and I can feel the heaviness in it. "My obaasan."

"That's 'grandma' in Japanese, right?"

"Yeah."

"The whole family basically disowned Audrey when she got pregnant, but her mom came to visit once. I must have been like, six or seven? She saw me sucking my fingers and slapped my hand, saying it was something only babies did. I remember going around the apartment, trying to hide from her, but she'd always find me and slap my hand away. Then an extra slap for hiding."

Violetta says it all rather casually, but I'm horrified nevertheless. I can't imagine Mama or Baba, let alone Ahma, slapping me for any reason—especially when I was small. I've always been the cherished baby of the family, breaking the stereotype of Taiwanese parents only valuing their sons.

"After she left," Violetta continues, "Audrey seemed crushed. I thought maybe it was me that had run Obaasan off, so I decided I was never going to suck my fingers again."

"Wow." I am often frustrated with myself for not putting

a stop to my thumb-sucking, but I just can't seem to break the habit. I clearly don't have Violetta's sheer force of will. "What happened next time?"

I feel Violetta shrug next to me, the movement letting a little pocket of cool air into the covers. "Like I said, she only visited the once. After a couple more years, Audrey stopped talking about her all together. I'm not even sure she brought photos of her when we moved down here. I never asked about it and Audrey never brought it up."

Violetta, it seems, is also coping with trauma.

"It's her loss," I reassure her. "She's missed out on so many great years with you and it's not because you sucked your fingers as a kid."

Violetta makes a noncommittal *hmm*. "Maybe I'd still be doing it too if she'd never come to visit. All I'm saying is it's no one's business what you do with your body. And if that's what helps you, then do it. You're not hurting anyone else."

"Thanks." I'm glad I made the choice to confide in her.

"Does your family know?" Violetta asks.

"About the thumb-sucking?"

She giggles. "No, sorry, I guess that too. But I meant the news about getting back into the tournament."

"Not yet." I chew my bottom lip, thinking about the match looming tomorrow. "I know I've had all day."

"You don't have to explain yourself to me."

But I want to.

"I guess I'm being a little spiteful. Like they kept things from me so now I'm keeping something from them."

Violetta muffles a giggle, a full laugh too loud for our close proximity. "Sorry, I am in complete support of your pettiness. I couldn't keep something from Audrey even if I *tried*."

Now it's my turn to giggle. I have yet to meet Violetta's infamous mother, but I hear the constant pinging of her phone throughout the day and see Violetta's reaction to the messages.

"Does she come to all your matches?" I ask.

"Every single one. Since she works for Bastille, they give her 'special accommodations.'" Violetta doesn't sound overly enthusiastic about it.

"Still, to have someone you can talk about this stuff with? Now that my dad is gone . . ." I trail off.

"I guess. She definitely understands how it is. But she was also in the top one hundred by the time she was my age."

"It was a different era," I argue. "Women don't even have to retire now when they get pregnant. You can't compare yourself to that. There are only so many Martina Hingises in the world."

"Except it's not Martina Hingis, it's my mom!" Violetta kicks the blankets up again and blows out a breath, scrubbing a hand over her face. "I'm just saying, the expectations for me are different than other people's."

I let the information sink in, trying to measure just how wide the divide is between people like Violetta and people like me. Surely, most do not expect much of me here. I slid into the main draw at the last second and without a real win. Whatever pressure I may have felt, trying to fulfill Baba's and my dream, is probably nothing compared to what Violetta feels.

I'm almost afraid to ask, considering her earlier story, but I do it anyway. "What happens when you lose?"

Violetta answers quickly. "Oh! She's not like, abusive or anything. She doesn't make me stay out in the sun and run a hundred laps or whatever. It's mostly just a debrief—a long debrief—of all the things I could have done better." She pauses and grimaces. "She takes notes."

Violetta is no longer stretched out, her legs now pressed against her chest, arms hugging her shins. I can see why armadillos do the same to protect themselves.

I want to know more, but it's clear Violetta isn't ready to talk about that so I ask something easier. "Why do you call her Audrey?" I'd never heard anyone call their parent by name until St. Aidan's.

"She always said being called Mom made her feel old. She was only nineteen when she had me; I think she just couldn't wrap her head around actually being a mom, even though she was one."

Mama, on the other hand, has been old for as long as I can remember. With slightly stooped shoulders and calloused hands, she looks nothing like Audrey Masuda, who, according to my calculations, is not yet thirty-five, and looks even younger.

I think of how lonely Violetta looks sometimes, even when she's surrounded by people. "She never talked about wanting another kid?"

"I'm not even sure she wanted the one she has," Violetta jokes, but it sounds humorless.

Though I've been hurt by Mama's silence, she's never made me feel like a mistake.

I reach over and squeeze Violetta's hand, hoping I'm able to bring her an equal measure of comfort she's brought me. "Well, I always wanted a sister."

She squeezes me hand back, fierce and warm. "Sisters. I like it."

MONDAY, JULY 10TH

MAIN DRAW, ROUND OF 64

31

ALICE

I PRACTICALLY SPRING OUT OF BED THE NEXT DAY, DESPITE STAYING UP far too late with Violetta again. Thanks to our chat last night, I am a new person, which reflects in my play.

All my shots come together and I am finally able to play the way I know I'm capable of doing. I frustrate my opponent into a number of swear words and a warning for ball abuse. She insults me for hitting moon balls and drop shots—telling me I'm playing like 12U—but it's effective so I continue doing it. I have no qualms about hitting shots that work. Just because most people our age play a different style doesn't make mine invalid.

Baba didn't know the proper mechanics of tennis when he started teaching me, so I never quite learned them. He simply suggested the racquet be gripped and swung in whatever way was most comfortable to get the shots I wanted to hit. Now, watching my opponent melt down over it, I feel a certain amount of satisfaction.

Anyone can hit hard, Ba would say. *Not everyone can hit smart.* We modeled my game off that of Hsieh Su-Wei, the Taiwanese player who hits with two hands off both sides and can out craft anyone, even now at age thirty-seven. By the time I joined the team at St. Aidan's last year, my strokes had been too ingrained to fix and too effective to bother.

I hit another sharp angled passing shot with a flick of my wrist and my opponent lets out a feral scream before launching her racquet across the net at me.

It lands somewhere near the service line, and I dutifully pick it up and walk it over to her. She can't even meet my eye when she takes it back.

Violetta passes by my court, balls in hand, heading to her own match, and shouts, "Let's go, Alice!" and I can't stop smiling through the rest of my match. I slice and dice my way to a clean two and two victory, and even my opponent congratulates me at the handshake. I know she's not upset with me, but at herself for not figuring out how to adequately respond to my shots.

For the first time in what feels like forever, I don't want to leave the court.

32

VIOLETTA

HOWEVER PROUD I ORIGINALLY FELT ABOUT QUALIFYING FOR TWO AGE categories, a long day of both 16U and 18U singles matches and 16U doubles match has quickly changed that. This isn't my first time doing it—ever since I can remember, Audrey has had me play up an age level "for extra practice." Not ever at an L1 tournament like Bastille, but enough times that I knew what was coming.

And yet I feel a little like dying on the court as drag myself through my 18U doubles match with Rachel in what must be record-setting one-thousand-degree heat. My ankle is still sore and I'm acutely aware of what's left of my makeup running down my face.

Audrey is watching, as she always does, perched in the corner of the farthest bench, practically hidden beneath a massive umbrella. As much as I try not to glance up at her, it's impossible not to. Between the umbrella, her hat, and her sunglasses, any expression she might have is completely hidden. But when I miss yet another easy volley, I see the umbrella tilt down ever so slightly, as if to show how disappointed she is in my performance.

"Sorry," I mumble to Rachel, who slaps my hand harder than usual.

"I'm serving down the middle so *be ready* this time," she says sternly.

Rachel can be intense but at least I'm familiar with her and her style of play. Even with my shitty performance, we're still up a break. If I had played like this in my earlier 16U doubles match with Oksana, we definitely would have lost already.

I flash our signals behind my back and Rachel serves down the middle as planned, my poach perfectly timed for me to slam the ball into the stomach of the other net player.

She crumples into a heap and her partner rushes over. "I'm sorry! I'm so sorry!" I cry. "Is she okay? Are you okay?"

"Stop apologizing," Rachel says, dragging me back to the baseline for a quick meeting. "It's her fault she didn't get her racquet up in time and you need to focus."

She's not wrong, but it eats at me anyway.

"It's rude not to apologize," I point out. Hitting people may be well within the rules, but ultimately, tennis is an etiquette sport.

"You could have just held your hand up for a second and that would have been plenty." Rachel shrugs. "That's what I do."

I don't mention that no one thinks of Rachel as a polite player. Or even a polite person, really.

She finishes serving out the game and I head to the bench, where I collapse in the shade with relief.

"Can you at least *try* to look a little less tired?" Rachel hisses, her skin flushed red from the heat. "It's not exactly screaming confidence if you look like you're dying over here."

I sneak a quick glance up at the stands but can't make out Audrey's expression from this distance. Still, Rachel's right. I spring up, doing a few hops on the balls of my feet to get energized. The next court over, Leylah and her partner are just starting their warm-up. I notice *she* doesn't look tired. Though she's only had her 18U singles match today.

Rachel and I end up closing out the first set, but the second set is much tighter. Our opponents start playing two back to avoid any more peggings and my legs are too weary to run down the lobs going over Rachel's head. They've identified me as the weak link and there's not a whole lot I can do about it except stay back myself, which still involves running.

I limp through the second set, which we lose in a tiebreak, and head to the ten-point breaker for the third. God bless the ten-point tiebreak. I usually hate it, because it more or less turns your match into a coin toss, but right now I could kiss Dick on the mouth for choosing this format. Ten points. I can make it another ten points.

Maybe if I say it enough times I'll actually believe it.

Just ten more points. Just ten more points.

Rachel's doing everything she can to motivate me, though her idea of encouragement is saying things like, "I'm going to fucking kill myself if we lose to these nobodies." I take a big gulp of lukewarm Gatorade and bounce on my toes again, before we head to our side to begin.

Just ten more points. Maybe a little more.

Rachel is still screeching her concerns with an intensity that borders on frightening. "We cannot lose to them, V. One of them is from fucking Iowa. Iowa! Is that even a real state?"

"We won't lose," I say with much more conviction than I feel. I'm not even sure why I'm so tired today. Alice and I went to bed at a relatively reasonable hour, especially compared to the partial insomnia I've experienced lately.

Is that why I feel so drained? Because I *didn't* pace around all night until I needed to smoke? Maybe Faded Violetta gets a deeper sleep. I imagine telling Leylah and just the thought of her reaction jolts enough energy through me to make me laugh.

I glance over at Leylah's court, where she is predictably hitting a perfect overhead. She's always so dialed in I doubt she's even noticed I'm on the court next to hers.

Two years, she's missed.

It's not like I never thought about her during that time. Of course I did. But everyone seemed so relieved that she was gone—to not have to compete against her anymore—that I guess I let myself believe the same thing. That it was better she was gone.

I never demanded that Audrey let me contact her. I never made any effort to sneak around Audrey's rules and reach out anyway. I never even checked in to make sure she was okay.

I botch a forehand return that lands way too short, but luckily my opponent overhits it. I sigh with relief and Rachel cuts me another look. If I don't get it together soon, I might need to sleep with my doors locked tonight. Rachel has never been a gracious loser.

Our opponents continue to make mistakes at the same rate as me, keeping things close, but slightly in our favor. Eventually, we come to match point.

One more point. Just one more point.

My brain is practically begging the universe for Rachel to hit an ace so this can all be over without me having to hit another ball. I don't know what happened to the thousands of hours I've spent on physical conditioning in my life, but right now I would surrender a kidney just to get out of this heat and lie down.

Rachel serves. It's not an ace. I'm so disappointed by this that I let the return fly past me down the alley. I should have gotten it—it was clearly within my reach. But I hesitated, and now all I can do is pray it lands out.

My head whips around just as the ball bounces; almost half of it lands directly on the baseline.

My heart sinks. We'll have to play another point. At least two, really.

I could cry right now, I'm so tired.

But a split second later, Rachel yells, "Long!"

The outrage from the other side of the net begins immediately.

"What?"

"Are you kidding me?"

"That ball was not out!"

"Look at the mark!"

Their shouts overlap each other, bouncing between anger and pleading—trying to appeal to our sense of fair play.

I replay the point in my mind. I watch it bounce in slow motion in my memory, like I have Hawk-Eye inside my head.

There's no sign of red clay between the white line and the edge of the ball, which means it must have landed on the line.

Hitting the line makes it in. The score will be 9-9 and we'll switch sides again. We'll have to play at least two more points so one of us can win by the required two-point margin.

I want so badly for the ball to have been long.

Rachel called it out, which means I will have to overrule her to call it in—to elongate this match I'm so desperate to end. Technically if partners disagree on a call, the rule is that the point goes to their opponents.

But I didn't disagree. I didn't say anything. After all, it wasn't my call. My partner on the baseline is responsible for calling the shots that go past me. I'm nearly forty feet away at the net, and the ball was moving away from me. I could have mis-seen it.

"Aren't you going to say something?" The girl at the net is staring at me like she can hear my thoughts.

I wish I had someone to tell me what to do right now. Cooper. Audrey. Even Leylah.

"I know you saw that land in," the girl's partner says, her eyes boring holes into me.

This is the *first* round of doubles. It's never even occurred to me that we might lose in the first round.

Rachel walks over and drags her racquet head in the red clay. The ball mark she's circled is well past the baseline. Clearly out. "It's *my* call," she asserts. "And it was out."

She says it so confidently. Like it *was* out. Maybe I blinked at exactly the wrong moment and that's what made it *seem* like it had been in but it actually wasn't. After all, Rachel circled a mark. Who am I to say it isn't *the* mark?

Six sets of eyes focus on me, waiting for me to say something. Anything. The moment seems to stretch on forever. Out of the corner of my eye is Audrey's cream-colored umbrella. It's completely still. Frozen, like everyone else, waiting to hear my reply.

I shrug weakly. "I didn't get a good look at it."

Both girls across the net mutter unflattering things only partially under their breath, but begrudgingly shake our hands over the net anyway. I can't bear to look at either of them, nor give my standard "good match" congratulations. They flee the court in record time and I'm left with just Rachel, who looks perfectly unbothered.

All I can think of is her match against Leylah two years ago. The girls on the other team today were just as outraged as Leylah was then. But just like that day, I say nothing as I walk off the court.

33

LEYLAH

GODDAMN IT.

I really, really wish I had some kind of Violetta-blocking glasses, like UV protection but to keep me from having to see her. Then I wouldn't have noticed how she froze when Rachel cheated.

It's ridiculous to feel disappointed, like I expected V to do the right thing. Overruling your doubles partner is always uncomfortable and might upset them, but the only other option is cheating.

I give myself a mental shake.

Of course Violetta's okay with cheating. She stole Peter from you.

She didn't deny it when I confronted her yesterday. Instead, she'd made it seem like she did it because she was jealous. Of me. Which is bullshit, of course. Violetta has always been good at telling people what they want to hear.

Mint, my doubles partner, hands me the balls at the end of our changeover. I need to snap out of my Violetta-induced coma.

It's not fair to Mint that my mind is wandering, even if the time is creeping into early evening and it's so hot I'm honestly concerned about dehydrating.

I was able to keep up my physical fitness in my two-year gap, but the mental game is a different story. I don't feel nearly as confident as I project. But acting like I am is just as crucial as feeling it. People believe whatever it is you show them.

Which is exactly what Violetta does.

Fuck.

I pause my thoughts while we play out the first point of my serve. It ends in a long volley rally between Mint and our opponents. I realize belatedly that I should have made my way up to net too. Damn it. Violetta is as much a distraction as Noah.

Naturally, Noah appears at that exact moment, walking down the path wearing stupidly bright neon-orange sneakers. God, I hope those aren't his actual tennis shoes.

Minus 5. You already know what his tennis shoes look like, you fucking nitwit.

I double-fault on the next point.

"Sorry," I mutter to Mint as she comes back to check on me.

"Come on, you can do it." She slaps my hand before flexing a skinny biceps in a show of strength—for me, I guess? She scrambles back to her spot and I wait for her hand signals.

Three quick points later, we hold my serve and toss the balls over the net to our opponents. Only then do I look over to where I last saw Noah.

He's looking at his phone. Why is he at my match if he isn't even watching it? And where are his friends?

Mint holds up her hand to pause the server as she pretends to have one last thing to discuss with me. Normally I hate holding up play but considering the number of shoelaces that've needed to be retied by the other team, I can live with it.

"Are you ready?" My partner is staring at me expectantly, even as she maintains a pleasant tone. I wonder how much of her ability to keep calm in irritating situations was learned from having to deal with others as a trans athlete.

I force my thoughts back to the match I'm supposed to be playing.

10 points if you can stay focused for the entire next game.

I can't believe I'm bribing myself with fake points like Mom and her goddamn sticker chart. Every single primary school teacher had insisted it would motivate me to read, like *ooh, a gold star that means nothing.* Even years later, I still have nightmares about that chart.

Fuck. I've wandered off topic again.

Minus 5 points.

I remind myself of everything that's at stake. It's my life, or death by parental suffocation.

I slap Mint's waiting palm. "Yes. I'm ready."

34

ALICE

I LANGUISH ON THE GROUNDS AFTER MY MATCH, TRYING TO SOAK UP as much of the atmosphere as possible. Everything seems a little brighter today. I wish I had someone with which to share my joy. Both my roommates are still on court, and though I am more comfortable now with Kevin and the other boys, we're not quite to the point of seeking out one another.

Still, I float down the tree-lined paths of the garden that's supposedly a miniature replica of the gardens at Versailles. Compared to the shrub maze around the perimeter of the Observatory, this green space is much more open—simply low, flat grass and tall trimmed trees with only people as the middling height. I'm not sure anything will ever seem more beautiful to me than the rows and rows of varying roses in Golden Gate Park, but this is definitely the second most beautiful.

Inside this garden, I can pretend to be royalty if I want.

I pull out my phone to take a photo and see I have an unread message. It was sent a while ago—just before my singles match.

Violetta: your objective today is to enjoy playing

Violetta: soak up every moment on court

Violetta: you deserve to be here

I think of Ba's messages, of how today was the first time I didn't check my phone beforehand, thinking I was on my own out there. But it turns out I wasn't.

Before I can overthink it, I snap a photo of the gardens and text it to David. I'll have to eventually tell him everything that's happened, I know—I've been avoiding his calls since Saturday— but for now, I take Violetta's advice.

I soak up every moment.

TUESDAY, JULY 11TH

MAIN DRAW, ROUND OF 32

35

LEYLAH

THE NEXT DAY DOESN'T GO QUITE AS WELL. I WIN MY SINGLES, BUT Mint and I lose our doubles to the top seed in what felt like ten minutes. We step off the court at the same time as Alice, who'd started her match an hour and a half earlier than us. Either we lost with record speed or Alice won in record slowness. Alice tries to console me but it's no use—all I can do is focus on tomorrow's singles, which now has even *more* pressure.

I can practically hear Mom's voice in my head, telling me I just need to work harder after failing. Bootstraps and all that.

Of course, she means it in a schoolwork sense, but it's probably why I spend so much extra time practicing tennis. Immigrant perseverance is ingrained in me like Texans and football. Or Puerto Ricans and their flag. I should be practicing my serves right now, not leaving the court until I fix whatever the hell it was that went wrong in doubles. But first I need a good sulk.

I throw open the door to the villa and am rewarded by two satisfying bangs—one when it hits the wall and one when it ricochets off and slams shut. I drop my bags and kick off my shoes as loudly as possible, heaving a grumbled sigh for good measure. The perks of being on my own: at home, I'd already be halfway through a lecture.

I take it out on Violetta's throw pillows. It's right in the name, after all. I *throw* each cream-colored pillow onto the ground as hard as I can. It's semi-satisfying.

The matching cream-colored blanket gives me nothing.

At least the couch is free now.

I flop down onto it, my head, arms, and legs all sticking well off the ends as I attempt to stretch out. If Bastille is going to shove three or four people into a room, the least they could do is give us a couch that can at least fit one individual.

I spot Violetta in the back of the room. She's lying in bed, one arm tucked under her head and the other holding her phone.

"I saw you and Oksana lost today," I call over. I feel just the tiniest bit better about losing, knowing Violetta did too.

Minus 5 points for being a terrible human being.

"Mm-hm," she hums, eyes still glued to her phone. The thumb of the hand she's using to hold the phone is doing all the scrolling. It can do both side to side and up and down. I'm mildly impressed—even with my long fingers I can't seem to manage that without my hand cramping.

"Don't you still have 18U doubles later?" I ask. Maybe I can get her to admit she knew that ball Rachel called out yesterday was in, but she's giving me nothing.

"Mm-hm."

"Did you see who you're playing?"

"Mm-hm."

I sit up and lean V's way to a get a better look at her. Her hair is still in a ponytail.

Violetta never wears her hair up unless she's working out. It's annoying how much attention she gets for her hair but I guess if I had hair like that I might be tempted to throw it around like I was in a shampoo commercial too. The fact that it's still up means she hasn't showered after playing three matches.

Ew. She's under the covers! In her sweaty clothes! It's as bad as watching actors put their shoes on the bed. Oh God, what if she's wearing shoes under the covers?

"Did you shower already?" I need to know. Of all the terrible things Violetta has done in her life, this might be what breaks me.

When she doesn't answer, I clarify. "I'm only asking because then I'll know if you're going to hole up in the bathroom for an hour to redo your makeup."

A beat passes. Then another. She's still staring and scrolling, but no reply.

"Hello? Can you hear me?"

V heaves a sigh, like it's a chore to have to talk to me, but her voice remains toneless. "What?" She still hasn't taken her eyes off the phone.

What the hell?

"What's with you?" I ask.

"Nothing's with me," she says in that bland voice. "I'm not the one who came storming in here and started throwing pillows because I lost."

I frown. "How do you know I lost?"

She doesn't answer that one.

It's starting to freak me out, this frozen-robot routine. What the hell is going on with her?

"Is this some weird attempt to get back at me?" I ask cautiously. "Like you're showing me what it's like to be cut off or something? Because I already know."

"Contrary to what you might believe, not everything is about *you*, Leylah." Her tone has no bite.

Getting off the couch and replacing the throw pillows and blanket on it, I head to the back of our room, where she is. I don't have fucking bionic eyes to have picked out the other changes in her appearance but now that I'm only a few feet away, I can see her eyes are drooping, sagging into dark smudges that tell me she hasn't been sleeping.

She looks like shit. Well, shit for her standards.

Violetta *never* looks like shit.

"What's been keeping you up?" I ask quietly. Alice mentioned hearing Violetta wake up at night, but that she just went to the bathroom and came back to bed every time. I rack my brain but come up with nothing she could be doing in there other than, well, going to the bathroom.

"Why should I tell you?" Violetta flashes her eyes up at me before going back to her phone. "Don't act like you care."

Do I? Care?

I don't know what else to say. So I leave. This time, I close the door quietly.

36

VIOLETTA

IT'S A RELIEF WHEN LEYLAH FINALLY LEAVES. THE WAY SHE WAS LOOKING at me was unsettling. Like she was really looking at me, instead of just the usual quick glare and dismissal. But more important, what did she see?

I open my camera app and peer at my reflection. I look terrible. But then I always do after a match. I'd only planned to stop at the room for a makeup touch-up before heading to Burgundy for a bite to eat so I'd have energy for my 18U doubles with Rachel. But then I decided to get a quick hit in beforehand. Just to relax my nerves.

One hit turned into three and I was barely able to climb off the windowsill and hide my oil pen before collapsing in bed. I hadn't intended to summon Faded Violetta in the middle of the day, but it seemed silly to waste the unexpected visit. So I've spent the past hour mindlessly flicking through cooking videos, trying to figure out why I'm so drawn to them.

It's not just because it stops me from eating in real life,

preventing any weed-induced munchies that might otherwise pack unmuscled pounds onto my frame. I think it's that each dish or cake or even cocktail represents a beginning. Surely after creating a masterpiece the creator is eager to share it with family or friends.

The cynical social media side of me knows it's all fake. Just like my crafted persona, most—if not all—are made only for digital consumption. For all I know, the dishes could taste disgusting.

But I like to imagine the type of family the dish was made for.

The beef stir-fry with Chinese broccoli and fermented black bean sauce? A happy family of four, where one kid sets the table and the other fetches everyone's drinks.

The lemon-and-rosemary soufflé with a dollop of rose-water whipped cream on top? A grandfatherly-type gentleman who wants to be on *The Great British Bake Off* and shares his experiments with neighbors and coworkers.

The carrot cake with raisins and pecans? A parent who throws big birthday parties in the backyard and loves her kid so much she'll put *raisins* in the birthday cake, knowing no one else at that party will like it.

As if she can sense my thoughts, my phone rings, the screen flashing *Audrey.*

I dismiss the call and roll onto my back, where I can stare up at the fairy lights crisscrossing the ceiling. I put those up only a few months ago, in an attempt to make this place feel homier and less like a sterile little apartment I've been living in for two years. How many different roommates have I had in that time?

Six? Seven? At least half a dozen people I've shared a home with, who I now only see in passing on social media.

Some of the players complain about having roommates, especially considering the price we all pay to be here. Well, the price other people pay. The only reason I can afford to live here full-time is because Audrey gets a subsidized employee rate—a benefit that I won't have if I ever leave and go somewhere else. Like college.

I guess it's a good thing I'll never go to college.

I recently looked up the stats: Less than 10 percent of high school–level kids end up competing in the NCAA. Of those, less than 2 percent make it to the pro level. Yet here we all are—all five hundred twelve of us in the tournament—fighting over a fraction of a percent chance of actually achieving what we're all training for.

My phone rings again and I don't bother to check it. I know it's Audrey, refusing to give up until I answer. She's calling to debrief my 16U doubles match—to go over in painstaking detail exactly what went wrong and how we can address it for the future. It's a useful resource, no doubt, but not always wanted the day of the match. Audrey insists the details be "fresh in my mind." Maybe I can blame it on my rolled ankle, still sore but firmly taped. But Audrey hates excuses. And even I know the ankle story is an excuse.

My phone starts another round of ringing and I'm too tired to fight it anymore. "Hello?" I answer.

"I've given you over an hour, darling. You can't expect to avoid me forever."

"People lose matches. It happens," I say.

"It happens to other people, Violetta."

Audrey only ever calls me Violetta when she's upset about something.

"Yeah, well, it happened to me today."

"Losing doesn't just happen, darling. You *choose* to let it happen to you."

Why am I not surprised to find that Audrey has the same attitude as Leylah?

"You forget I watched you out there, Violetta. You chose to lose today and for the life of me I cannot figure out why." Audrey is definitely trying to make this seem like a casual conversation, but the tension in her tone tells me she's upset. "I suppose it *was* too much to expect, let alone *hope* you could bring home four trophies from one tournament at this level," she continues, chattering nonsensically as if just to herself. "And if your results are any indication, the field seems to be stronger this year. You'll need a quick 18U doubles match so you can save your legs for tomorrow's singles."

I wish I hadn't put my oil pen away. I could use another hit just to make it through this conversation.

"Have you eaten something yet? You should have some protein. Maybe some eggs, or you could ask the chef to make you that lentil stew they have sometimes?"

"I'm not going to ask them to cook me a special meal."

"It's not special—they already make it. I'm sure it would be no problem for them to whip you up a bowl. They're here to ensure you're prepared and well fed for your performance."

Despite what Audrey and Leylah think, I don't believe the entire world is at my disposal.

"Fine, whatever," I say. I just want to get off the phone and relax for the few remaining minutes I have before I'm forced to get out of bed and go play again.

"Not whatever. I'm trying to talk to you about your nutrition, making sure you're ready for every match. I wouldn't be doing all this if I didn't have full confidence in your ability to bounce back."

I'm sure she thinks she's doing something with these words, but I'm even more sure it's not accomplishing what she thinks it is. The more she discusses tennis, my next match, or anything about the future, the more I want to lock myself in the bathroom and smoke myself into absolute oblivion.

"Now. Let's talk about your poaching. During your match with Oksana, you missed . . ."

She drones on but I tune her out, scrolling silently while she prattles on about something I'm not doing or should be doing or need to learn how to do. It doesn't really matter. It's not like I'm magically going to develop new skills in the next thirty minutes.

"Well," I cut in, not much caring whether I interrupted her midsentence. "Thanks for the pep talk. I need to go play now."

My tone conveys exactly how *not* thankful I am.

I expect another scolding for my attitude, but instead she backs off. "I can see you need some time and space to get focused so I'll check back in on you later."

"Don't bother," I tell her before hanging up. "I'll be the same."

WEDNESDAY, JULY 12TH

MAIN DRAW,
ROUND OF 16

37
ALICE

I AM EXCEEDINGLY GRATEFUL MY MATCH IS SCHEDULED FOR THE FIRST time slot of the day, 8 a.m. Though I've been back to myself the last two days, the temperature of early morning somehow propels me to a level previously unachieved. I hadn't realized just how much the humidity and heat were sapping my energy reserves.

The cooler weather also allows me breathing room to look around. Tennis is such a solitary sport, with no team to cheer you on when you're tired. Even at St. Aidan's, where there was an official team and therefore teammates, it never felt that way because at the end of the day, it's still only me on the court.

Still, I check my phone.

Violetta: your challenge today is to win!
Violetta: then come cheer me on so I can win
Violetta: so we can play each other in the next round :)

The messages are time-stamped just after 2 a.m., long after I was asleep. That she thought to pre-send best wishes so I'd have them at this early hour makes me fluttery inside, like walking into a surprise party.

It would be an honor to play Violetta, not unlike going up against an established legend. I've been watching her matches here, of course, but everyone's game feels different from the other side of the net. To be able to stand out there as an equal would clear my status as an outsider who lucked into getting in here, instead marking me as a real contender others should be concerned about.

I'm asserting my existence. Taking up space.

I smother the court with my presence, tidily taking a 6–4, 6–3 win over the number one player from Türkiye. I'm indestructible.

When we finally shake hands at the net, I realize telling Violetta my good news is no longer enough. I'm so happy I need to stretch it further, filling a balloon with this . . . this *hope* that seems to have sprouted within me.

Already I'm dialing David before I step off the court. He picks up on the first ring.

"Hey Alice, what's up?"

David's voice is always upbeat when he talks to me, but this time it sounds even more so. I've called him for the first time, instead of waiting for him to call me.

"I'm back in the tournament," I tell him. I explain my loss on Saturday and the lucky-loser situation.

"Yeah. I already knew."

"What? How?!" I clamp my hand over my mouth, giving a quick look around to make sure I haven't just disturbed someone else's match. I tiptoe off the court and close the gate behind me. "How?" I ask again.

"I saw it on the tournament website. You know, the internet?"

Right. The same way I'd even applied to the tournament.

"So you know I'm in the quarterfinals?"

I have to pull the phone away from my ear as he whoops and hollers.

"I do now," he cries. "I've been following your scores, but the tournament only updates them at the end of the day."

I can't believe he's been tracking my progress this entire time.

"Why didn't you tell me you knew?" I ask.

"You haven't exactly been picking up my calls," he points out.

Right again. Even after I texted him the picture of the gardens the other day, I skipped the call that came in immediately after. It's on the tip of my tongue to apologize, but I swallow the urge. I'm not ready to smooth everything over just yet.

"I was mad at you," I confess.

"I know."

"How?"

"You stopped picking up my calls."

"You didn't think I was lying dead in a ditch somewhere?"

I want to take back the words as soon as I say them. It's too soon. It's too close.

David pauses for only a beat. "I can tell when I'm being screened, Alice. This was your first time really stepping out on your own and I didn't want to repeat the mistake of treating you like a little kid. I figured you needed space and that if you wanted us to know what was going on, you would've told us."

Us. He's doing it again, talking for the entire family.

"Are you just saying that because you have to?" I ask.

"No, why would I have to?"

"Because that's the same logic you used when you didn't tell me . . ."

I don't finish the sentence but I don't need to. I've forced the conversation anyway. We're finally going to talk about the one thing we never talk about.

The silence drags on a few more beats before David speaks. "It wasn't about what we *wanted* you to know," he says quietly. "Of course I didn't *want* to keep things from you."

"And yet."

I hear shuffling and the muffled sound of voices, only catching the tail end of the sentence, the gruff voice barking out, "This better not become a habit." More shuffling and the creak of a door being opened before David returns, his usual cheerful voice back. "Sorry about that. I'm at work so I just needed to let my boss know I was stepping out for a couple minutes."

This time I am sorry. "Are you going to get in trouble?"

I hadn't even bothered to consider what he might be doing before making the call. Meanwhile, he's been looking up my results every night.

"Nah. Besides," he adds, "I'm legally entitled to a fifteen-minute break. I'm just taking it a little earlier than usual."

He says it so cheerfully I almost believe it *is* no big deal. But I check my watch and adjust the time for the West Coast. It's then I realize: David's upbeat attitude is my thumb-sucking.

He's always been an optimist—he wanted to be a doctor, after all. If he could, David would help everyone. And since Ba's death, he's been a one-man life preserver, trying to balance the rest of the Wu family on his back. As if he can bring us all back from the semi-dead if he were only buoyant enough.

Maybe David didn't tell me about Baba not because he thought *I* couldn't handle it, but because it was the only way *he* could. Maybe he needed me to stay the same—the one part of his life untouched by sadness and despair. By holding himself over me like a shield, it protected his squishy insides so they could go on keeping him alive.

"It's okay to say you're hurting too, you know. Carrying that secret around for as long as you did." I don't say it in a condescending way, but in a way I hope conveys my understanding.

David remains silent for a few beats, before clearing his throat several times. "I've had a lot longer to wrap my head around all of it, so it wasn't as bad for me. I'm sorry we kept it from you."

"Grief isn't a contest. And who knows, maybe if I'd known all this time, it would have made watching it happen all that much worse."

I don't know if I really believe that or if it's just something I say to make David feel better, but it feels nice to be the one to soothe for once.

"Thanks, Alice. That means a lot."

I can hear David's voice thickening and I don't want to upset him while he's still at work, so I pivot. "How's Ma doing?"

He clears his throat again before attempting an answer. "She's good. You know, the same. She misses you."

I'm skeptical. "She said that?"

"I know she misses you."

"Did she tell you that? Did she say those exact words to you?"

"Alice, you know how she is. You know she loves you. She's just not as good about, you know, expressing it . . . verbally."

It's the understatement of the century. She speaks only when necessary, using as few words as possible. Baba always did the talking, which is why the house is so quiet now.

In a former life, I think she would have flourished in a monastery.

Maybe we are more alike than I ever realized. After all, David is the Baba, chattering his way through tragedy as if he's unaffected, while Mama and I shrink ourselves into tiny pebbles, taking up less and less space. Maybe one day we can learn to communicate like the mother and daughter rocks in *Everything Everywhere All at Once*.

"Did you know about Mrs. Conrad?" I ask. I need to know.

David hesitates. "Don't tell Ma you know."

"Why?"

"Because she would hate it if you knew."

"I meant why did she accept the money in the first place? Ma's always been against taking gifts from clients."

"I told you. She loves you."

I've never thought Mama didn't love me. But I guess I didn't realize how *much* she did, going against her own beliefs and swallowing her pride for my benefit.

Now I'm the one needing to clear my throat to keep away the tears. I swipe them with the back of my hand just to be sure. "I've got to go report my score now, but tell her hi from me."

"Sure thing," he says, his tone back to that of the cheerful cruise director of the Wu family ship. "I'm glad you called."

"Me too."

38

VIOLETTA

I'LL ADMIT IT: I DIDN'T EXPECT ALICE TO MAKE IT THIS FAR. I KNOW
I told her I wanted to play her in the next round, but the fact is
I'd sort of hoped she'd just lose today. Then the issue of having to
play her head-to-head would've resolved itself—drama free.

Instead, I'm going to have to beat her tomorrow and end this
fairy-tale run of hers.

If I could give her the win, I would. I don't need it. I have lots
of wins.

I think about my argument with Leylah from the other
day—how she accused me of needing to win everything in life.
It's why she thinks I kissed Peter. Who knows? Maybe she's
right.

It didn't feel like it at the time. And I didn't go into it with the
intention of getting back at her in any way, but subconsciously I
resented her. I knew I did. I was never going to be able to beat her,
and it slowly poisoned our friendship.

I can't stand the thought of that happening with Alice.

Finally, just when the universe gives me something good, it immediately takes it away from me, as if to show me what I'm losing. Another sacrifice to the tennis gods. A test, I suppose, to see if I *want* it enough.

Sitting on the bathroom counter with my feet in the sink, I inhale another puff from my oil pen and blow the vapor out the window. I never meant for this to become a nightly routine, but there are only three more days until this tournament is over. Then I'll scale back.

I rest my forearms across the windowsill, looking out onto the blackness of the cypress trees that nearly block the moon. The world out there feels empty. Like there's space to breathe. Space to create.

If I'd had the chance to design an entirely different life for myself, what would I have made? What parts of my current life would I have kept?

But no matter what scenario I dream up, it's impossible to imagine Audrey supporting anything other than what I'm doing now. Tennis was her entire life. And *I* was the one who took it from her.

It's not like I hate tennis. And I'm clearly really good at it. Leylah said I'd never have gotten this good if I didn't love it but I'm not so sure. When I'm on court, I'm not usually thinking about the exhilaration of hitting an ace or winning a set—I'm thinking of Audrey in the stands, marking those down as little victories to be celebrated afterward. Because winning makes *her* happy.

I've seen the footage of her when she was on tour. She was all business on the court, but the second she'd win, it was all smiles. When she played, she looked like she'd rather die than give up.

I'm not sure I have that same passion in me.

I feel my stomach starting to roil so I take another hit. It seems like I'm having to smoke more each time to reach actual relaxation. Even now I still feel a little jumpy, my arms and legs tingly like they're falling asleep.

I try to shake out my feet and end up banging the top of my foot on the brass faucet. "Fuck," I mutter to myself. That hurt. A lot.

I take one more hit, hoping it'll stem the pain in what is definitely going to be a bruise tomorrow. Except I'm distracted by trying to rub the spot on my foot and I inhale a little too much. I start coughing violently and almost slip off the counter, trying to make sure I don't drop my pen but also not kick the sink again.

Maybe I've had enough for tonight.

I climb down and stick my mouth under the faucet to give my throat some much needed hydration. But in keeping with the theme of the night, I nearly drown myself and end up coughing again. I scramble to the toilet and lift the lid just in time to puke my guts out. I hadn't planned on doing it today, but I always feel just a little bit better afterward. Reset. Like there's no mistake I can't just quickly undo with the press of a finger.

39
ALICE

THE SOUND OF MUFFLED COUGHING DRAGS ME FROM SLEEP. I TRY TO ignore it, but as soon as I'm about to drift back to sleep, it comes again. It's raspy and low, and I immediately look to Violetta's bed.

It's empty.

There's a sliver of light coming through the bottom of the bathroom door. It's still dark outside, but my watch indicates we're in the wee hours of the morning.

A tiny knot of dread starts to weave its way into my stomach. She's been getting up to go to the bathroom every night. I wasn't certain before, but now I know. The cough happens every night too.

I wait for her to emerge but instead I hear the flush of the toilet. Scrambling down the ladder, I reach the door at the same moment Violetta opens it. In the harsh light of the bathroom, she looks haggard. Her eyes are bloodshot, her face drained of color, a light sheen of sweat along her hairline and down her neck.

It's a shock to my system, she usually looks so . . . alive.

But then I smell it. It's barely there, but I'm not mistaken. I know that smell. The truth hits me all at once and suddenly, the pieces about her that seemed mysterious fall into place.

"I wasn't feeling well," she says, not waiting for me to ask the question.

But I know what a lie looks like now, and Violetta is lying. And I suspect she's *been* lying. The familiar scent of betrayal.

I fix her with a hard stare. "How long have you been doing this?"

"I don't know what you're talking about."

The liar's favorite phrase.

"How long?" I demand.

Violetta rolls her eyes, pushing past me and heading for her bed. "It's not a big deal. You just did it on Saturday, remember?"

She can't possibly think it's the same. "I didn't have a match the next day!"

"So what?" She gives a defensive shrug, like I'm attacking her. "It's not like I'll still be high when we play." She climbs into her bed but remains sitting, one leg tucked under her and the other hanging over the edge.

I step closer and lower my voice even more so we don't wake Leylah, but try to keep the hardness in my voice so Violetta will understand how upset I am with her right now. Of all the irresponsible, reckless teenager decisions!

"It's not a big deal," she protests, and I have to remind her to keep her voice down. "Lots of tennis players smoke pot."

"How many of them do it every day?"

Violetta looks surprised, like she hadn't expected me to know.

"It's the lavender," I tell her, disgusted and not triumphant. "That's why you're always covered in it, isn't it? Lavender lotion, lavender detergent, lavender deodorant. You suffocate yourself in lavender so no one can possibly smell anything else." I think of Baba's sunglasses and how he'd started wearing them to hide the bulging of his eyes near the end.

"You're such a drama queen! You act like I'm doing meth. It's just pot."

I shake my head at her complete naivete. "Do you think weed isn't addictive? Or harmful? Do you have any idea what it can do to your body, especially long term?"

It's clear I have struck a nerve because Violetta huffs and I can see her gearing up to argue back. "You didn't even notice before today, which means it hasn't negatively affected me in any way. You're freaking out over nothing."

Another piece of the puzzle falls into place with a tiny *click*.

"This is what started your fight with Leylah, isn't it?" The night I said I wanted to be reckless, Violetta had been about to offer me something and Leylah reacted right away. Violetta told her she was freaking out over nothing. Leylah had to have known what V's suggestion was going to be.

"That wasn't my fault," Violetta insists. "I'm not the one who's supposed to know how to manage type I diabetes."

I can't help but shake my head. "How many friends are you going to lose over this? Is it really that important?"

"You're really going to stop being friends with me over this? Even though you've done it too?" Her voice is indignant. "I already told you, I don't even do it that often. Don't you think you would have noticed if I was always on the couch, snacking? Not to mention, I would be a lot bigger. You've seen me eat while I'm high."

Click.

"You've been throwing it up." I say it aloud as I piece together the rest of Violetta. I'm in the end stages of the puzzle, where everything gets easier. I press my fingers into my temples, trying to force the thoughts out like frosting. "It all makes sense. The cooking videos! And the salads! God, you're killing yourself."

"Overdramatic much? Puking every once in a while isn't going to do anything."

"Did you not learn about disordered eating in health class?"

"Eating salad doesn't mean I have an eating disorder."

"You don't have an eating disorder *yet*," I correct her. "Where do you think all of this leads? Do you really think you're going to just stop one day? Because I know what happens to people who develop eating disorders. We watched a lot of first-person interviews about it. Wiki summary: it ends in organ failure."

Just like Ba.

She's slowly killing herself. She's *been* slowly killing herself.

Flashes of pain rip through me and I relive Ba's death all over again. Lies upon lies upon lies. He'd been killing himself. He had a choice and he chose death.

Just like she's doing.

I can't go through this again.

"You need to tell Audrey."

Violetta looks at me as though I've just told her to jump to the moon. "Tell her what? That you're overreacting to very normal teenager behaviors?"

"This isn't normal, V. Most teens don't need to smoke weed just to make it through the day."

"Yeah, well, most teens don't have my life," she snaps.

"No, but the other people here do. Do you really think they're all doing the same things you're doing? Every single one of them is smoking pot in the bathroom at three o'clock in the morning? How about puking after meals? If it's so fine and good, are you going to explain the finer techniques of sticking your finger down your throat to a younger player who doesn't do it yet?" I don't bother waiting for her to answer my rhetorical questions. "This isn't normal and it isn't healthy. You either tell Audrey or I will."

I'm done standing on the sidelines, watching people kill themselves.

Violetta jumps up, full of righteous anger. "This is none of your business. You think what, just because you follow my social media and you hung out with me for a week that you suddenly know me? That you can come and interfere with my life?" She pulls out a fluffy purple robe, the kind that's shown in movies. "You're such a hypocrite. What happened to letting people do what they wanted with their bodies? Is that only for you? Because you didn't hear me talking down to you because you still suck your thumb."

The words land like physical blows.

Hypocrite, boom.

Only for you, bam.

You still suck your thumb. Knockout.

I trusted her with my deepest, darkest secret, and she used it against me. I can feel the tears coming, but I fight it, trying to keep my voice steady. "At least I told you about it. I didn't keep it a secret and then *lie* to you about it."

"Oh, grow up, Alice," she snaps. "No one lied to you. They just didn't tell you everything. No wonder, if this is how you always react."

She whirls around and marches out the door, her exit a fittingly perfect goodbye.

Because after I beat her in our match, I never want to see Violetta Masuda ever again.

40

VIOLETTA

I TAKE A PAGE OUT OF LEYLAH'S DRAMATIC HANDBOOK AND STORM out of the villa. It's hard to seem quite as intense considering I'm dressed in pjs and a fluffy robe, but I couldn't just stand there and let Alice threaten me like that. Who does she think she is, anyway? She's not even older than me! She's in no position to lecture me about anything.

Unfortunately, I didn't think to grab anything useful on my way out, like my phone. Or car keys. Or even shoes. All I have is this robe and my oil pen, which I shoved into my pocket. I'm so worked up I'm tempted to take another puff but I don't want to prove Alice right.

I decide to head for the beach, where the warm sand and gentle breeze will make my hideout more comfortable. The last thing I need is to somehow run into someone when I look like this—no makeup and my hair in an *actual* messy bun, not one I've artfully crafted to look good.

It's late—or early, I guess—but the sky is light enough for me to make my way without any trouble. I'm not moving particularly fast without shoes, so I pull out my pen and take one last drag just to pass the time. Forget Alice. I don't need to prove anything to her.

I'm killing myself? Ha.

Alice acts like she's the expert on eating disorders. Well, I too know how to use Google. I've seen the pictures of eroded esophagi and yellowed teeth and ragged knuckles from repeated purges. Or the emaciated skeletons with brittle bones and dull, lifeless hair that falls out by the handful. I'm none of those things, with none of those side effects. I eat—oftentimes completely normal, healthy meals. Despite what Alice thinks, I don't eat salad *that* often. And my salads always have a protein. I'm an athlete—does she really think I'd starve my body of important nutrients? At most, the occasional puke balances out my chocolate chip cookie addiction or anything I inhale when I get the munchies. That's it.

What's that saying? *Everything in moderation.*

Part of me knows it doesn't apply to this. Throwing up your food can't be good for your body. But is it really *that* bad? After all, we puke when we're sick. And people skip meals all the time. Someone created intermittent fasting based on this exact idea! If I were really on some kind of slippery slope toward certain death, wouldn't I be doing the other things like forcing myself to work out for hours on end or taking laxatives? I've never even *considered* taking a laxative. Gross.

I haven't shed a single pound in months. At least, my clothes aren't fitting any looser than usual. I don't know for sure because I don't ever step on a scale. I don't even *own* a scale! How can it be considered a disorder if I don't even care about losing weight? At most, it's a bad habit.

As I reach the sand, I pull my robe tighter around me. It's only a little windy and I'm sure the temperature will shoot up as soon as the sun breaks the horizon, but right now I feel cold. I stay a safe distance from the water and plunk down onto the sand, burying my feet up to my ankles.

I've never really loved the ocean. Sure, it's pretty to look at, but it's also unpredictable. Dangerous. A wave could sweep you away at any moment, drowning you in the turbulence of the riptide. That's how I feel now—standing on the edge of something that could kill me, but only if I let it.

But it's not what Alice thinks. In fact, most of the reason I smoke is because I'm so fucking lonely. I'm a deep, gaping, bottomless pit of *need*.

Leylah was right: I *need* people to like me.

It's not really a surprise she treats me the way she does. In her mind, I'm a sellout, if such a thing is possible to be at our age. But she doesn't realize how lucky she is to *know* who she is at all times—to know exactly what she wants from life. Maybe having to overcome her parents, her grades, and her diabetes is what's made her so laser focused. Like a non-immigrant version of "the struggle." It can't be a coincidence that so often the standouts in any field of life have traversed massive obstacles to succeed. Look at Leylah's parents! If I'd had more real struggles, would I be a stronger person too? Or would I just have collapsed sooner?

I draw swirls in the sand as the sun rises, the dark oranges and purples fading into the blues of daytime. Burgundy is probably open by now—it extends its open hours during the invitational for kids who are jet-lagged and keep odd schedules while trying to adjust to local time.

It's sick to be jealous of someone else's illness, I know. I can't imagine the nightmare task of having to manage every single calorie, every single minute of the day, at risk of death—especially with a life as active as hers. I can't even manage my calorie intake now and there's nothing wrong with me. Nothing real, anyway.

The pressures of social media and an overbearing parent are not *real* problems. Feeling like I need to put on makeup before doing anything because of low self-esteem is not a *real* problem.

Once upon a time, I was someone different. At least I remember being different. Sure, I've always loved dressing up and looking pretty, but I used to care about other stuff.

Didn't I?

Now it feels like less like something I *want* to do and more like something I *have* to do. Without it, I'm not just naked, I'm weak. My looks are my armor, distracting people from what's beyond—or more accurately, *not* beyond—that. Because Leylah's right about that too; I'm a shell of the person I'm supposed to be. Or that Audrey wants me to be. It's hard to know now where her dreams stop and mine begin.

I pick at the glue that holds my hair extensions in, scraping each one off with my fingernails. They were Audrey's idea. To give my ponytail more bounce. She told me they took my hair from "nice" to "memorable." When people meet me, the thing they will remember about me is my *hair.* Half of which isn't even mine.

It's not all Audrey's fault. It would be easier if it were. And I know she means well, trying to give me the life she lost.

I watch the sun rise higher into the sky, feel the air beginning to warm, and hear the waves mellowing. Under the glowing light of the sun, the ocean doesn't look nearly as menacing as it had earlier.

"How did I know I'd find you here? You're such a cliché."

Even before I turn around, I know it's Leylah.

She sinks down into the sand next to me, her knobby knees propped up as she leans back on her hands, casual as can be. I can't help noticing her thigh to knee ratio. See? I don't have an eating disorder—I don't want to be *that* skinny.

Ugh. Even thinking about it puts me into a bad mood.

"Did you come to insult me some more?"

"When did I insult you?" She pulls back. "Is this about the *pillows* again?"

I shoot her a look. "I'm not in the mood for another fight."

Leylah sighs. "Fine. Sorry I called you a cliché." The apology sounds like it was coerced by a teacher or other supervising adult, but it makes me feel a tiny bit better anyway.

I'm pathetic.

"Did Alice send you?" I ask. Part of me hopes she did; the other part of me is still furious at her for her ultimatum. Real friends don't threaten to rat their friends out to their moms.

"No."

I furrow my brow. "I don't understand. What are you doing here?"

"You had a fight with Alice, yes?"

"Did she tell you that?"

Leylah rolls her eyes. "You left without the phone you go *nowhere* without and Alice is back to moping? It's not exactly solving a murder."

Still, that doesn't answer my original question. Why is she here?

"Anyway," she continues. "I woke up to this fun little divorce." She points between me and campus, where I assume she's referencing Alice. "I figured my choices were either to tell the creepy coach who hits on teenage girls to find you or come do it myself."

"Cooper isn't creepy!" I exclaim. "And he doesn't hit on anyone—they all hit on *him*."

"The fact that you knew exactly who I was referring to kind of proves my point."

Damn it. Leylah is a lot smarter than her parents give her credit for.

"That's what you came here for?" I ask skeptically. "To talk about Cooper?"

"Absolutely not. But someone probably should, at some point. The guy's like, thirty. He has no business texting teenage girls."

"He's twenty-five. And we're friends."

"And you're sixteen. He should get friends his own age."

I look away. "Whatever."

It's not like I don't grasp the significance of Leylah coming out here and trying to help, but I definitely don't need her weighing in on my other friendships.

"Anyway," Leylah says, pushing herself to standing, "I assume you lost track of time because your match is in like"—she pulls out her phone and checks the time—"forty-five minutes."

That snaps me out of things. "What?!" I'm still in pajamas. I have sand sticking to all visible parts of my body. And I'm over a mile away from campus. "What am I going to do?"

I scramble to my feet and she gives an exaggerated eye roll. "Guess you'll have to settle for only one coat of mascara instead of five." She looks down at the clumps of hair I've scooped up and her eyes light up. "I knew it! I *knew* that couldn't all be your hair! No one has that much hair!" Her voice is triumphant as she jumps around, pointing like I'm going to try to deny the physical evidence in my hand.

Of course she noticed before this. My hair was memorable. For once, I want to be memorable for another reason. I want to be a tennis player first, the girl everyone wants second. I want to be more than just fake hair and a constant smile. I want to prove I can do at least one thing right.

I shove the nest of hair into Leylah's hand while she protests, but before she can give it back to me I'm already running to campus.

THURSDAY, JULY 13TH

MAIN DRAW, QUARTERFINALS

41
ALICE

VIOLETTA ARRIVES ON TIME TO OUR MATCH, BUT IT'S CLEAR SHE'S NOT in top form, the dark circles beneath her eyes visible despite concealer. To an outsider, she looks perfectly fine, but I sneak a closer look during the racquet spin and notice her foundation isn't blended all the way in at the jawline, her eyelashes look thin, and she seems to have skipped any kind of lip treatment. Even her hair is limper than usual.

I wonder what she ended up doing last night after she left. If she slept at all.

I give myself a mental shake. She used my secrets against me. That falls into the unforgivable category—even worse than what Baba did because she lashed out at me. There was no lashing out with Ba because I never had the chance to confront him.

I steel myself. I need an objective. That'll keep me focused.

Tennis objective: no soft thoughts about Violetta!

Every time I'm tempted, I'll have to remind myself that she betrayed me. Then she took it a step further and told me to grow up. Insinuating what? That I'm a child while she's an adult? Why? Because she flirts with inappropriately aged coaches?

If she thinks I'm a kid, I'll play her like a little kid.

I moon ball. I drop shot. I hit lobs so high they make Violetta's eyes water from having to stare directly at the sun. I hit slice after slice after slice, forehand and backhand, my balls skimming low to the ground.

I play every single point with 100 percent effort, running for every ball, no matter how improbable it is I will reach it. I play the best I can possibly play—considering the circumstances.

In the end, it's not enough.

But there's a humbling truth in sports that is easier to ignore in the real world: some people are just going to be too good for you to beat. It doesn't mean you should give up or always fear them, but that losing isn't shameful. By Baba's standards, I've succeeded beyond anything I could have imagined.

If only it felt like that inside.

We shake hands at the net—a necessary ending for every match. Perhaps this is the ending I, too, needed to free myself from here. Vacation is over.

42

VIOLETTA

BEATING ALICE IS A COMPLETELY MISERABLE EXPERIENCE. SHE BARELY looks at me afterward. I try to hold her handshake just a second longer, but she wriggles out of my grip and bolts.

I don't know if she's still angry about last night or the match or both, but I've never felt this terrible in my life. Not even when we moved and my dad didn't come to visit me in Florida because there wasn't a tournament nearby.

I take my time on the changeover bench, peeling off my socks and shoes before stuffing my feet into more comfortable sandals. Alice has made it clear she doesn't want to talk to me right now so there's no point in rushing off after her.

Besides, the rational part of my brain reminds me I need to conserve energy for my 18s matches later this afternoon—singles *and* doubles.

I sit there for so long the next set of players come out for their match—two boys so young their voices haven't dropped yet. They must be in the 12U.

I drag myself out of their way, already exhausted by their excited energy to play. I can't believe I have to go back on court and do this again today.

Twice.

Rachel already texted me four times while I was on court, wanting to go over strategy and general readiness check-ins. I suppose it's fair, considering how checked-out I've been in our last couple of matches. She lost in singles yesterday, so now she can devote her full attention to our doubles chances.

Yay.

I return Rachel's text, telling her I'm headed to the Panthéon to ice my foot. Her reply is almost instantaneous.

Rachel: what the hell happened to your foot?
Rachel: did you just hurt it in your match?
Rachel: and don't you have 18U singles before our match too?
Rachel: fuck, we're screwed
Rachel: how bad does it hurt?

I don't answer any of those questions, instead hobbling down the hallway and into the training room Cooper took me to last time. My foot really only hurts when I flex it, because of the bruise from the sink yesterday, but this is a good place to hide out. You can only be in here if you have an injury or are helping someone with an injury.

Coop's back is to me when I come around the corner. Through the windows, I can see he's standing next to one of the training tables, his hands and hips bracing his body as he leans into the person sitting there. I can't hear what he says or how he looks as he says it, but I hear the ensuing laugh from the player on the table. It's definitely a girl.

I make it a point to hit my bag on the doorframe, to alert them of my presence. Coop turns and I see the girl who was just laughing like he was the funniest person on earth. She came to Bastille not long ago, from Wisconsin, I think.

A stab of jealousy makes me think ugly thoughts about her. But then I see Cooper straighten and head toward me. He helps me set my bag down, then helps lift my legs onto the table, just like he did the other day.

"I haven't heard from you in days. What's going on?" He places a hand on my bare shoulder. Out of concern. But then he teases, "I thought maybe I'd been replaced."

"I could say the same."

Coop swirls around for a quick check that yes, I'm referring to the girl who has suddenly been flanked by two other giggly 14Us, no doubt to get close to him. He tips his head at them. "That?" He looks amused. My jealousy is amusing to him. "Come on, V. You know you're my number one girl."

He clasps my ankle with his hands in a brusque, businesslike manner, but it doesn't matter. Electric currents shoot through me like he's tracing a line up the inside of my leg. "What's going on here? Is the ankle still giving you trouble?" He's asking . . . like a coach.

But then I lock eyes with him and I see the concern in them. He's businesslike because he *cares*. Also, his hands are still wrapped around my ankle—the correct ankle! Because he remembered!—which has scrambled my brain into mush. He's staring at me, holding the rest of the world at bay until I answer the question: *Am I okay?*

There's a power in this—in holding the attention of someone like Cooper Nelsen. His *whole* attention.

I'm sure he knows this. I think that's why he does it. Power is the most addictive thing there is—what better way to hook a girl's affections?

Even knowing this—hearing it in Leylah's voice—I tell Cooper that yes, my ankle *is* still bothering me and could he get me some ice?

Breaking eye contact helps, allowing me to finally draw a full breath while his back is turned. "You never answered my question," he says over the crunch of scooping ice. "Why haven't I heard from you? You leaving me for a girl? What's her name? The one you're always talking about—Alice."

For some reason I want to slap the name out of Cooper's mouth. I don't want to talk about Alice with him. It feels too . . . personal.

"I'm busy," I tell him. "I'm still in three draws, you know."

I hold up three fingers and wiggle them for effect. I also want to puke. Violently.

Cooper pauses and grins at that. "That's why you're my number one girl."

He jostles the ice bag and sucks the air out, just like last time. He also holds my eyes while he does it—just like last time. It takes him four full seconds to take the air into his lungs.

I wonder how many numbered girls he has. Is there a number two or number three around here, ready to step in at a moment's notice if I'm indisposed?

"Don't you ever get sick of being here?" I ask as he ties off the bag and positions it on my ankle. "Always surrounded by teenagers?"

As if on cue, I hear more giggling from the 14U girls across the room, followed by furious whispering back and forth.

He smothers a laugh of his own at the poorly concealed conversation behind him. "Nah. You all keep me young. What can I say? I live for the drama."

"You say that like you're fifty."

"I might as well be. I'm surrounded by teenagers, remember? I'm just an old man to all of you."

When I don't respond, Coop fusses with my ankle again, seeming to examine it with both hands. "This is the part where you're supposed to be all, 'No, Coop, you're still young and spry to me.'"

I raise my eyebrows. "Spry?"

He slides his hands just above my ankle, shooting me a devastating grin. "Attractive? Fit? The most attentive personal trainer?"

He wants to play the game; I know from his eyes. He wants to see how far he can inch his fingers up the back of my leg before I say stop. He wants to wind plastic wrap around me again, casually brushing my skin to see which one of us breaks first. He wants me to flirt with him and edge ever closer to that line we've never, ever crossed because deep down we both know it's wrong.

I think I've always known it. But it took Leylah pointing it out to finally make me rethink it. Why? Alice had said essentially the same thing to me, but I didn't listen then. For some reason, I hadn't respected her opinion as much as Leylah's.

Because I didn't treat her like an equal.

I owe Alice a very big apology.

Cooper gives my calf a little squeeze and I realize he's waiting for me to answer a question. "Do you need some help with your ice?" he repeats patiently, waiting expectantly.

He's asking, but I've never said no. I've never wanted to say no.

This time I pull back, grabbing the ice pack with my own hands as I firmly slide my ankle out from his grasp. "I've got it."

For a split second, I see the confusion all over Coop's face. The sense of rejection.

I've never said no before.

He recovers in record time, shifting back into the familiar smile I now recognize as his mask. No wonder I thought we had a special bond—we wear the same costume.

"Congrats on your win," he says, backing away from me in a carefully timed way that seems neither too fast nor too slow. "Catch up with you later, okay?"

He doesn't wait for me to answer before he leaves.

Even though it's what I expected, it still stings. Just another relationship that was based on appearance.

43

ALICE

I AM TRUDGING ACROSS CAMPUS, LICKING MY WOUNDS—META-phorically—when I hear someone call my name.

"Alice Wu?"

I turn and find a Black woman in a blue polo shirt, khaki shorts, and yellow baseball cap summoning me. I'm so baffled I point to myself just to be sure she hasn't mixed me up with someone else. "Me?"

Blue and yellow. Blue and yellow.

My brain scrambles for why those colors seem important when I finally see the word on her cap: *Cal.* Written in the highly identifiable *Cal* script.

The woman holds out her hand as she introduces herself. "Sah'rai Morrison, head coach of the women's team at Cal Berkeley."

I shake her hand, still in a bit of a daze as she continues: "I watched your match today and I was very impressed."

"But I lost."

She smiles. "True, but you showed tremendous fight out there. The variety of your shots—and your range!—is impressive, especially at your age. Between yesterday's match and today's, I see a lot of potential in you. I understand you'll be a junior this fall?"

My eyes widen and she chuckles again. "Sorry, I usually remember to remind people that it's my job to keep an eye on top talent, especially if they're in my own backyard. I'd been waiting for that darn June 15 deadline to pass so I could finally reach out to you and then my mother fell ill . . ." She trails off and waves it away. "Never mind about all that. When I get going a train can't stop me. The point is, I'm interested in getting to know you and you getting to know Cal. I'd love to have you out for a visit this fall. You know, meet some of the team, see how things work."

She's talking so fast I have a difficult time keeping up. What was she saying about June 15? The confusion must show on my face because she pauses. "Do you . . . know what a visit entails?"

I shake my head.

She takes a deep breath and I brace myself for another blizzard of information.

"Are your parents here?" She cranes her neck around. "I'd love to give them the rundown as well, maybe walk them through all the steps we'd need to take to get you to come play for Cal? See if I can answer any questions they might have?"

Parents. I wonder when hearing the plural will stop hurting.

"No, it's just me."

She stops looking. "Oh, okay. That's fine too. The short of it is, you're allowed one official visit per Division 1 school, but coaches aren't allowed to contact you before June 15 of the summer before your junior year—which has passed so that doesn't concern you anymore—and you can start your visits any time after August 1. You'll just want to make sure you certify with the NCAA first."

It takes me a moment to even remember what month we're in right now. I'm exhausted, doubly so after that match with Violetta, and while I want to be excited about this woman talking to me, I'm having a hard time summoning the energy to keep up.

"Official visit?" I echo. This is so much more complicated than I thought it'd be. Last time, at least I had Ba to go through my Bastille application with.

Somehow, after all this time here, I am feeling like I'm back to day one.

"That's where the school covers any or all of the costs of the visit. Since you're so close to home that won't be a big thing— we'll probably just send a car to pick you up and take you across the bridge. Usually I like to have recruits stay with one of the girls in the dorm so you can get a first-hand view of what life is like on campus, ask any questions you might have, et cetera. We'll be out of season but you'll observe a practice, maybe sit in on a class if you want. At Cal, we really prioritize the *student* portion of student athlete."

I'm only catching every third word or so at this point, but I'm not sure it matters. I'm already going to have to spend some time researching how all of this works anyway.

What I *am* noticing is Coach Sah'rai's energy. It's a little chaotic—the opposite of Baba's calm demeanor—but I like it. She smiles a lot and seems relentlessly enthusiastic. I try to imagine myself playing for her. I think I would like her more than my coach at St. Aidan's, who is polite but mostly aloof.

Maybe at Cal I would finally find a team.

When Coach Sah'rai is finished talking, I try to brighten my face like I've been listening the entire time. "Maybe I can give you my brother David's number? He's, um, he's the head of household."

It's not that Mama isn't. I'm just not sure she's ready, or willing, to assume Ba's old roles. She may have signed off on the money from Mrs. Conrad, but the fact that she didn't tell me about it signals she'd prefer to remain in the background.

"Yes! Sure. Of course." She holds out her phone and I enter the details, double- and triple-checking I've gotten my own brother's phone number correct. I'm so nervous right now my fingers are shaking.

"So are you planning to stay at Bastille until the final or are you headed home?" She asks it casually as she tucks her phone back into her pocket and straightens her cap, but the mention of leaving sends a riot of emotions through me.

I feel like a year has passed instead of a week.

"My plane ticket is for Saturday," I say.

She nods with understanding. "Of course. Go. Get some space. Ugh! Sorry I attacked you right after you got off the court."

We shake hands again and head opposite ways. I wish I had someone to talk to.

44

LEYLAH

THE GOOD NEWS IS THAT I WIN MY SINGLES MATCH. WINNING IS ALWAYS good news. Especially in a tough match, which this one was. It takes nearly three hours, but I scrape out a win against a girl from Brazil.

The *not*-good news is that I manage to break three strings doing it. I go straight to the pro shop afterward to get them restrung, but they're backed up because someone is sick or out or whatever. It doesn't matter. What does matter is that I need my racquets restrung ASAP.

I text Kevin. Even if we're not friends anymore, he's *that* guy—the one who just knows how to get stuff.

Leylah: hey do you know where I can get my racquets restrung?
Leylah: pro shop is backed up
Leylah: and I have 3 that need stringing

I have no idea if he even still uses this number, but I really don't know who else to ask. Besides Violetta, I guess. But I'll at least try Kevin first.

Kevin: bowl round my room
Kevin: villa 26, Place du Tertre

Breathing a sigh of relief, I head straight there. But when I knock on the door, it's not Kevin that answers.

It's Noah.

Why didn't it occur to me they might be rooming together?

He looks as shocked to see me as I am to see him. I double-check the number on the villa to make sure I've come to the right place.

Thankfully, Kevin's head pops up over Noah's shoulder. "Hey Ha Lê! Chur, cuz? Come on in."

I've been upgraded to cuz. Does this mean we're friends again? Still, I'm a little stiff as I enter their room. "You said you had a stringer?" I ask. Best to get straight to the point.

Kevin gestures to the machine on the coffee table in the middle of the room. "Yeah nah, yeah," he says after a pause. "It's Noah's but it's good as, aye?"

That sneaky motherfucker. Whatever it is he said, I understand that he's set me up. His barely hidden grin doesn't deny it. But before either of us can respond, he sails out the door, cackling. "I better be invited to the wedding!"

The door shuts behind him and Noah and I are left alone, staring at each other. I don't need to look around to know this villa feels a lot emptier than mine. It turns out, I hadn't fully appreciated how much of a difference Violetta's cozy little creature comforts made.

"I had no idea you'd be here," I blurt out.

"Or what, you wouldn't have come?"

Welp. I guess he's noticed I've been avoiding him.

"I just meant that Kevin didn't tell me it was your stringer."

Noah shrugs and moves out of the way for me to walk ahead of him. "I lost on Tuesday anyway, so I don't need it. Strings are in the bag underneath the table. Knock yourself out."

I don't know how to string a racquet. I mean, I do in theory, but I've never actually done it. And I could YouTube the instructions, but there's the chance I'll fuck it all up. I can't afford that.

Any points Kevin earned for finding me a stringer are obliterated by him stranding me on this island nightmare. To think I'd been planning to bribe him to string them for me.

Noah's standing with his arms folded across his chest, waiting for me to admit this.

"Are you going to stand there and watch me the whole time?" I ask.

"It's my stringer. I want to make sure you don't break it."

I roll my eyes. The thing is solid metal and weighs as much as a small car—I wouldn't even know how to break it if I tried. I take my time, removing each racquet from my bag and cutting out the strings. But if I hoped he'd get bored enough to leave, I'm out of luck.

Finally, I can't stall anymore. "Okay, fine, I don't know how to use it, are you happy?"

Noah crisply takes the racquet out of my hand (and not one of the other two that are sitting on the couch) and places it into the stringer, moving all the little levers and knobs until it's locked in place. "Now, the string," he says, pointing to a bag full of strings of varying material, thickness, and color—a traveling pro shop of his own.

I choose three packets of a four-sided poly blend, opting for sixteen gauge so I won't have to come back here tomorrow.

"Tension?" he asks.

"Forty-two."

His eyebrows shoot up and he makes a little sound of disbelief. "Seriously? Forty-two pounds? How do you hit a ball off that? It's practically a trampoline."

Now it's my turn to shrug. "I have good timing. I've always played with loose strings."

It's so much easier this way—just talking about tennis. If we can keep this up for the next couple of hours, or however long it'll take him to string my three racquets, we won't have to go back to that awkward silence. Because I can't just leave them with him and come back later to collect them. Right?

But then he hands me the string. "Mark off six feet," he instructs.

"Huh?"

"You didn't think I was just going to do it all for you, did you?"

I definitely did. I'd even started thinking of what I could possibly offer him in exchange.

"Come on," he coaxes. "It's a life skill. If you're planning to go on tour, you're going to want to know how to string your own racquets. You never know when this might come up again."

After I ignored him at Ping-Pong the other day, why would he go through all the effort of convincing me to learn this? Especially if he's the one who has to teach me.

Is this what being a good person looks like?

Plus 50 points for Noah.

He leads me through the first few steps, pointing to where things go and how to check my clamps to make sure I don't lose tension. He stays across the machine the entire time and I hate how preoccupied I am that he doesn't come closer.

Goddamn it Leylah, you're supposed to still be mad at him. Even if I don't hate Violetta quite as much as I did on Saturday.

I dock myself 100 points.

The whole racquet goes this way—only a few words here or there about stringing technique. Aside from the clicks and scrapes of the machine, the entire procedure is silent. It's like being in school, where I'm uncomfortable for six continuous hours and people only talk to me when necessary.

It's brutal.

When I finally tie off the last of the string and pop the racquet out of the machine, I've had enough. I can't survive another two racquets' worth of this awkward silence.

"So. How was your weekend?" My voice is only on the edge of accusatory and I avoid having to look directly at him by starting my second racquet.

Noah furrows his brow. "My weekend?"

"Saturday night?"

His frown deepens. "What about it?"

God, he's really going to make me say it. I try to keep my voice as normal as possible. "You have a good time with your *acquaintance* Violetta?"

I sound exactly as petty and immature aloud as I do in my head.

Noah shifts his stance and rests his hands on the machine. I continue to avoid eye contact. "I don't really do passive-aggressive so why don't you just tell me what this is about?" he asks.

I didn't think this through. Now I'm going to have to admit I was spying on him. "I heard you were with Violetta," I hedge. "And that the two of you were pretty cozy."

Noah tilts his head. "You heard?"

"I saw," I admit begrudgingly. "I went to the beach that night and saw you with her."

"Saw me what, exactly? You know there were other people there, right?"

The longer this conversation goes, the more I regret it. I should never have said anything. This is worse than bringing up the Peter thing from two years ago.

I silently keep stringing my racquet, trying to remember each step and hoping I'm not forgetting any. But Noah is annoyingly patient and offers no rebuttal. If I don't say it now it'll eat me alive, which is *more* distracting than liking him is.

"Violetta has a history of swooping in and taking things from me."

"*Things.*" Noah is unimpressed by my argument.

"People," I correct. "You said you weren't really friends with her, but then you were out with her and I saw her leaning on you and . . ." I trail off.

"And you got jealous?" Noah prompts.

10 points for him. He's really drawing this out to torture me.

"Maybe," I say. My eyes stay glued to the task in front of me.

"So you decided that instead of just asking me about it, you'd completely blow me off and shoot death glares? Do I have that right?"

I am in actual hell. The nuns didn't do a good enough job of decribing just how miserable it really is.

"Pretty much."

He settles back into his folded-arm stance. "Okay, so ask."

"I don't want to."

Noah rolls his eyes with so much exaggeration I can see it even though I haven't looked up once. "Yes, you do. Clearly."

"No, I don't," I insist. "It's not my business. I just wanted you to know that's why I was annoyed and avoiding you. So now it's out there."

"I see. Well, thanks for telling me."

I'm being consumed by a thousand fire ants inside, convincing myself I don't care he's not volunteering more. It doesn't mean anything and I don't need it to mean anything.

Because I don't care. He's a distraction.

I string in silence and Noah stands across from me the entire time, overseeing my work. When I finally tie off the string and release my second racquet, I practically collapse with relief. I feel like I've just finished the longest match of my life.

"Maybe two is enough," I murmur, debating with myself whether I can really tolerate being here for another forty-five minutes to an hour.

"You really want to avoid me that much, huh?"

My head snaps up. Of course he heard me. I don't know what I was thinking.

This is the problem! I'm never thinking when I'm around him.

Noah sighs and grabs my third racquet from the couch, fastening it into place on the stringer. He's still safely on the other side of the machine but I take a step back anyway. He notices. "If you're really dying to get out of here, I'll string it so it'll go faster." He sounds almost resigned.

Did he expect *me* to keep talking?

"I'm not dying to get out of here," I lie. "I just figured you had other places to be."

He shoots me a look. "A clandestine appointment with your nemesis?"

Okay, I deserved that.

"I'm not saying you can't hang out with her," I say, more than a little defensively. "It's none of my business what you do."

"As long as I don't do it with her, right?"

Even hearing the words *do it with her* is like a punch to the gut. But I don't let it show on my face when I say stiffly, "If that's what you want."

Noah shakes his head like he knows I'm lying but keeps working. He's amazingly fast at this.

"You're really fast," I remark.

"That's what she said," he quips, almost like a reflex. It's the first joke he's made since I arrived.

My chest eases a fraction. Maybe this is a step back toward normal for us?

There is no us.

"This is my job back at home," he explains. "I get paid by the racquet so I learned to be pretty fast at it."

He's flying through this and when he's done, I'll leave. These are probably our last few minutes together. *Ever.*

"How long does it take you to do one racquet from start to finish?" I ask.

"Fifteen minutes, maybe twenty if I'm tired."

"Wow."

It's clear stringing racquets isn't what's been occupying his free time. So what's he been doing that I haven't seen him in this many days? And why is he suddenly fine with me ignoring him now, when he'd refused before? *He* was the one who practically chased me down from the beginning. Another couple of minutes and he's done, twirling the racquet a few times before handing it to me. "You need the logo on it?"

Players who are sponsored, like Violetta, have to stencil their strings every time they get their racquets restrung as part of their contract. Unsurprisingly, my parents were against anything and everything that might help build me a professional career.

"No." I shake my head. "Thanks. This was a lifesaver."

I carefully tuck each of my racquets back into my bag, stalling for time, until I can't stall anymore. I zip the bag closed and lift the strap onto my shoulder, shuffling my way to the door.

"It's not, by the way," Noah says. "Spending time with Violetta. It's not what I want. I went with Kevin on Saturday because I thought you'd be there."

I don't know how to respond, so I just say, "Okay." And then I bolt.

45

VIOLETTA

WHEN MY LAST MATCH OF THE DAY FINALLY WRAPS, I STUMBLE BACK TO the villa and fling myself into the shower. I haven't had time to process everything that's happened today and even though the room is empty, the bathroom lock ensures me privacy for as long as I need it.

I pour a generous dollop of shampoo and my body relaxes a tiny bit as the lavender scent fills the steamy shower. Even in hot weather, my showers are always hot. As I scrub, I try to replay the day in my head but I can't seem to remember much. I have no idea how I managed to get through two matches after that awful one with Alice—let alone win them both. I must have been on autopilot.

Last night, Alice said I was *killing myself*.

At the time, it seemed . . . overdramatic. But now? Now I think she might be right.

I've felt like death this entire day. This entire week. If I'm being honest with myself, I've felt like this on and off for months now. Sure, I've put on a smile and pushed through it. I really wanted to win the tournament. I wanted to win all the tournaments. Or at least I thought I did.

But Alice is right. I'm killing myself.

What's more, I'm killing myself for a dream I'm not even sure I want. I'm not sure I ever truly wanted it.

I close my eyes and let the hot water run down my hair and over my face, enjoying the way it blocks out even my closest surroundings. As long as I stay in this tiny waterfall, I don't have to think about the fact that I'm in three separate semifinals but still stuck on my loss in 16U doubles.

I'm good, but not good *enough*.

Whether I would play tennis was never a question—I was born into it. But once I showed potential—once it was clear I was blessed with all the makings of a champion—Audrey and I made *The Plan*.

My entire life, everything has been examined from the angle of: Will this help or hinder my future career? What I eat, what I wear, how I interact with others. I've been molded to be the complete package—while still standing out as unique—right down to my purple contacts.

I reach for my shampoo and pour it directly onto my hair, lathering vigorously, like it can clean the inside of me too.

The Plan used to be aspirational. We always talked about it as a given, but I never realized how close it really was. How close *I* was.

The lavender is starting to overwhelm me, my stomach churning from the smell and the steam, so I quickly rinse my hair and crack open the shower door to get some fresh air. I'm not ready to get out yet but I know better than to puke here. Especially since I ate a whole sleeve of chocolate chip cookies from Burgundy earlier—they'll be especially disgusting coming back up and I don't want to ruin cookies for myself.

This is killing me.

I gulp down one more breath of fresh air before diving back inside the steamy shower, pouring myself a heap of shampoo to wash my hair. It feels almost pointless. Tomorrow I'll wake up and do this all over again. And then the day after that. And the day after that. Six days a week, this is my life.

My entire future is one long tournament, where no win lingers longer than the start of the next tournament. Even if I end up winning the 16U singles and the 18U singles and doubles, what does it matter? What do I get, other than the chance to do it all over again? I do that already.

The sharp desire to puke comes back and I have to quickly rinse my hair and poke my head out again for air.

This is killing me.

I know it's unhealthy. And I'm not naive enough to believe I can continue to purge indefinitely without consequence. Already, I can sometimes summon the urge without needing to stick my fingers down my throat. I'd convinced myself it was temporary—first as a way to get through a stressful week, then a stressful tournament, and now the Bastille Invitational. It's helped, but I'm only inching closer to the point where that stress will be *all* the time.

The ITF circuit. Then the WTA 125. Then the WTA. Top

one hundred. Top ten. Top five. Number one. Even then, there are only more goalposts. Tournament titles. Grand Slam titles. Record-setting numbers of Grand Slam titles.

It's the one thing Leylah and I have in common: exceptional mothers. And exceptional parents expect exceptional things from their kids.

It's killing me.

I wash my hair and only now do I realize how much shampoo I seem to have used in this one shower. I can't even manage to keep my thoughts together long enough to remember if I've washed my hair already. My brain feels fractured, like it simply buckled under the weight of all this expectation. I don't know what I'm supposed to do. It's killing me.

By the time Leylah comes home, I've pieced myself together enough to get dressed. A quick smoke is mostly responsible for my stability now, but I think I needed the courage of Faded Violetta to do this anyway.

She's sitting on one side of the couch, humming to herself while regripping her racquets. It's a weird reversal, seeing Leylah upbeat and somewhat relaxed while I suppress my jitters.

Post idea: facing your biggest fears

Faded Violetta calmly picks up the pile of throw pillows and the blanket and tosses them onto the floor, creating an empty space next to Leylah.

She arches a sharp eyebrow at me as I sink down onto the sofa. "I thought you had *feelings* about your throw pillows on the ground."

I shrug. "They're just pillows."

It's funny. Now that I've made up my mind, I no longer feel anxious about everything else. I truly do not care in this moment that my throw pillows are on the ground.

It's killing me.

Leylah pauses what she's doing and frowns at me, but it's not her normal frown. She looks almost . . . concerned.

"Is everything okay?" she asks.

"I'm pulling out of the tournament." The words feel foreign in my mouth, but once I say them I already feel the pressure on my chest easing.

Her eyes bulge out of her head. "What?!"

"I'm withdrawing," I repeat.

"Are you injured? I thought you were just playing up that ankle thing."

I was, but that isn't the issue at hand.

"It's not an injury," I confirm. "Not an external one, anyway."

Leylah is still frowning, like she doesn't understand what I'm saying. "So you're pulling out? Of which match?"

"From all my matches."

Her eyes go wide. "Oh my god, Rachel's going to kill you!"

I don't know if it's because I'm buzzed, but her reaction strikes me as completely hilarious. Instead of thinking of herself first, or what it would mean for our semifinal matchup tomorrow, she thought of Rachel of all people.

I laugh so hard I have to clutch my sides, thinking of the animosity between Leylah and Rachel. Somehow I'd decided that Rachel was worth keeping as a friend and Leylah wasn't. It's funny.

When I finally pull myself together, Leylah is still staring at me the same way she had the morning after Alice's and my fight. "I feel bad about Rachel," I say. "And I know she probably won't understand—or you, either—but I just . . . can't anymore. It's killing me."

"The pressure?"

"Everything. The lifestyle." I gesture around the villa, the lights and decorations now a suffocating reminder of my solitude. "I lived here *alone* for three weeks until you two moved in. I've had seven roommates in two years. People constantly cycle through here and you never know if you're going to see them again. It's impossible to get close to anyone because at the end of the day, we're all competing against each other."

"You just described my second-favorite trait of tour life."

"What's the first?" I ask.

"The tennis. Duh." She says it like it's the most obvious answer in the world. And maybe it is—for someone who wants to play professionally.

"That's another thing," I add. "I don't love tennis. Not like you do."

Leylah shakes her head, finally turning her attention back to wrapping her grip with determination. "No one gets to your level unless you love it."

"I might have loved it at some point," I concede, "but that hasn't been the case for a long time now. I mean, I play it. I try as hard as I can at practice and at every match. And until recently, I didn't *hate* it. But even *thinking* about having to get up tomorrow and play again makes me want to set my hair on fire."

Leylah wraps the finishing tape around her newly gripped racquet before setting it in her lap. I can tell she's gathering herself to say something.

"V. We all get tired at some point. You're just burned out. It's a phase. You've worked at this your entire life. You're in the semis of *both* the 16s and 18s draws, and *this* is when you decide you're sick of tennis?"

It sounds so logical when she says it.

"Would it be any better to wait until the end? Why put myself through more of this if I'm leaving either way?" I fold my arms across my chest. Resolute. "I'm not going to change my mind."

Leylah leans close, her dark brown eyes assessing me. I don't realize what she's doing until I hear a distinct sniff. She's smelling me.

I lean back uncomfortably.

"You can't make this kind of decision when you're high, V," she says.

"I'm not. I made the decision and *then* I got high."

I collapse into giggles again and even Leylah has a difficult time keeping a straight face. Something has definitely gotten into her today.

"Seriously, V. You can't just quit."

"Why not?"

"Because I haven't gotten to beat you again yet!" Her sudden burst of intensity makes even her laugh this time. "I don't need your pity default," she manages to choke out between reluctant giggles.

"I believe I told you the other day, not everything is about you?"

Leylah raises both eyebrows. "Okay, then tell me what it *is* about."

"It's about me. And how this life is killing me. Maybe I can push through it for now, but how long can that last? Besides," I add, using my most serious voice, "the tour conducts regular drug tests."

She shakes her head away from me, trying to cover her laugh. "I can't believe this is happening. You're sitting here cracking jokes when you're about to make the biggest decision of your life. Just you and me. How is this real?"

She's right—it doesn't feel real. Even though my normal buzz is keeping me from falling apart, it's been ages since I've actually been this relaxed. Because I know when this wears off, I won't have to go back out on the court.

"Who else have you told?" she asks.

I lean back into the sofa, enjoying the slouch of my shoulders and neck against the cool leather. "You're the first."

"Me?!"

It hadn't even been a question in my mind. Maybe because we sort of started this together. She, Rachel, and I had all met when we were ten and managed to stick it out on court until now. Rachel, I'm sure, will make it to the tour too. Leylah and I may not be friends anymore, but I feel like she'll be the one to understand best just how badly I must be doing to walk away from it all.

Maybe, just maybe, I'm also looking for her forgiveness—for giving up the life she would have killed to have.

"You realize you're basically a drug PSA now, right?" she asks. "You started smoking weed and now you're dropping out."

"Don't blame this on Bob, he's done nothing wrong."

"I thought her name was Cheryl."

"Cheryl is my pipe. She doesn't get out much these days. Once I started having roommates, I had to switch to an oil pen for less smell. He's kind of boring and but gets the job done. That's why I named him Bob. Basic, but functional."

"Wow, I can't believe I possibly got those mixed up," she says sarcastically.

"That's okay. Luckily for you, Cheryl's a groovy girl who just wants peace and love in the world so she won't hold it against you. Bob, on the other hand, definitely will."

Leylah just shakes her head. "My mom's biggest dream in life is for me to have a brain like yours and you're slowly suffocating it to death with that shit."

"My mom's biggest dream in life is for me to be you on court."

Leylah snorts. "Oh yeah, I can see how that would go. I'm sure Audrey would be really proud after she saw one of my meltdowns."

"I think Audrey would forgive anything if I just kept winning."

We sit in silence for a few seconds, the mood sobering.

"I hope she does," Leylah says. "Forgive you."

Me too. Me too.

FRIDAY,
JULY 14TH

(THE ACTUAL) BASTILLE DAY

MAIN DRAW,
SEMIFINAL

46
ALICE

JUST LIKE YESTERDAY, I SPEND THE ENTIRE DAY AT THE COURTS WATCHING other matches. And just like yesterday, I spend a large portion of that time dissecting my argument with Violetta.

I had been so *angry*. But I wonder how much of that was really with myself?

After all, I was the one who decided to fill all my waking moments with her. I made the decision to open myself up to such a degree that I could be hurt in the first place.

"Alley-Oop!" Kevin and a few other people are climbing into the bleachers and when he sees me, directs the group toward me.

A sliver of panic shoots through me at the thought of suddenly being surrounded by all these people who might want to make conversation. I may have managed to be comfortable with Kevin, but that doesn't extend to others. And on top of all that, I'm really not in the mood to socialize.

None of this matters to Kevin as he plunks himself down

next to me, looking around at our sparse surroundings. "What are you doing way out in the wops?"

"Knitting a sweater," I deadpan.

Kevin bursts out laughing, before all his friends turn to shush him, moving away from us. "You're a crack up," he says delightedly.

I don't respond. It's not Kevin's fault I'm in a foul mood and I don't want to accidentally take it out on him.

But still, he wants to converse. "Where's the missus?" he asks. When I don't immediately respond he prompts, "V? Tall girl, smokes a lot of pot?"

I know Kevin is joking around, but he hits a sore spot.

"Is that how you two became friends?" I ask.

"It's how you and me became friends, aye." He grins.

"That was a onetime thing."

He shrugs. "Your loss, mate. But you look like you could use some right now to put you right."

I glance around the bleachers to ensure no one is overhearing our conversation. The seats are sparsely populated and no one seems to be paying us any attention. I suppose this is why I decided to watch the 12U doubles in the first place.

I haven't spoken to Violetta since our fight the other night. I even went so far as to hide out in the library yesterday after dinner, aka Mont Saint-Michel, just to avoid her until bedtime. If I had any other friends here maybe I could have asked to stay over, but as it is, I really only know the two people I'm rooming with.

Still, I have questions I need answered, and Kevin seems like the next best person to answer them. "Why do you do it?" I ask.

"Do what? Smoke?"

I nod.

"Why'd you?" he asks.

I've been asking myself the same thing. "I don't know," I admit. "I felt overwhelmed and I just needed a time-out from all of it."

He nods with a little shrug of agreement. "Hard out."

"You're really *that* stressed out all the time?" The impression I got from Saturday was that Kevin did it as often as Violetta—maybe even more.

"Yeah nah, sometimes I'm just keen as. But I'm not hurting anyone and it sets me right. So why not?"

"It hurts *you*," I point out. "You're an athlete. How can smoking be good for you?"

"I didn't say it was *good* for me, mate, but this lifestyle gets boring and it's bloody stressful. My mental health's got to be sweet as too."

I can detect a note of defensiveness in Kevin's tone, probably because I am treating him like a suspect in an investigation. It's not fair of me, to project my anger at Violetta on him. Especially when he has tried to hide nothing.

"Do your parents know?" I ask.

Kevin laughs. "Are you taking the piss? I can't even have a sip of alcohol at dinner, even if everyone else is munted and Dad's got heaps left. Mum would literally rather chuck it than let me have any. She thinks it'll turn me into my dad."

I frown, not really understanding why Kevin assumes he'd be entitled to drink until he clarifies, "Everyone drinks in New Zealand. The legal drinking age is eighteen but no one follows that. Except my mum, I guess," he adds.

"So if she knew you were a pothead . . ."

Kevin pretends to gasp. "We just became mates and nek minute you're ratting me out to Dick?"

Somehow in all of this, Kevin has lightened my mood and I find myself smiling. "If I never have to talk to that man again in my life, it will be too soon."

He chuckles. "I see you got the minority special. Or was it the 'young person talking back' package?"

It seems Dick is well known and well disliked. "I think both," I say. "Plus a tax for being poor."

Kevin howls at that and gets shushed again. "He must be packing a sad over you! Don't let him get to you. When I first started here, he called me to his office. Said I needed to 'review' the dress code because I was wearing basketball shorts. Told me to remember which sport I was here for. He's legit racist, aye."

I hate the underlying sense of resignation in it all, but I also understand it. These are just the kinds of things to expect on occasion in a wealthy white environment. It makes me question whether or not I really want to return to St. Aidan's in the fall.

"Are you rich?" I blurt out. "I'm sorry, I guess I'm just wondering . . ." I don't know how to verbalize what it is I really want to know: Is there anyone else like me here? Or will I always feel out of place?

Luckily, Kevin doesn't take offense. "Yeah nah. We've got money but not like, *money* money. My dad's a car salesman. Mum works at a bank. Straight up, my grandma pays for most of my travel, aye. She's sweet as—owns a couple spas in Queenstown."

More and more, I'm finding the life of a professional athlete seems to be out of reach.

"Do you think you'll go to college?" I ask.

Kevin shrugs. "I reckon. If I tried to go pro at this size I'd get carked. I need at least ten more centimeters or ten kilos in the next couple years, then she'll be right. You?"

"I got an invitation to visit Cal," I say shyly. I don't know why I choose this moment to share, or why Kevin is the person I tell.

But his face lights up for me and I realize I just wanted someone to share my happiness. "Far out! That uni's mean as, aye. Choice, cuz."

Despite not grasping any of those words, it's clear he's congratulating me and I manage a small smile. "Thanks. I hope it works out."

"You ring your mum yet? She'll be stoked, aye?"

Kevin doesn't know my mom. She's definitely not a stoker, if such a thing exists. But that he remembered I only have a mom means something to me. I was so angry at Violetta for disappointing me, but maybe I expected too much. I relied on her to fill all the holes in my heart when the truth is, there are other people in the world both willing and able to take on part of that task too.

Just because Ba was everything to me doesn't mean the next person has to be too.

47

VIOLETTA

IT TAKES ONLY ABOUT TWO MINUTES AFTER I LEAVE DICK'S OFFICE FOR MY phone to start ringing. I'm almost impressed it took him that long to notify Audrey. I send it to voicemail, still trying to find the right place to break the news to her. She wouldn't want anywhere public, of course. And I don't want anywhere enclosed.

I ignore her call, instead texting her to meet me in Provence—a section of the grounds that grows nothing but lavender. A lot of people avoid it because the smell is so strong, but it also means the space is almost always empty.

I don't have to wait for long.

Audrey approaches with a speed that borders on jogging, slowing down only once she spots me among the tall plants. She's still dressed in her work clothes—cream slacks with a beige sweater and gold flats. I always wished I could wear gold, but it doesn't suit my coloring.

When she gets closer, I see tiny beads of sweat along her hairline. A miracle!

Before she can say anything, I point it out. "You're sweating," I say.

Audrey delicately pats a spot on her forehead with three fingers before pulling them away to examine them. "The air-conditioning in the office is always on too high."

She pulls a tissue out of her purse and blots her hairline dry before turning her full attention on me. "Now. What's this I hear about you quitting?"

There it is again—*quitting*.

With Audrey, the word is said more sharply and with more judgment. I should have expected that.

Leylah insisted I do this sober, so it takes all my courage to hold my chin up. "I prefer to think of it as starting something new."

Audrey looks at me as though I've lost my head. "What on earth are you going on about? Did you or did you not withdraw from the tournament?"

The stalks of lavender around us quiver and I have to press my hands together to stay steady. I am not lavender. I won't be frightened.

"I did."

She just stands there, blinking at me. "I don't understand. Why would you do such a thing? Are you having a health crisis? Is it because you're afraid to face Leylah? I—"

I cut her off before she can finish.

"It's not about Leylah."

"Then tell me what the hell it *is* about, Violetta!"

All my words seem to fail me. Even having had this conversation twice already—last night with Leylah and an abbreviated version with Dick earlier—I'm somehow unprepared to do it all over again with Audrey.

She stares at me expectantly as I try to form a coherent sentence. "I . . . I just can't do this anymore."

It would be easier if she asked me questions—if she directed the conversation and I could simply respond. But she's surprisingly silent. Maybe she's still in shock.

"I know you sacrificed a lot for me—" I begin.

"I sacrificed everything for you!" she bursts out, a rare show of emotion slipping through her normally impenetrable mask. "Everything I've done has been to build you a better life."

"But you never asked me if that was the life I wanted."

"Why would I? You've never complained before now. And now, out of nowhere, you decide you want to give it all up? All the years of hard work? For what?"

Even though I expected it, the accusation hits hard. "I never complained because I didn't want you to be upset with me," I argue, unable to keep my voice calm. "I thought if I could just do everything you wanted, *be* everything you wanted, that . . ." I trail off, not wanting to say the rest.

"That what?" Audrey asks.

"That . . ." My voice drops to nearly a whisper. "That you wouldn't regret having me."

She flinches at the words, covering her mouth with a hand. "What made you think I regretted having you? I've never said anything of the sort."

"You didn't have to. I saw our life growing up. I saw *you*. Working around the clock, just so I could get lessons or new shoes or travel to a tournament. You never had any time for your-self. Even your parents didn't help! Everything you had was gone the second you got pregnant with me."

Audrey fumbles for a cigarette and lights it with trembling hands, waiting until she's taken a puff before attempting to speak again. When she does, she's back to her cool, calm, and collected self: The Audrey that doesn't sweat or curse or cry. The Audrey I've been measuring myself against.

"I made the choice to have you and I knew the risks associated with it," she says. "Perhaps not quite all of the risks, but the point is I *chose* you. I'm not religious; I had other options."

She takes another puff, blowing the smoke upward in a long, steady stream.

Watching her makes me wish I had something to soothe my nerves as well, but I also recognize that's part of the problem. I suppose we learn our coping mechanisms from our parents.

"I worked to give you every opportunity, not because I didn't have them, but because I did choose you. You're my life. What other purpose should a mother have besides giving their child the world?"

When she says it, it sounds almost . . . maternal. Which makes my heart hurt even more when I tell her, "That world is killing me."

"Darling, don't you think you're being overdramatic?"

This is it: this is when I'm supposed to tell Audrey all the things I've been going through so that she can help me heal. But looking at her detached demeanor, the cigarette between her fingers demanding her attention, I'm not sure I can.

I love my mom. But I'm not convinced she's the right person to lead me through this particular battle. I don't think she's even dealt with her own demons yet.

"I . . ."

I want to tell her. I've always wanted to tell her.

But that's not the relationship we have.

"I just can't do it anymore."

She takes another long drag as she considers my confession and I know in my heart that when I first started smoking it was because I wanted to be like her. I just didn't know it at the time.

She pulls a small, flattened pouch from her purse and I can't help exclaiming at the sight of it.

"Kuchisabishii!!" My voice is practically a screech with the unexpected childhood nostalgia. Audrey's cigarette-butt receptacle had fascinated me for hours on end as a kid. The way it could be snapped open and shut with only two fingers; the way it swallowed the still-burning cigarettes and extinguished them as if it was nothing.

My childish glee puts a trace of a smile on Audrey's face. Just one corner of her mouth is turned up but she looks amused. "I forgot you'd named it that."

"*I* named it?" I don't remember that.

She busies herself digging in her purse as she answers. "You overheard me talking to it and thought that was its name."

"What does it really mean? It's not just what all of those portable-ashtray things are called?" Even now it's strange to think of it as anything other than a silent, mostly hidden third member of our family.

She pauses. "The word *kuchisabishii* means 'lonely mouth' in Japanese. People use it to describe stress eating or eating out of boredom."

My mom, it turns out, understands a lot more than she's able to articulate.

She drops the still-burning cigarette into Kuchisabishii's mouth and snaps it shut before stuffing him back into her purse. "I need to head back to the office but I'll be finished at five. I'll bring boxes."

48

LEYLAH

I HAVE AN ENTIRELY FREE DAY. MY BRAIN HASN'T FULLY PROCESSED THAT Violetta really pulled herself from the tournament. Or that I'm in the finals because of it.

It seems . . . too easy?

It's unsettling, like I'm just waiting for the other shoe to drop. Is the universe going to curse me tomorrow? The next day? It can't possibly be this easy.

Not that anything until now has been *easy*.

I decide to watch the other girl's 18U semifinal match and take notes to keep my mind occupied. Bonus: not thinking about Noah. Not thinking about how he said he was only with Violetta because he came for me, and not thinking about how I then *ran* from his room. I don't need that encounter playing on loop right now.

I jot down a few observations about each player, along with notes about what to research on whichever one wins tonight. The problem in school isn't that I don't know how to do shit (okay, sometimes it is)—it's that I don't want to. No one will ever convince me that knowing the date Washington crossed some stupid river is more important than the date women earned equal prize money at the Slams (US Open, 1973; Australian Open, 1984 (but with the weird exception of 1996–2001); French Open & Wimbledon, 2007). Or the date Nadal won his mind-blowing fourteenth French Open (June 5, 2022).

I'm so deep into this internal argument that when Noah unexpectedly appears, I skip over any awkwardness by pulling him directly into it. "Which do you know better: famous battles or historical tennis stats?"

"Uh, hello to you too," Noah says, perching himself one bleacher in front of me and turning carefully like I might be ready to attack him. "I know . . . both?"

Ugh. I should've known better than to ask a nerd.

"Hey, what's *your* plan?" I ask. "You going to do the college thing? Or what?"

Noah shoots me a coy look. "Is this your way of putting out feelers for the future?"

I roll my eyes but inside I'm dying. That was not at all what I meant and having him here like this only reminds me that we all go home in two days and Noah lives in California. It's kind of a now-or-never situation.

Best get it over with. But not here.

I stand. "Come on."

"Where are we going?"

"You'll see."

"How far are we going?" he asks a few minutes later. "Like

should I have packed a snack? An overnight bag? Are you going to human-traffic me?"

"Traffic you to whom?"

Noah shrugs. "I don't know, but if suburban moms can be worried about it so can I. Half the friends on my mom's Facebook have some story about how they think they might have been almost trafficked in the grocery store parking lot or something."

Even through my nerves, he gets a laugh out of me.

His ridiculousness makes it hard to pivot the conversation to a serious topic. I wish we could just keep going back and forth like this forever, but I can recognize a miracle (him still talking to me at all) when I see one. At least walking side by side instead of being face-to-face makes it easier. I decide to just blurt it out. "I'm sorry I took all my shit about Violetta out on you. I was a being a dick."

"That's an interesting word choice."

"I don't like using the word *bitch*. It seems sexist."

"Your dedication to gender equality is admirable."

"Smart-ass," I mutter, and Noah chuckles.

"Well, thank you," he says. "For both the apology and the insult."

"Okay fine, sorry for the insult too." We walk another few steps before I ask hesitantly, "Why aren't you more mad at me?"

"Do you want me to be?"

"No. I just . . . I guess I don't really get why you even came over to talk to me today."

"Again, is this your way of telling me you didn't want me to?"

"No!" I exclaim. "I'm just saying that if you treated *me* like that I would probably never speak to you again."

"Ah. Well, this is where I tell you we're two different people."

I give him a look.

Noah shrugs. "It's not exactly news to me that you can be mean sometimes. Pretty sure I told you as much the day we met."

"And that doesn't bother you?" I can't help feeling like this is a trick. Someone who just . . . accepts my prickly attitude?

"I know not to take it personally. You only act like that because you have a crush on me."

My jaw drops and my face heats approximately two thousand degrees. I could bake pottery on it. "I'm not . . . I don't . . . that's . . ."

I desperately flail around, searching for a coherent response. Any response, really. Noah quiets me by stepping closer, wrapping his hands around my upper arms. "Leylah. It's okay that I know you like me. I like you too."

I'm simultaneously mortified and relieved to have it out in the open. But he's so very close and he's staring into my eyes—clearly waiting for me to say something—except my brain is no longer functional.

This feels like the time for a joke. To make this moment a fraction less serious. Fraught.

I pull my head back an inch. "I'm uncomfortable."

He leans even closer and I wish he would just kiss me and get it over with. Then I can shut the hell up. Instead, his eyes lock on mine and the moment grows even heavier. "I know you are. But it gets easier."

His mom must be a hell of a therapist.

Before I can overthink it, I close the gap and kiss him.

49

VIOLETTA

I FIND ALICE IN BURGUNDY. I'M SURPRISED TO SEE SHE'S NOT ALONE. NOT that I think she doesn't have any other friends. It just underscores the amount of time she spent with only me, and that I basically told her her opinion was worthless.

I swallow hard and make my way over. I have a new sympathy for those bumbling boyfriends in movies, having to go apologize after you've done something stereotypically thoughtless like undervalue the other person.

When I reach the table I stay standing, waiting for Alice and her companion to acknowledge me.

"Hi," the girl says. Alice nods at me, but says nothing.

"Is it okay if I join you?" I'm following the script line for line, it seems.

They nod and I take the chair next to the friend so Alice will be forced to look at me, which she does only sparingly. It's diffi-cult to read her face like this—it feels like we're back at day one when I didn't know anything about her at all. Her posture is stiff, but not particularly upright; her features flat and without any spark of life. I can't tell if she's sad or mad. Maybe both.

We make awkward small talk until the girl excuses herself and I'm finally alone with Alice.

I begin with, "I'm sorry."

Alice nods like she knew this was coming. "I'm sure you are."

It's not sarcastic, but there is an undertone of *you should be* in it. A tiny part of me is proud of Alice for standing up to me like this, even as it hurts me.

"I said some horrible things the other night."

Alice doesn't disagree.

"Unforgivable things," I add. "I wasn't the best version of myself then and—"

"You were high," she says bluntly.

I have never been more thankful to have listened to Leylah. I'm not sure Alice would forgive me if I was trying to have this conversation while buzzed. I'm not even sure she'll forgive me *now*.

"I didn't do it to hurt you," I explain. "I'm going through so much stuff right now and it's the only way I know how to cope."

Her eyes look sad. "Exactly. You never told me. You never told me any of it. It probably didn't even occur to you! Your problems are yours to deal with, but somehow I should share mine with you? You can be my friend but I can never ever be yours because you don't even think to tell me you're *leaving Bastille*. I found out by looking at the draw!"

Her voice is raised and her cheeks are flushed—she's clearly so angry at me—but all I can focus on is the fact she said *leaving* and not *quitting*. How, if I hadn't shared anything with her, is she able to understand the importance of the difference?

I know it's not enough, but I say it again anyway. "I'm sorry."

She repeats, sadder this time, "I'm sure you are."

She stands to clear her tray and something like panic seizes me at the thought of our friendship ending right now. I need to do something quickly. Something big. How do I convince her I've really learned my lesson?

I rip my chest open without a second thought.

"You're right," I confess. "I wasn't telling you everything. Because I barely knew what was wrong myself! I thought it was just burnout and considering what you and Leylah went through to get here, I wasn't going to complain about not wanting to play. But then it just sort of spiraled and I was so used to always dealing with it myself that I didn't think to tell you."

I know she already knows this—I'm basically parroting her own words back to her.

"But I think it was more than that. I think maybe deep down, I knew this was hurting me and that if I told you, you'd want me to stop."

I can't bear to look at her as I admit this. I went from Violetta Masuda, social media influencer and rising tennis star, to a girl who hides on a windowsill to avoid life.

Alice's expression softens and she sits back down, this time next to me. "Would that be such a bad thing? Having someone care enough to want you to stop?"

"Not *someone*. You."

I shake my head, trying to piece the words together as they come together in my mind. "When you first got here, you looked at me with this like, reverence, you know? I guess I didn't want you to think different of me."

"That's a *fan*, not a friend. You know, the thing you accused me of being?"

The hurt in her voice is so sharp it elicits a tear from me. "I know."

"You're not supposed to be trying to impress me."

"I know." I wipe away another tear as it trickles down and Alice hands me a napkin. "But if you told me to stop, I'd want to. And I don't think I'd be able to." Another tear cascades down my face. "I think that was the same reason I didn't want to admit what was going on with Coop."

Alice's eyes widen. "What *did* go on? Did he—"

"Make a move on me?"

Alice nods, and I shake my head. "No. Not anything . . . I don't know. Illegal?"

Framing it like that—in a strict good vs. bad paradigm—makes me realize that Coop knew it was wrong too. That's *why* he was so careful not to cross certain lines.

We're startled by the crash of someone dropping a tray and it reminds me we're in a crowded cafeteria and not somewhere more private. I stand and hold out my hand to Alice. "Come on, let's get out of here."

I pull Alice to standing but she's looking at me warily. "No more cooking videos."

Shaking my head, I lead her to the dessert bar. "I'm just getting cookies to go. Now I can eat whatever I want."

Walking away from tennis won't solve everything but even if just for today, I want to believe it will.

SATURDAY, JULY 15TH

(UNOFFICIAL) BASTILLE DAY

MAIN DRAW,
FINALS

50

LEYLAH

I CALL "5–4," HOLDING UP THE BALL SO MY OPPONENT CAN CONFIRM SHE'S ready for me to start the game. The *last* game of this match.

I hope.

My back is to the sun and I bounce the ball exactly five times with my right hand.

Five for first serves. Two for second serves.

Just like Serena Williams.

Before she started chasing history, Serena Williams was the greatest closer in the history of women's professional tennis. She won finals because she walked into every single one fully expecting to win.

I'm going to win. Of course I'm going to win.

I serve and it flies wide. Fault.

I will win this.

Only two bounces this time. I only need two bounces because I'm confident. I'm going to win. It's why I'm not panicking at the thought of double-faulting. Because I'm going to win. Definitely.

I hit my second serve almost as hard as I hit my first serve. It ends with her burying a backhand in the net.

I don't fist-pump. I'm not a fist-pumper. I don't need to cheer myself on if I'm confident.

It's the secret, really, to a big serve. It's serving every single ball as if you expect it to go in and never second-guessing your own ability. More confidence equals more relaxed muscles, which results in a better performance. Which then runs on a loop.

It makes sense then, really, that cis boys tend to have bigger serves than girls—boys have that kind of unfounded confidence ingrained in them from birth.

The second point is a short rally that ends with my approach shot winner into her forehand corner.

The third ends exactly like the first point, my serve and her return nearly carbon copies of earlier. The other secret to a big serve: knowing your opponent. Like how she loses confidence in her backhand after missing a few. And knowing that I've been practicing that same damn into-the-body serve the entire time I've been here.

Then there's *my* personal secret to serving. It's spite.

Dick is just to my right, looking more unhappy by the minute as he realizes I'm going to win this damn thing. Instead of looking at Alice, Noah, and Kevin in the bleachers, I stare at Dick, holding my serve until he makes eye contact with me.

I don't do anything over-the-top like wink or give him my villainous smile, but I know he sees it in my eyes anyway. It fuels me.

Five bounces. *I'm going to win this.*

I serve an ace to clinch it.

I try to soak up the minutes—to relish my victory. But the shock of actually, finally, getting this *thing* I've wanted for so long, sends me into autopilot. I know I talk to people and accept their congratulations. I know I eat some mango and check my blood sugar. But it all goes by in a haze until I'm standing next to Dick for the trophy ceremony.

Two years ago, I was defaulted on this exact court. Now I'm being handed an eighteen-inch trophy in the shape of the Eiffel Tower. Dick looks like he's going to be sick. Alice, Noah, and Kevin cheer enthusiastically from the bleachers. I'm invincible right now.

"Hope you enjoyed the match," I say to him. My smile is so big he can probably see my molars.

Dick offers me the most perfunctory handshake ever to exist. "Congratulations on your win," he says stiffly.

"Bet you didn't think you'd be saying that to me eleven days ago," I volley back. There are so few opportunities in life to say *I told you so* to an adult and this is the sweetest-tasting one yet.

He doesn't say anything and we stand silently next to each other for pictures, keeping the trophy between us like a safety bumper. Eventually, his eyes not moving from the cameras, he mutters to me, "I'll assume you mean that colloquially, as gambling on matches is quite against the rules."

It's actually a decent joke. And if he's serious, it's even funnier. If he so much as touches this trophy again, I'm pleading justification at trial.

Out of the corner of my eye, I see movement. My friends, I assume. But I have to wait until all the pictures are done before I can turn my head. I don't know how Violetta takes so many photos of herself. I've been doing it for a minute and a half and my face is practically cramping.

Except the person within arm's reach isn't Alice or Noah or Kevin.

It's someone much, much shorter.

Mom.

Holy shit. Mom is here.

I quickly sampeah.

She greets Dick first, pressing her hands together with a tiny bow. She gives him a chest-level sampeah, not a chin-level one. I'm sure he has no idea what that means but I gloat inside.

5 points to Mom.

But then she opens her mouth.

"Mr. Duncan, congratulations on the tournament. Thank you for letting Leylah enter and for overlooking her past here."

Is she really thanking Dick for *letting* me play?

Minus a thousand points. Minus ten thousand points.

She keeps dipping her head to him, the silver strands of her hair bobbing up and down like he's worthy of any kind of consideration. The sight of it makes me ill.

"Mrs. Lee." Dick addresses Mom with one of his oily smiles, nonexistent lips disappearing behind the flash of overly white teeth. He's probably loving this.

"It's Lê." I jump in to correct him. "*Doctor* Lê."

I see the exact moment Dick realizes he's been mispronouncing my name wrong for years and I'm pleased to see this bothers him. Probably because my subtext just called him a racist dumbass.

"Well, I'd love to stay and chat, but I have to talk to my mom about which WTA event I'm going to enter." I smile at Dick as Mom shoots me warning glances not to be rude. Well, rud*er*. I've never smiled this much in my life.

I give him a sampeah this time—the real kind. I'm playing the good Khmer daughter. Mom smiles at my obedience. "I hope you have the life you deserve," I say to Dick, perfectly gentle and sincere.

The minute I step away, I'm attacked from behind by Noah, Alice, and Kevin, who have snuck up behind me. Alice's eyes are wide, her hands clamped over her mouth. "Did you really just say that to Dick?"

"And I meant every word." I smirk.

"Lê Ha." Mom's sharp voice calls me back to earth. The happiest moment of my life and she couldn't even let me enjoy it for ten fucking seconds.

With a grim look, I send them away. They don't need to see me get a dressing-down from a sixty-year-old Khmer woman half my size. Noah flashes me a thumbs-up and Alice crosses her fingers. Kevin gives me the Mockingjay salute.

I take a gigantic breath, using the time to pull together my cheeriest, most deferential face. I hadn't counted on having *this* match right now, but this is how it's going down.

I have a death grip on the Eiffel Tower and I sampeah to nose level again. Well, sampeah *with* the Eiffel Tower between my hands, which I hold far enough away to make sure I don't poke out my own eye with this trophy. "You surprised me."

I hope my voice sounds neutral and not accusatory even though her actions are the very definition of an ambush.

Mom's eyeing me warily like she doesn't trust my calm demeanor. "You're always saying *Come see me play, you'll change your mind.*"

I'm terrified to ask. I do it anyway.

"And?"

"And . . . you were right. You're very good."

I'm holding a championship trophy after not competing for two years while managing my type 1 diabetes in one hundred-degree heat under the threat of never playing again, but sure, I'll take *good*.

"I already know which tournament I want to submit for," I say optimistically, hoping my positive attitude might miraculously rub off on her. "My wild card. There's one in DC in two weeks. Two top-twenty players have already committed to it."

"Two weeks?! Why so soon?"

The real answer is that it's before school starts. I'm hoping if I do well in DC, I can scrape together enough money to enter another tournament. Then another, and so on, until it's clear that high school is only holding me back. This has always been the plan. I'd just believed—naively—that Mom and Dad might come around if they saw me win Bastille.

I can tell Mom's gearing up for her usual "education is important" speech, which means I need to buckle the fuck up. She's going to drag this argument the whole three sets; no easy tiebreaks here.

"Mom." I place a hand on her soft forearm. "We talked about this. We had a deal."

It's clear my parents never expected me to actually win. I bury the disappointment. I'll deal with that later.

"We worked so hard to provide all this for you," she scolds. Mom doesn't have to raise her voice for me to know when she's upset. "All that work, for what?" she continues. "So you can run off and play sports? Become part of the fifty-four percent of Cambodians who never graduate high school? Is this what you want?"

"Yes! But not the way you mean," I hastily clarify. "School is impossible for me. You know this."

"You just need to study more. The way you practice tennis."

Deep breaths. *Deeeeep* breaths.

"Mom." I set my trophy on the ground and put my other hand on her arm. Maybe I can transmit my reasoning via osmosis. "School just isn't for everyone. You already know how much I study. It doesn't make a difference. We're not lazy. You can't *possibly* think fifty-four percent of an entire ethnic group just doesn't try."

I'm pressing my luck, talking to Mom like this. But she's smart enough to stop imagining I'll become some kind of star student if only they push me harder. She just won't admit it.

"It's not about trying. Education is important. Without it, the communists—"

"Mom. Don't you think there are ways of getting educated that *don't* involve sitting and reading in silence? We have the internet now. There are tons of jobs you don't need a degree to do."

Mom scoffs. "Playing sports isn't a job. You might as well be an actor."

I don't point out the obvious: both of those are totally jobs.

But I need to dig deeper. Because at the heart of it, I think my parents don't trust me. They don't think I can be successful at this.

And as much as it's going to hurt, I need her to say it to my face.

"Are you worried I'll fail?" I ask tentatively.

"We raised you better than that. I know you won't fail."

A compliment, I guess, except for the fact that I've failed multiple classes. I forge on.

"Are you worried . . . I won't succeed?"

Mom looks away and I have to pretend it's not fucking killing me. When she finally turns back she says, "What is success? To me, it's supporting my community. Supporting my family. Doing good in the world. Showing our culture. How do you do this just playing tennis?"

"You want better visibility for Khmer Americans? Well, here I am." I spread my arms out. "I just won a very big, very prestigious tournament. When you came in, there were people taking my picture. Reporters. I'm going to be put in newspapers. Online. Talking about who I am and where I come from. You don't think that counts as visibility?"

Mom frowns dubiously. "Athletes aren't *role models*. You think we need more kids trying to do the impossible? Hoping for dreams that will never come?"

I never knew Mom was so disillusioned. Especially considering her own background.

"You did the impossible," I point out, putting my hands back on her arm.

"And I was lucky! So was Dad! Not everyone will be so lucky."

How do you defend against a hypothetical future?

Mom looks troubled and I have to remind myself just how old she is. How much she's seen in her lifetime. Maybe that sense of doubt—that it could all disappear in a moment—maybe when you've seen the things she has, it never quite goes away.

"Your parents wanted you to have more opportunities and a better future than they had, yes? That's why you worked so hard to go to medical school? To keep trying until your device worked?"

Mom frowns and I take advantage of her silence.

"You and Dad always tell us how you did this for us. And I appreciate it. But isn't the reason you did it so *your* kids could have more opportunities? *Choices?*"

"Not this choice!"

Mom's reaction is so sharp, so visceral, that I yank my hands away to keep from getting stabbed. Even after all my calm, rational arguments. Even after proving I can win. She still says no.

My life isn't my own.

For the first time, I have no fucking clue what to do. I never actually considered the possibility that I would give up tennis. But what else can I do? Run away? Cut off my family over this? My entire community? At what point are there just too many obstacles to overcome?

Maybe I'm not strong enough to make it after all. My parents went from refugees to doctors and here I am, stuck at seventeen with no future.

I wrap my arms around myself, trying to quell the chill that's come over me. Maybe it's the ghost of my tennis career passing through.

"Con Ha." This time Mom is touching me, her thumb wiping away a tear from my cheek.

I hate that I'm crying here, where anyone and everyone can see me. But it really doesn't matter. In the end, Violetta is the brave one—the one following what she really wants.

I'm the quitter.

"Con Ha." My mom cups the sides of my face and turns me to her. "Do you know why I came here today?"

I sniffle pathetically, swiping a hand across my eye, only to accidentally rub salt into it. Now my eye stings *and* I'm crying even more. "To crush my dreams in person?"

"Someone called me yesterday. A friend of yours."

What?

"We had a long talk. She convinced me to come watch you before making decisions about your future."

"I don't understand." How could Alice have gotten my mom's number?

"Your old friend, Violetta. She called very early. Too early, I think. But she was convincing."

I'm stunned.

Or not, though. Because Violetta's the only person I know who would go behind my back and do something that drastic. She's also probably the only person who could flatter and charm my mom into doing something completely out of character, like jump on a plane and fly down to Florida just to see me play.

"What did she say?"

"That was our private conversation." Mom's hands are still cupping my face, but her eyes have softened. "I don't like your choice. And I worry with your diabetes. I don't think it's a good lifestyle for someone with your health."

"At this point, I know more about how to manage my diabetes than any doctor," I point out.

Mom gives me a disapproving frown. God forbid anyone know their own body better than a medical doctor.

"You could . . . send a doctor . . . with me, on the road?" My feather of a suggestion lands silently on the big red nuclear button of my remaining hope. "I know you and Dad have money stashed away for my future."

I'm careful not to detonate everything with the c-word.

College.

I practically shudder just thinking it.

"I worry about you being on your own all the time," she muses.

I can see her thinking about my suggestion and I hold my breath until I'm about to pass out.

"Your friend Violetta said you like to be alone."

This isn't the time to dwell on the fact that Mom is listening to a virtual stranger over her own daughter. This isn't the time to think about Violetta winning yet again.

My abs are starting to spasm from holding my body so stiff after playing eleven matches in thirteen days and I'm still shivering like there's snow on the ground but I refuse to move until Mom finishes that thought.

"That isn't true, is it? You like being by yourself?"

I'm holding back a flood of tears—the stakes of this conversation higher than anything I've ever experienced in my life. I don't know if I'll ever get another chance at this.

"I always have," I tell her.

"But you're always with us all at the gatherings and the cele-brations and parties." She keeps frowning, like this is one of those complicated word math problems needing to be solved. "Is this why you're so angry whenever we go?"

I nod. "It's too much for me. I can't be around a lot of people for very long."

Mom's face fractures, like she's realizing I'm a completely different person than she thought I was. I'm even less the good Khmer daughter now.

She steps back, taking her hands off my face, and I can finally breathe again. I gulp down air by the gallon. "So is this a yes?"

Her head moves only a fraction of an inch, but it looks like a nod. It's almost nothing, but it's not a no. And I'm smart enough not to push her any more right now.

Mom effectively closes the discussion anyway, changing topics. "This friend of yours," she says seriously, "you should keep in touch with her."

51

ALICE

IT'S OVERWHELMING, THIS SMELL. A FULL ASSAULT ON THE SENSES. VIOLETTA has insisted we close our eyes to get the full experience. Standing to her right, I can hear her inhaling deeply, a sigh of satisfaction on the exhale.

We open our eyes and the interior of the store seems nondescript. White tile everywhere and a wooden facade on the bottom of the display case.

"Hello, old friend," Violetta says. "I've missed you."

Next to her, Leylah rolls her eyes. "It smells like a sugar factory. Just order your cinnamon roll and let's go."

"Not cinnamon roll," V corrects her. "Cinna*bon*."

It smells nothing like the bakeries back home, which are sweet but more yeasty than sugary. Maybe because those bakeries offer a variety of buns and baked goods, whereas this is wall-to-wall cinnamon rolls.

"I can't eat anything here. I'll get a table," Leylah says with a wave, heading into the seating area of the food court.

"I've never been in a mall before," I confess. "It's a little overwhelming."

Violetta looks shocked. "Really?"

I shrug. There's only one mall in all of San Francisco, not that I've ever had reason to go.

She orders three different kinds of buns for us to share, along with a metric ton of napkins, and we make our way to Leylah.

"You're going to die when you taste these," Violetta promises as we settle into chairs.

"Ah, so *that* was your plan."

Violetta rolls her eyes at Leylah's little quip. "Not you, obviously. Don't eat these. They really could kill you."

"Thanks for the heads-up," Leylah says dryly.

It's funny to notice now, how many similar facial expressions they make. They have the easiness and tension of siblings. Maybe one day that means Leylah will be my sister too.

I take a bite of the pecan caramel bun and Violetta is right. It's confectionary heaven. Still, I don't have time to savor it.

"We can't stay long," I warn. "My flight is at four thirty."

"Mine is at six," Leylah adds.

Violetta frowns. "I can't believe you're both leaving."

Leylah hands me a napkin as I rescue falling caramel from my bun and attempt to lick the stickiness off my hand. "Technically, so are you. When did Dick say you need to move out by?"

"End of day tomorrow."

"I can't believe he's really only giving you one day," I say.

"Technically three days," Violetta clarifies. "Since I told him yesterday morning."

I try a bite of the churro swirl. Definitely not better than actual churros. I talk while the food is still in my mouth. "Still, he could have some compassion."

Leylah snorts. "Dick? Go soft?"

I choke on a laugh and churro swirls come flying out of my mouth. "Sorry! Sorry!"

"Who knew Alice had such a dirty mind?" Leylah asks.

"You're the one who said it," I protest.

"And you're the one who laughed at it."

"Only because it surprised me." I turn to Violetta. "Really? No reaction?"

Violetta pretends to disapprove, shaking her head with a little tsk. "You kiss your mother with that mouth?"

"You kiss your mother?" Leylah volleys back. The two of them laugh.

"Do you?" Leylah asks me.

"Do I what?"

"Kiss your mom."

"Uh. No, I guess not." I'd never really thought about it.

Leylah shrugs. "Sometimes I wonder if stuff is just a Southeast Asian thing or like, an all-Asian thing."

I think about Mama and how different she is from Baba, who told me all the time how much he loved me, how proud he was of me, et cetera. I used to think it meant he loved me more. But being here—knowing the sacrifices Ma made to get me here, and without saying a word about it—I realize she simply shows it in other ways.

Like making sure our clothes are always washed, folded, and mended. Keeping our house calm, even during the stress of Baba's illness. Mama has been a rock in a sea of turbulence. And yet.

"We're not really kissers," I say. "We're more of a hugging family."

"Do air-kisses count?" Violetta asks. "Because if so, I'm coming out way ahead."

I know Violetta is joking and I'm glad to see her more relaxed, but I still hear a twinge of sadness in her voice. I reach over and set my hand on her forearm and she covers it with her own.

"Maybe it'll change as she gets older," Leylah says. "If you think about it, my mom is old enough to be Audrey's mom, so in another twenty-five years or so . . . "

"I'm okay with it," Violetta says resolutely. "Really. Audrey and I are good for now. She's coming to the villa tonight to help me pack up my stuff."

I still don't fully understand Violetta's complicated relationship with her mom, but then again, neither do I with my own. I aim to change that when I get home. This week has shown me how it's only too late to make amends once one of you has passed. And I still have three family members I wish to have better relationships with.

Leylah picks at a tiny corner of the regular Cinnabon and tastes it. "Blech. That's disgusting. You might as well just inject sugar straight into your veins."

"I told you we didn't need to come here," Violetta says, though her mouth stuffed with the pecan bun indicates otherwise.

"Yes, we did," I insist. "Now tell us your big announcement."

Violetta, understandably, wasn't able to watch Leylah's match. Instead, she waited until we retreated to the villa to tell us she had important roommate business.

She reaches down to the giant bag she's been carrying and fishes out two wrapped packages.

"When the hell did you have time to wrap presents?" Leylah asks.

My question is even more basic. "*Why* did you get us presents?"

Violetta can barely contain her grin. "Just open them. It's a parting gift. As a thanks for putting up with me for this last week."

"Seven years and a week," Leylah mutters under her breath, but she's already ripping off the paper.

We open our boxes at the same time.

They're full of old Bastille Invitational T-shirts. An entire stack of poorly designed prison shirts, dating all the way back to 2004.

"There's a storage room with all of them," she tells us. "This was all I could find."

Violetta cackles as we pull each one out, comparing designs and collectively deciding that 2007 was definitely the worst design. Leylah pulls the T-shirt on over her tank top, standing and twirling for effect. "What do you think? Am I ready to be an influencer?"

"Can you imagine?" Violetta laughs. "You'd get banned the first day for arguing in the comments."

"Are you going to keep your social media?" I ask Violetta. I know how much time she's spent building her platform—it would be difficult to simply give it up. At the same time, it can't be good for her mental health.

Her face scrunches. "I haven't decided yet. I just posted that I'm going on hiatus for a while, while I figure out what I want to do next."

We finish our buns in silence, processing the fact that we are all figuring out our next steps. And they may or may not intersect with one another's.

But I've spent so much of my time recently being sad. I don't want to end my week this way. So instead of letting the tears fall, I pull out the 2023 Bastille Invitational T-shirt from the bundle and pull it over my head.

"Break free," I tell them with my most serious of faces, the printed neon-yellow *break free* shirt echoing my words across the front.

Leylah lifts her water bottle in a toast. "Remember the Alamo."

Violetta closes it out. *"Liberté, égalité, fraternité."*

Liberty. Equality. And a fraternity of sisters, forever bound together by these past eleven days.

ACKNOWLEDGMENTS

IF YOU'VE NEVER HEARD OF PATSY MINK, GO LOOK HER UP RIGHT NOW. (No, seriously. Do it. Talk about the ultimate overachiever Asian American archetype.) Though she's passed on, she's the reason I'm now an author. (Stay with me.) Growing up, Title IX was the goal. As in, "We're training with the express intent to earn a college athletic scholarship, only possible because of Title IX." My dad drilled it into our heads—Title IX was our ticket to higher education and, therefore, a more prosperous future. I probably knew about Title IX before I knew about the Bill of Rights.

I am now years past doing anything that could be reasonably described as a "sport." I write about people playing tennis instead of doing it myself. (Those who can't do, write?) But it relies on the same skills I honed over the years of working toward that Title IX scholarship—my ability to push through the hard parts; to keep striving for improvement; to finish no matter what, if for no other reason than to prove to myself that I can. Being an author means you need to finish the damn book, conquering the blank pages over and over again.

Point being: thank you, Patsy Mink, for standing up in a world that teaches women to sit down. It seems fitting that all three girls in this story are Asian American too.

As for the currently living, thank you to my agent, Kiki Nguyen, who somehow always understands what it is I'm trying to write, even when I don't. I am forever grateful for my editor, Ashley Hearn, who doesn't shy away from the work of making *me* work, regardless of scope or timeline. And the entire team at Peachtree/Holiday House, who were so wonderful to me during the release of *Boys I Know*—especially Sara DiSalvo, Michelle Montague, Darby Guinn, and Terry Borzumato-Greenberg. And Fevik, whose beautiful cover illustrations attract more readers than I ever could on my own.

I've noticed these things tend to get shorter the more books an author writes (and I used most of it on a history lesson!), so I'll whittle down my thanks to Naz, my forever (non)writing partner in crime, the rest of my writing friends (you know who you are), and all the bloggers/YouTubers/BookTokkers who read and promoted my debut. The publishing industry would not exist in its current form without your labor and I am grateful for every drop of your love, time, and effort.

Lastly, thanks to my real-life people outside the publishing world, especially my former editor, Sonya Abrams, who taught me the correct usage of "myriad," Cici and Nate, my unwitting tennis consultants, and all the coaches I've had in my life—whether I loved or hated you, I learned something from each of you. And to my family, who is prouder of me than I dare to be. I hope my kids find happiness and stability in whatever path they choose in life.

ABOUT
THE AUTHOR

Anna Gracia is a former Division I athlete and tennis coach who now excels at snacking while yelling advice at the TV. Her weaknesses include crying at movies, running long distances, and temperatures over 70 degrees. Her debut YA novel, *Boys I Know*, was both an ABA Indies Introduce and Indie Next pick, and was featured in the *New York Times, Paste, Seventeen*, and more.

FIND HER AT **ANNA-GRACIA.COM**
OR ON INSTAGRAM AND TIKTOK
@GRAHSEEYA